DOUBLE STANDARD

"What happened?"

Bluish blood flowed liberally from a cut across Aniel's forehead. He stepped forward into the light. "A massacre, Gol. An unprovoked, unmitigated massacre."

Golanlandaliay's lip curled. "How many?"

"The whole hamlet, my liege. Young and old. Male and female. It was the Darklings."

The king of the wood elves rose from his throne. "I cannot believe it. He has never done anything like this before."

"The Erl-King is out of control, as the Sisters said. You wanted proof. You have it."

"How could he do this? Killing humans is one thing, but to declare war on the rest . . . what could he be thinking?"

JASON HENDERSON

THE IRON THANE

Copyright © 1994 by Jason Henderson

A Baen Books Original

Baen Publishing Enterprises
P.O. Box 1403
Riverdale, NY 10471

ISBN: 0-671-72203-4

Cover art by Darrell K. Sweet

First printing, January 1994

Distributed by Simon & Schuster
1230 Avenue of the Americas
New York, NY 10020

Printed in the United States of America

Dedication

For Robert Page, Jr., who can run now, and for Cedric Messina, who kept the bard alive.

Acknowledgments

For various verses in Scots Myth, legends and religion, I am highly indebted to Anne Ross' *The Folklore of the Scottish Highlands* (Batsford: London, 1976), especially for "Bless O Chief of Generous Chiefs," "Thou man who would travel lightly," the incantation against the evil eye, and the Bride's Day Hymn. For support both moral and practical it would be criminal to forget my troops of friends, that gold mine David Banchs, Dennis Vranjesevic, Ruth and Oriane Messina, Steven Loomis, Mark Lehmann, Pat Hykkonen, Mary Jane Miller and Win Hooper, David Sexton, wherever you are, Kim Rosenthal, Mom, Dad, Bekki, Matt, and the inimitable Julia Guzman. Con tres palabras, amor.

"Here is a test to find if your mission on
    earth is finished:
If you're alive, it isn't."

— Richard Bach

"I have supped full with horrors;
direness, familiar to my slaughterous
    thoughts,
cannot once start me."

— Shakespeare

PROLOGUE

A.D. 1057

DUNFERMLINE, FIFE, SCOTLAND

It was dark in Scotland and over the smoke of the dying campfire MacDuff could see down the hill to his home. He churned the coals with a stick and watched gray and red mix. The wind tossed his hair as it sped up the hill from the castle. *I cannot sleep there.*

It was a soldier that had first brought the troubles: a soldier and friend named MacBeth, who trafficked with the devil and became King of Scotland. MacBeth had fought and schemed and murdered to seize the throne. Once he had it, he fought and schemed and murdered more to keep it. And he was told by witches that no man of woman born could stop him.

MacDuff watched the gray and red tumble. The ashes were bleeding fire and he could taste the soot. He had left Scotland then, to find allies in England, to gather an army and overthrow MacBeth. It was while he was gone that MacBeth had sent his men to Dunfermline. Only MacDuff's family had been there.

I am running through a hallway at Dunsinane looking for the mad king. I have returned with an army to strike at the heart of MacBeth's kingdom. As we swarm the castle,

*frenzied men shout to my left and right. Hired kerns are
screaming and swinging their swords, blood is flying
everywhere, but my sword remains sheathed. I am saving
it. Once, I considered the king a good man. I am going to
kill him.*

Somewhere in MacDuff's brain, his love screamed. He
could see it all in the folding coals, could see the soldiers
of the king sacking his house and cutting the throats of his
children. His wife screaming his name as her throat was
ripped asunder. Cursing him as a coward. He was not
there.

*Find the king. My God, my God, if you will lead me to
the king, I will ask no more.*

Through the blood I can see the master is at home.

Turn, hellhound! Turn! The bastard does not stir. Turn.

*He recognizes my voice as I visualize taking off his
damned head. MacBeth turns calmly to me. If I could
praise him I would say he looked brave. If I gave a damn I
would say he looked sad. The bastard tells me to leave. Get
thee back, he says, My soul is too much charged with
blood of thine already. My wife and children are screaming in agreement. I let fly my blade and his rises to meet
me. The clash of the metal is just another scream.*

*You cannot harm me, the king says. I bear a charmed
life which must not yield to one of woman born.*

Of woman born. His wife and children were still
screaming in the metal as it sparked and danced in their
power. Now another scream joined, in the castle and in
the sword and in the churning red and gray, that of his
mother, his first memory, of a woman whose child was too
much to bear. The scream was muffled in sackcloth,
throbbing with the swish of blood and pounding of heart
surrounding him and in his brain. *In the memory it is dark*
until *it is dark* until *it is dark and blood is pounding* until
and she is screaming until *you DIE, King!* MacDuff was
not born. MacDuff was RIPPED.

In my mind I am being held up, swathed in blood, and cannot stand on my own, and now the king's head is rolling like the ball I sewed for my son before he could walk. A doctor is holding me aloft by my right foot as I hold the king's head by its matted hair and set it fast upon a spear.

MacDuff, the screams sang, in the quiet way that remembered screams do. All of the screams were there in the churning gray and red.

I am MacDuff. My voice is in my sword.

MOUNT CHEVIOT, THE CHEVIOT HILLS

The Erl-King stood still and felt the cold wind in his razor teeth. His eyes crackled bright and icy as he stared northward, to the kingdom he would soon devour. It was open to him, fresh, weak, and ripe for violation. So many. So perfect for a beginning. He threw back his glistening, silver mane. He smiled. He could taste blood.

So many. So perfect for a beginning.

"And never, since the middle summer's
    spring,
Met we on hill, in dale, forest, or mead . . .
To dance our ringlets to the whistling wind,
But with thy brawls thou hast disturbed our
    sport."

— Shakespeare

"Dost not see the Erl-King, with crown, and
    with train?"
My son, 'tis the mist rising over the plain . . .
"My father, my father, he seizes me fast,
Full sorely the Erl-King has hurt me at
    last."

— Goethe

PART I

CHAPTER 1

There are witches; this we know, and there are many things which the average man will not believe if he does not have to. It had happened, in the time of which we speak, that "nature" in Scotland had gone or been forced awry. There were those who said that the moment the good King Duncan breathed his last, time itself, the world as it had been known, was upset. This aberration, this beguiled time which found voice in the political upset among mortals, did not end with the death of the tyrant who slew Duncan. The imbalance that lay across the land was larger, as if all that had gone before were the distant rumblings of a very nasty coming storm. It was because of this that a man like MacDuff came into contact with the likes of the supernaturals. The troubles were not over. The beguiled time was not over. And whether he wanted it to be or not, MacDuff's service to the capricious whim of fate was not over.

MacDuff absently flipped a coin to a beggar woman

outside the doorway of the timber castle at Dunsinane.
The Thane of Fife sniffed; it had rained that morning and
the air crackled with energy. He walked briskly, his red
cloak flapping behind him, boots clacking violently against
the cobblestones, and he barely noticed the people jumping out of his way as he maneuvered through the market
that surrounded the castle walls. The journey home to
Dunfermline would take at least fifteen hours riding, and
he was anxious to get on with it. First, however, he had
business to attend to in Dunsinane. The woman had only
caught his eye because he had to step over her. A sentry
began to bark at him when MacDuff moved past the
threshold and into the courtyard, saw MacDuff raise an
eyebrow in annoyance, and promptly fell silent. He, too,
moved out of the way. MacDuff was going to see the king.

MacDuff took in the courtyard in a glance. He who
wore the crown naturally led a life of greater comfort and
ease than the typical lowly Scotsman, but luxuries were
not plentiful in Tacitus' "Caledonia stern and wild." The
way the king lived was never far from the way the earthy
man of the field would live. But luxury is a subjective
term. Where thousands sleep in thatched houses which
let in the wind, a castle's walls are a luxury, cold though
they be. When the king was little more than the most
powerful and most charismatic of a loosely knit country of
local chieftains, then the throne was a precarious seat
indeed. A Scot might laugh at the very English notion of
royal divine right: only Hell seemed to have a steady hand
in choosing Scottish kings, but MacDuff always felt that
God might at least want to work through the throne. He
simply hadn't found a good method of doing so as yet.
Caledonia was still stern, long after the fall of the Roman
Empire, and not nine years before the Duke of Normandy would come in and change the world all over
again, it was still wild.

Had MacDuff wanted to, he might have become king

himself; whether he wanted to or not, his removal of the previous king's head led many — especially Canmore, the young King Malcolm III — to wonder exactly what the former Thane was planning. But King Malcolm's fears were displaced. As head of the MacDuffs and executor of the Law Clan MacDuff, as foremost judge over the land, with the power to act with king's authority in the king's absence, with immunity in case of warranted — and when, one wondered, might *that* happen? — murder, MacDuff was no ordinary chieftain. *Deus Juvat*, proclaimed the lion that held aloft a great broadsword on the metal badge that clung to MacDuff's cloak. *God helps.* Yes, well. Maybe He would help King Malcolm understand his errors. Kingship was the last thing on MacDuff's mind. MacDuff was different. MacDuff was leaving.

Having frightened away yet another useless guard outside the royal dining hall (who knew better than to cross this particular nobleman, this day or any), MacDuff threw the door open and strode in. He stopped a short distance from the door and stood, staring at King Malcolm. The king sat at the end of the gargantuan table, devouring his roasted duck, while the ubiquitous and doglike General Dukane, and the king's chief server, stood by. The server stared sheepishly, as if wondering what to do and not wanting to do anything. Dukane practically growled and moved a quick hand towards his belt. The king raised a hand to stop whatever Dukane had in mind. Malcolm frowned, and his young, petulant face betrayed his annoyance. The Earl of Fife had just barged in on a perfectly important discussion.

Malcolm looked at MacDuff and found he couldn't help but survey the man completely. As much as the king resented him, MacDuff had the air of a statue that had somehow chosen to move with life, but might never move again if one took one's eyes away. He stood tall, at least six feet, with black hair swept back from a high brow. Here and there streaks of iron gray had intruded, but not detracted; they only served to make him look more *other*, as if MacDuff were slipping away and being replaced, bit by bit, with iron. The iron was in his eyes, too, which bore into the boyish king more than Malcolm was comfortable with. *No*, he was certain, *no, I don't like you. And I don't trust you.*

Malcolm was the son of Duncan, the late king of Scotland, who had been killed that fateful night some two years previously by MacBeth, Thane of Glamis. Malcolm deserved his throne. Was he not called by the Scots *Canmore*, the great leader? It wasn't *his* fault that there were circumstances that kept him from avenging his own father's death, wasn't *his* fault that MacDuff had done it for him. It had simply worked out this way. After all, Malcolm thought, MacDuff wasn't so wise, was he, if he could desert his family to go traipsing off to England? But here MacDuff was. The hero of Scotland, and a king-killer besides, who thus far had made no move for the throne. Perhaps because he doesn't want it? Perhaps he just likes to kill kings? Perhaps because he wanted to vanquish MacBeth first, and then plot his ascension? Or aid Donalbane, the second son of Duncan, now lounging drowsily in the English Court, in his ascension? Malcolm feared all these things, none of which were true, and yet could only barely glimpse through the haze in his passionate young mind that which he hated most — that MacDuff, after all, would make a good king, and a better king than most. Rather than dwell on this he had rushed to the second conclusion: MacDuff was a threat. Such is the hatred of a small man for a great one, with or without ambition.

"I am leaving," MacDuff said, shattering the silence. "Today."

"Leaving?" The king tried to look official and felt small for his robes. "Scotland? And where does our good MacDuff intend to go?"

"Away, Malcolm. I am tired."

"*Malcolm* am I called? I am your king, man, do you forget?"

MacDuff was not impressed. He strode over to the table and leaned on it, staring hard into the eyes of Malcolm. "You are king," he said, "because I have made you king, boy. Do you forget?"

Malcolm smiled nervously. Dukane snarled. Malcolm flicked his right hand to quiet him. "I spoke . . . hastily," said the king, "I meant nothing. Yet you are much respected here, as the liberator of Scotland, and slayer of the tyrant MacBeth." He poked at his duck. A tousle of reddish hair fell over green eyes. He slumped in his seat. He was a twenty-two-year-old king who looked like a watering boy, and for an instant MacDuff marveled that *this* was that for which he had gone to so much trouble. *This* on the throne.

MacDuff did his best to swallow his disgust. "You know reputation means little to me. Even so, many already ascribe the 'heroic' deed to you."

Malcolm grinned stupidly. "To myself? The killing of the mad king?"

Aye, thought MacDuff. *After your own men reported it thus. Fine, then, Malcolm, take the credit. Try to gain courage from it. I care little enough, and my leaving will make it that much easier to spread.* "I know what you are doing, Malcolm." MacDuff picked up a chalice and poured himself some ale. "With all your . . . stories."

"And what stories would those be?"

"Don't patronize me, whelp. The campaign I gathered in England — your organization. The camouflage we used — your genius. The storming of the castle — your brain-child. And last of all, the killing of MacBeth — your sword. Your hand. Very nice."

"I don't see what you're getting at."

MacDuff grinned for a second. "What are you afraid of? Of what they'd say about a boy king who can't fight his own battles?"

"See here!" The boy actually changed. He flicked his wrist at the two observers and the server scurried out. Dukane eyed MacDuff suspiciously, then followed. The door swung closed and Malcolm breathed coolly, levelling his gaze to meet MacDuff. "I am king. Rightful king. What you say, MacDuff, is . . . fable. That is all. Oh, I know about your vengeance upon MacBeth, about your family . . ."

"Do you?"

". . . your brilliance. But you see, it really doesn't matter. I am king. Truth is mine. I pass a story here, a tale there, and soon enough the truth — my truth, the new truth — is known. It is better that my truth be known."

"Because you need it?"

"Because I wish it."

MacDuff realized he could be watching a serpent growing in its lair. And for all his disgust, he couldn't bring himself to give up completely. "This is wrong, Malcolm. You are capable of much more than bending simple truths for the sake of public approval."

"No truth is simple. I will be vindicated by history."

"History should tell the truth. It is our only record."

"History is a fable we can all agree upon, Earl of Fife. Would not that be more accurate?"

Some little tendril within MacDuff snapped. His body whipped and uncoiled and became one long arch of movement as the tall man slung his chalice clear across the hall. Hundreds of tiny crystal shards sang out and died as MacDuff turned his eyes upon the king. "I am *not* . . . an *Earl*," he hissed, "nor have I ever been one or seen one in all of Scotland. Malcolm, what in God's name are you doing to my country? Glamis, that ineffectual bastard you appointed last week is not — should not be — an Earl! Cawdor is not an Earl. We are *Thanes*, for God's sake, King, Thanes of Scotland. Your Scotland! We lead our clans and keep your castles and guard your country with our lives. What, did you spend so much time in England that you forgot what your homeland was like? Do you think an Earl can play the *ceol mor* on the pipes like a damned typhoon and sing the songs of the old Scots, dead in the eye of his ancestors? Can an Earl bear the cold of these moors, stand through even near the din of metal a Thane can? Will an Earl stand against all Hell at his house's door and defend it with his own blade?"

"Did you, MacDuff, as a Thane?" Malcolm whispered, waiting for the blow he was sure might take his young head off. He looked at the table, as if compelled to go on the defensive. "It is only a name."

"No," MacDuff said, losing his gaze out the window for a moment. "It is not only a name. I admit, my liege, for you perhaps even Scotland herself is only a name. You care not for our heritage, our proper titles, or our past. You trample on these, you cannot understand them, and so you use them and waste them as you please. Enough. Time was a good king ruled, who cared for peace and truth and law. You have brought a momentary peace. You create your truth. I will not wait for your law."

"Afraid of losing the Law Clan MacDuff? Ready to kill another king, Fife? Regicide becomes you, doesn't it?"

"Enough, boy. It's yours." *Watch the wall. Forget the boy. Forget MacBeth. Forget the Clan.* "All yours. I have nothing here. All I held dear is lost. My castle is quiet and cold as a tomb. My food is tasteless. My country is no longer herself. I am ready to leave."

"Where?"

"It matters not to you, nor would I tell you if it did. You, Canmore," he said, gazing in the eyes of the boy king, "take care of my country. But take her to Hell if you must; she will come back without you. Make her great, if you can." Now MacDuff stood straight and turned to go. "She may take you with her."

"And where may I say you have gone, MacDuff?"

The Thane of Fife did not look back. He did not answer, and the ironic truth was that, at the time, he actually believed he was leaving.

The king's eyes followed the Iron Thane out the door before he called in Dukane.

All of that had been a week ago.

It was dark. MacDuff rode silently southeast along what is now the Firth of Forth, which pours into Scotland from the North Sea along the South of Fife. The ride had taken longer than expected to return to Dunfermline. He had found it no easier to bear than he had remembered, had finished his business and quietly slipped away. Undoubtedly, Malcolm would soon be appointing a new Earl, some other clansman like the new Glamis would be taking his post, and the Thane felt his title passing like an ebb tide. Moonlight bounced off the water and lit the shore, here and there bathing man-sized rocks in moon-glow as they jutted from the beach and froze there. *The ghosts of the Firth.* MacDuff remembered coming here as a child, climbing on the rocks and swimming. Wasting time.

He recalled the old talebearer to whom he and his companions had occasion to listen, and the tales the old man had told. There were ghosts along here, he had said, lost soldiers and lost men from ships, lost people. He spoke, in a throaty old-way voice, a thick Scot/Pict mix even older than that of MacDuff. MacDuff understood this tongue, and spoke it, but as the years had passed he found he spoke less than he remembered. But the teller's language suited him, as did his looks. MacDuff would say the old man played the part "exceeding well." He had a patch over his left eye, and a head of sea-gray hair that met his beard and surrounded his face.

MacDuff tried to remember one story . . . oh, yes . . . *it is in these parts*, he used to say, *that you may see a bonnie*

*lass by the rocks in the rain, soaked to the bone and chilled
to the core. She will seek a ride on your horse or wagon,
and . . .*

Even at fifteen, the future Thane knew how the story
ended. The poor wretch who helped the lass always
arrived at her home to find she had disappeared. Some re-
liable witness at the house would explain that she had died
long ago on the rocks; her ghost was now striving to come
home again, yet somehow she could never make it. Something in it spoke to the boy and made him shiver even
now. It was an ageless story, of course; in fact it is still told.

The wind shifted and blew more fiercely. It licked
spitefully at the rocks along the shore, flashing white and
iridescent in the night, bringing mist. MacDuff felt the
hairs prickle at the back of his neck. The mist was cold and
stinging, and now he watched it and it looked like a huge
snake of fog, winding towards him, like nothing natural he
could imagine, hissing . . . no, whispering. It was whispering something as it curled around him and spread across
the path and over his head, sliding serpentlike into his
brain, filling the Thane's mind, throbbing with pain and
terror which he could not identify. *MacDuff.*

It was a woman's voice, soft and silky and cruelly familiar to his ears. And then, shifting in and out of view in the
fog, unreal and yet as real as MacDuff could hope for,
there on the rocky path stood his wife. *MacDuff,* Lady
MacDuff called, and her voice struck him with the force
of a kick in the chest from his own horse. The figure was
wearing a white gown, silky and long; she spread her arms
and where she lifted them, before the folds of her sleeves,
appeared two boys, one some eight years old, hair brown
and mussed, going shirtless as boys do, the other, four
years at most, reddish of hair, mouth agape at all he could
see.

*My sons. My boys whom I will raise to be men, who
will hunt and fight, who will make me proud, who are*

noble sons, who come from a Thane's family, who will be
educated and fed and clothed in the MacDuff tradition.
In a time when families send their sons into the field
because it must be done to survive, I will not sacrifice my
sons to poverty or greed. They do make me proud, would
do so even if they were born half-wits, would make me
proud even if I could never see them . . . *MacDuff!*, one
sang . . . never see them . . . *Fife-Thane!*, the other. *Say it!*
Say it! Never see them again . . . who will make me — oh,
my Lady, *I am sorry, so sorry* . . . proud even if I . . .

MacDuff felt his stomach knot and his chest tighten
and his eyes sting, but he stood still and watched Lady
MacDuff with his boys. The fog swirled through them and
through MacDuff's brain as the lady took each one in her
arms. She moved fluidly, as through water, as she turned
first to the older boy and softly held his head, hands over
his ears, and bent low to kiss him on the forehead. She
brought her hand down to his shoulder and noticed the
blood which suddenly issued from his throat, and now the
boy was vomiting blood on her gown. *Sorry* . . . She
screamed and turned to the other, who reached out to
take her by the neck, to be picked up, and as the boy held
out his arms he threw back his head and it came off, tumbling like a ball, tumbling like a clown at court, tumbling
and throwing blood like the head of MacBeth. *Sorry* . . .
Now the boys were on the ground, bathing in blood and
mist, that mist, and only she remained.

She had been a good woman, a strong woman, whom
MacDuff loved because she had never fully needed him,
but seemed to have only chosen to. He had left her alone,
and here she was, looking at him, waiting for him to help
But no, you were in England, weren't you? Again she
cried, *MacDuff, my husband, why have you left us? Why*
have you turned your back on us? Why have you betrayed
us? MacDuff!

And now the cry was joined by the eight-year-old, who

turned his semi-detached head and gurgled *MacDuff!* in a *dying* eight-year-old voice and the head of the youngest opened its eyes and looked at him and cried *MacDuff* in a *dying* four-year-old voice and he who was MacDuff threw his hands over his ears and closed his eyes and screamed like a baby. "No!

"No!"

No.

And then they were laughing, somehow, chattering in a laughter that took the humanity out of them, and MacDuff opened his eyes and saw what they were.

Witches. *Sisters.* The wind swirled around them and they took their forms, sick and greenish and beyond, *other.* The middle creature began to bend in form and fell forward to rest on her staff, and mould grew over her gossamer, blood-soaked gown to drown it green and cover the rancid body of the First Sister. The head of the boy drifted to the shoulders of the putrescent, rag-covered form that had replaced his youngest son and deflated, went green, then shifted and stretched and changed into the hideous and ancient face of the Second. The eight-year old's body boiled out like flowing, flesh-toned lava and swallowed his arms and moulded over with bad cloth and grime and dried blood. The body stretched and inflated and the skin flowed out to envelope the bloated, ancient body in a hanging, wrinkled mess. The Third. Of course.

"What is this?" yelled MacDuff, as he tried to lift his voice over the howl of the wind.

"Why," spoke the first witch, "a visit."

"An introduction," cackled the second.

"For those who have not seen what they should see," giggled the third.

The earth hath bubbles, a good man had said. These are of them . . . MacDuff was trying to regain his composure. Just a vision. Just another dream. A cruel hoax. "What are you? Women? Devils?" Or both . . .

The first simply laughed. Her laugh changed every moment or so, from that of the rotting old corpselike creature that she was to something else, something younger, something that, if the rot and boils were hidden, would be enticing. "MacDuff! Fortune is thine, Fife-Thane!" and she twisted her head and looked at him sideways, grinning full of drool.

The second sister laughed and shrieked, "MacDuff! Fortune is thine, slayer of MacBeth, loser of love!"

"MacDuff," joined the third, "Fortune is thine, where thou wilt find it, if you know where to look and when."

MacDuff slid from his horse and drew his sword, toying with its weight. The realness of the metal set the world a bit more in order. "Do you toy with me? Make clear your message, what fortune? Answer MacDuff or answer to his sword," he lied. In truth he feared them, one and all, as any superstitious Scot would. He was already telling himself and not completely believing: the vision was not real, it was a witch's conjuration. Shake it off. Cross yourself. *It is my own eye, it is God's eye, it is the eye of the Son of God which shall repel this.* Shake it off and face them.

The Third Sister simply giggled as her sister had before her, that same, disgusting, enticing laugh, "MacDuff! Slayer of tyrants, yet not much wiser!" She cocked an eyebrow and spoke in the voice of the red-haired son. "Aye," the voice from the mouth said, "Aye, what fun we shall have. A warning, Fife-Thane. From the Sisters who care."

"And we do," cackled the drooling First Sister, "we do, we care so deeply!"

"All right, then. Your warning," cried MacDuff, "what is it?"

Thou man who would travel lightly . . .

The voices were different now, soothing, almost singing.

There is red blood upon thy shirt;
Not the blood of roe nor blood of deer,

But blood of thy body, and thou full of wounds.

MacDuff thrust his sword into the ground and rested on the pommel a long time before looking up again. *But I have plans. My service is finished.* "How do I know this to be true?"

"You do not," smiled the First. "But we occasionally do favors as well as curse. Take the advice as you like: We are all of us sheep, MacDuff. We are led whether we like it or not. Go where you will. There is a game afoot." And she giggled again and was joined by the other two, moaning high and shrieking and laughing and suddenly, completely, gone.

Except the fog, which remained, and the lone Thane, who remained as well.

MacDuff mounted and guided his steed up the path. Through the mist he could vaguely see a strange landmark, two rocks some twelve feet long and at least as high, spaced by at least six feet. He stalled before entering the throughway, his senses wild. *Unreliable. Shake it off.* He shrugged and shuddered and tried to blink the witches from his mind. *Fortune,* he thought, as he entered the rocks. *Where thou wilt find it. We are all of us sheep. It is my own eye, it is God's eye . . .*

His horse stopped now, quizzical, uneasy. The moonlight glistened on the steed's black hide. It shifted its weight, lifting its hooves and scraping the ground. The horse snorted fearfully. MacDuff raised an eyebrow but determined to go on, laying his hand on the hilt of his sword as he nudged the mount's flanks.

Between the rocks there was nothing to see when MacDuff glanced around, however many times he looked. He pushed the horse on, clearing the rocks, and they plunged into the abyss of shadow cast by the rocks on the far side. MacDuff looked west, toward the hills, east toward the Firth. All at once he heard a scuffling from behind and something heavy had him by the shoulders. The horse thrashed and pitched out from under him as he was wrestled to the rocky ground.

They had jumped off the rocks.

Damn fool Scot, MacDuff cursed himself as his head struck the ground. *Pay attention. You rode into this like a child.* He rolled to put the weight of his attacker underneath him. The assailant seemed to be having trouble getting a good grasp on his knife and MacDuff took advantage of the borrowed time. He could make out the second attacker moving around the horse, which was beginning to right itself. MacDuff wanted to laugh as he felt at his own sword. He was a soldier; he had engineered many such ambushes in his day, and this one was being handled badly. He drove his elbow into the man's ribs and sprang to his feet, sword ready. MacDuff could picture the orders these men must have received: an easy job killing an old man in the dark. This old man waited for the young fool to lunge with his dagger and gave him a good slash across the chest. A scarlet line opened across the fabric of the man's tunic and he staggered in pain.

MacDuff gasped as he felt a leather cord wrap around his neck. He resisted staggering. *All too easy.* He took the broadsword in two hands and deftly heaved it clear over the back of his own head, cleaving that of the strangler. The head produced a truncated cry. MacDuff spun back with the weight of his sword and knew his arms would hurt a little in the morning. Wonderful feeling, that.

He laid his blade against the neck of the first attacker and took a better look at him, his eyes having adjusted somewhat. "Your wound will not kill you. But I could if I wished." He stared into the stranger's eyes and saw that he was too young for a good beard, much less a good attack. *Might still become king*, MacDuff mused. He was suddenly sorry he had killed the other one.

"Malcolm sent you, yes?"

"Aye," the youth choked, as he tried to keep from

vomiting from the stench of his own blood and the sight of his partner's spilt brains.

"Tell his majesty not to meddle in my affairs. I wish not to deal with him in the future — ever, perhaps. Tell him I have gone as I said I would." It suddenly occurred to Mac-Duff that, if the witches were correct, this may not be the truth. "There is no need to attack me, nor — if you understand me — to waste men." He lightly increased pressure. "Aye?"

"Aye."

"Good. Now drag your partner's body home and be glad you're alive." As MacDuff rode on, the young guard silently took away the mess that was his friend.

"Damn," MacDuff said aloud, hoping it was not true, knowing it was. Scotland was in danger. But how, and from whom? And if so, how to find out? He would have to turn back. "Damn," he said again, and the North Sea howled at him as he looked for a place to camp and think.

CHAPTER 2

A lone figure smiled down from Mount Cheviot. He was called the Erl-King. He would take humanity's young, because it pleased him.

He would take their suckling infants from the breasts of their women and he would talk to the babes as no human could. He would entice and seduce the children, taking their souls, leaving only the limp, useless carcasses of which the filthy humans were stupid enough to be so proud. He would visit the burial places and call to those who had died unbaptized, shamed by the humans who had no idea what goodness or evil was, and draw them to his side, giving the unnamed babes a place with him. He would visit the forests and call to those babes the humans had exposed, the bitter, angry spirits whom the fool humans did not want. Not because he pitied them, but because *their* hatred was pure, he would give the spiteful and confused infant spirits a channel for their anger. He would take everything the humans held dear and twist it, turning it against them. As he destroyed the humans with his children, those he spawned and those he took, he would feed upon their sadness and revel in their sorrow. He would take all that the humans feared and he would make it personal and close and cold and splitting; he would hurt them, and watch them suffer and die at his behest, stripped of their lives by his brood, the pure, young spirits of what had been their innocent ones. Their last hopes.

Because it pleased him. And then the humans would all be gone and he would rule his family alone, in his world. And he would drink the humans' flowing, bloodlike, lingering fear forever. He was what men called the Prince of the Dark Elves. *Der Erlkönig.* The Erl-King.

But first, he had to call out to his own.

"My children!" the Erl-King cried, lifting his voice and his thoughts out, down from the mountain, across the dark land, across the moonlit sea. "We have waited long enough! Hearken to me!" And he knew his cry would be heard. He could see them, all of them, the small, young Darklings playing their games at terrifying the living children, the older ones, spying upon humans in their houses, moving random items, sowing fear. Taking a child, here and there, if they were brave enough. He could see those under ground, under the lakes, in the trees. He could feel them like a rush of cold air, feel their hatred and black mischief, and the feeling elated him. All across the British Isles, all across the mainland, their ears perked and their smiles grew with the lust that is only known to the very, very intensely evil. Thirst, thirst like no other.

They saw his mane of brilliant white hair, his crystal eyes which shone like a dying star, his lithe, long body of chalky white. He stood against the Scottish sky and flared, enticing and quick and deadly. His leggings and tunic clung to him and flowed with the blackness that flowed through him. His open train flew behind him, the color of all of his clothing and of his shimmering wings, the color he and his children were called, not because of how they looked, but how they were at the soul. Black. Absent light. Absent any light at all.

"My liege," a voice spoke beside him, deliciously, familiarly evil. "My father. It has been a long time."

"Belial." The Erl-King did not turn. He was listening to his brood.

"Yes."

"They appear eager."

"We are eager, *Erlkönig*. What will it be this time? A house has angered you? A city, perhaps? Shall we destroy a city?"

"Oh . . ." the Erl-King sighed, his eyes shining. Somewhere he could see a bonfire being lit, and his Darklings were dancing around it, listening to their king. "Oh, more than that. Much more."

Belial chewed upon this for a moment. The Erl-King would know. "And it begins here? This country?"

"Yes."

"Why?" he asked, hoping the Erl-King would not be annoyed at his question.

"Oh, you wonderful Darkling!" the Erl-King said, turning to Belial and gripping him firmly by the shoulders. "So kind of you to worry. Why? Because . . ." He turned again, looking down at the dancing Darklings. "Because she is a perfect start. Ripe. And small. And so full of delicious pain. We will feed off her, and when she is dead, we will move on."

"There is a problem," Belial said. He looked down the mountain beside his king. He was the second-in-command, and he looked it, younger than the Erl-King by centuries, but nearly as hard of skin, with nearly the same crackle. His hair fell grayish over his ivory brow. His crystal eyes darted as he scanned the troubles in his mind. "The wood elves like this place, as do the Syth. They may not take to an attack upon the humans that inhabit it."

"Oh, yes. Hadn't I told you, darling Belial?"

"What, father?"

"I do not expect to have them around when this is finished," he smiled, and Belial would have answered then, but the King was talking to his legion. He threw back his head and began his call, and they answered him. The Darklings knew the responses in their hearts and called them out from where they were.

"My children, you have waited."

We have waited long.

"We have watched the humans grow."

They grow in number.

"But we will rule."

With you as our king.

"We will crush them."

Crush them all.

"Steal their young."

Steal them all.

"Fill them with terror."

Fill them all.

"And all will die."

All will surely die.

The Erl-King turned to his general. "Belial," he said, "find me two Darklings. I have a special mission for them."

Humans, Susan told herself, had to be handled by their emotions. She had done the right thing; she was sure of it.

On a lonely, fog-shrouded heath near the highland town of Forres, a black cauldron boiled. The cauldron gave off an aroma known to few, scarcely indicative of the bizarre ingredients found in its blackened walls. Each ingredient was carefully chosen to afford sight for its owners, to reflect the powers within the persons who stirred the murky waters. Many men had walked by the place, but few had ever seen those in the habit of gathering there.

Silhouetted against the moon, three figures conversed. One stirred the cauldron, intent upon its message. Another sat, poised upon a stone, caressing the cat that lay in her lap. The third figure sat cross-legged on the moist ground, feeding seeds to the owl perched on a short stand at her side. The owl ate greedily and tried to keep from catching the attention of the cat.

"Some game is afoot, isn't it, Sister," mused Susan, the First Sister. Graymalkin licked his whiskers as she scratched his head absently. The cat sat in Susan's lap, watching the heath, waiting for mice, ignoring the owl. The owl was *other*. Graymalkin listened intently and took in all that was said, quiet, barely noticed, all-noticing. He might, he felt, be needed.

"Aye," answered Ruthe, the Second Sister, and she looked at Susan, whose auburn locks flowed freely past her shoulders, setting off her chestnut eyes beautifully. So beautiful she was, Ruthe thought, or could be. She whisked the air and watched Paddock the Owl flutter his wings, startled by the sudden force.

In human terms, Ruthe was comely herself. Her eyes were blue and bright, her skin pale, but fleshly reddish at the cheeks, with a handful of faint freckles scattered on her face. Her golden hair was cropped short, and now it stood up a bit in the air, tousled and static-charged. She was tall and graceful, never overcome by her height, and her cream-colored gown flowed over her curves beautifully. She was the picture of seductive innocence. It seemed a pity that the First always wished for them to take such rancid forms when meeting the humans. But, Susan had once explained, they react so amusingly to it. We are, after all, witches.

Joly stirred the cauldron and tried to see. She was shorter than the other two by at least half a head, but not ill-proportioned. She had the small, tightly strung body of a dancer. She toyed with no familiar spirit. Her sisters had

Paddock and Graymalkin, but Joly, being the Third, the best seer, took more time with the cauldron. And today she was having a difficult time of it. Something was happening with the dark elves and the Erl-King.

It was not for the humans that they were particularly concerned. The humans were self-propelled toys, really, fantastic puppets which danced for them as they watched. Mortals whispered about the Sisters, called them by different names, *Norn* and *Moirai* and *Wyrd*, but never understood. Some said that the Sisters could alter the past and the future; not true: they could only see it and take part. Naturally, the future of humans was easily seen; it always followed the same pattern. They played with the humans because they could. They toyed with them, watched them run through their little lives as if any particular moment made any human any more important, as if his life would ever be any but that which it was: mortal. Soon to end. Occasionally Joly or Ruthe or Susan would grow bored and stir up the nest, give a bit of solid advice here, bad advice there, lead this one to his death or that one to greatness. Kill a few sheep. It amused them.

They did not hate the humans. The humans were perfectly useful. They cultivated fields to run through, made ships to blow off course. Humans herded swine, which were such fantastically stupid animals as to have no real value at all except for the intermittent joy of driving a handful of them over a cliff. The humans were impossible to understand for the Sisters, or rather, seemed so simple as to defy explanation. They were so small, yet felt so large. On occasion their sheer gumption was positively inspiring, if a witch may use such a word. The humans were amusing to the Sisters because they cared. That word, Joly snickered to herself. To care implied an understanding of order. The humans cared so much about so many things that were almost *out* of order. And they were so small, so easy to drown. "As flies to wanton boys are we to the gods," some human would say, "they kill us for our sport." And that was right. Exactly right.

And now, it looked as though they would be saving them, and not for sport. Put better, even the humans would even be needed. She had seen it first that morning, as she awoke upon the heath and watched the dew fall from her strawberry hair. Something unclear was happening: the Erl-King had, somehow, for some reason, decided to break the mold. She could not tell how, but she knew he was going after the humans. *All* of them.

This was out of order. Everything the inhabitants of earth did followed its pattern; even the Sisters' seemingly random games were in keeping with what they were. The dark elves were the same way. They stole the souls of children and frightened humans. They seemed, in fact, to live for little else.

"You could make the same comment about us," Ruthe had said, to make a point, as she was wont to do. Ruthe was the most rebellious against the order of things, her Sisters knew, but even she had to accept it. The Sisters lived for themselves, therefore the elves must as well. But now the Erl-King had a plan. He intended to destroy the humans, one and all.

"He can't," laughed Ruthe. "Even we can't do that. Well, we could, I suppose, a few at a time."

"Right," Susan answered. "Yet we do not. We toy with them, we don't want to kill them all. But the Erl-King has a thousand children. I fear he has taken his passion out of its bounds."

The dark elves were similar to humans in many ways, but in none so fundamental as their passion. And their passion was distinctly destructive. Not mischievous, though it often displayed itself so. Destructive. Evil. They were not simply amused by the harm of men, they loved it and thrived on it. And that the Erl-King had decided to kill all of the humans would not even so disturb Joly as the fact that the cauldron's vision of the future had become so unclear. That could mean one thing: more than humans were involved. The Erl-King, for some reason, out of whatever incomprehensible hatred drove him, was going to try to destroy all of the other inhabitants of the upper echelon of sentient beings. And the fact that he wanted to, and had his own particularly malicious way of fighting his foe from all sides, meant that he might be able to do it. The fact that she could not see how far he was going to succeed disturbed Joly all the more. But whatever he had planned, it was going to be big, and it was going to start here.

"What do we do?" she looked up from the cauldron.

"That seems clear enough," Susan answered. She had seen as well. "We stop him."

"Alone?" Ruthe asked.

"No," answered Susan. "This is unusual; if the Erl-King insists upon gumming the wheels, we shall have to meet him with a resistance." *Not that unusual*, she had to correct herself. Hadn't he at least hinted at these sorts of aspirations before? "We could go to where the Syth next meet —"

"Syth?" Joly could not fathom it. "You expect us to work with the Syth? What difference shall that make?"

"Some. They are extremely resourceful, the little devils. And given this, I imagine the wood elves will make an appearance."

"Do you expect their help?"

"They are distinct from the dark elves, cousins though they be. Especially given the Erl-King's . . . adoptions. They may help. Golanlandaliay should decide, and they will do as he decides." Susan chewed her lip. "We will need them. The most difficult part is that we need the cooperation of the humans."

"They are disjointed here," Ruthe observed. "Are there enough in Scotland to bring together a good army?"

"Plenty, and only they could pose a serious threat to the dark elves in physical combat." They had watched Scotland for the past years with much amusement, what with the Scots tossing one king after another into the grave. The counties were constantly quarreling. Now, Susan wished the humans could be a little less human.

Ruthe scampered to join Joly at looking into the cloudy cauldron. "They keep changing kings. Perhaps we should have him at the meeting. I still don't see why we —"

"Their king is weak," Susan answered. "At least Mac-Beth had backbone . . . No, if anyone can bring the Scots together, it will be the one who seems to least want to do it."

"The Thane of Fife?"

"Aye. MacDuff, the man of no woman born."

"But," countered Ruthe, "the Iron Thane intends to leave."

"Forget the Scots without him. We must stop that, if we can. I pray our visit this evening helped," Susan said. They had perhaps gone a bit far with the lesson on leaving, but there seemed no better way. "And we must get him to find his way to the meeting. Perhaps the Syth can be of service in that."

"Oh," moaned Joly, staring into the waters and seeing something come clear. "Oh, no."

"What?" Susan looked at her youngest sister.

"If what I see is true, MacDuff is going nowhere." Her sisters stared over her shoulders and saw it now. Something huge and black and coiling and stretched over heath and glen, out into the sea and around the entire country. "And neither are we."

"It's a wall," Ruthe almost cooed in admiration at its completed form. It was tall, so tall that physically flying over it would be impossible. The Syth would not be able to jump it for long, either. But there was something more about it. It seemed to ebb and flow along itself, like a moving belt of . . . yes. Life. It was alive. "Damn him. Can he do this?"

Susan spoke softly, reviewing what she knew of the Erl-King, just what he was capable of doing. "He can and he will."

"Can we get past it?"

She looked now, using the vision with which she was blessed as best she could, staring out to the borders, towards England, towards the Orkneys and Shetlands to the north, to the Hebrides in the southwest. Just a beginning, now, just a thin line of blackness, creeping, moaning, layering itself, still invisible to any human who might chance to walk upon it. *Goddess, how did he learn this?* Susan thought she must immediately alert the Syth, but dismissed this. The Syth would know. Graymalkin reached up and deftly batted a fallen lock of hair from her left eye. "Once it is up?" she whispered, silently calculating how long it would take. "Not a chance."

Julia counted the coins again. They lay strewn along the small table, a meager handful of gold and silver. They had not changed in number. *How,* she thought, *how are we going to survive at this rate?* She had spent the entire fall, going out of Oban each morning in her small boat, onto the Firth of Lorne, fishing like any other Oban fisherman the whole day through, and returning that night, and for what? Now, when it was beginning to get cold, and fishing was not going to get any easier, she had little more than that which she had had at end of summer. Each season brought promise of perhaps having a little left over, with maybe the ability to leave, to go somewhere else. The end of each season brought the realization that it would be, if ever, *not now.* Later. Next season. She should have learned, she grimly thought, from her father, who taught her to fish and finally left her alone, or even from her mother, who preceded his exit by so many years, who watched him fish his life away and learn the same lesson she did: something always comes up. If you leave, you will come home or something will keep you from leaving. Something will stop you and hold you back. So why come home?

The townsfolk didn't make it any easier, either. She grimaced, rubbing her hands. They were tired and aching from handling the blasted net all day and bringing in the boat and cleaning the catch, what there was of it, and trying to trade it. Julia reflected that her hands weren't getting any younger, and neither was she. The townsfolk did not like her, she knew. In fact, put more correctly, they feared her; she heard them whispering amongst themselves as she walked in the market, hawking her fish, making her meager living, and making it alone. She heard the rumors, and ignored those which she knew to be untrue. Those that struck most closely at the truth, she might stop and listen to, perking her ears and pretending to be fascinated by some seamstress's shawls, trying to find out: *What do they know? How much? And when am I leaving?* Sometimes it was as if the town wanted to drive her away, not to see her because she lived alone and had no man and worked with her hands. At the same time something kept her: the promise of a good catch, a bright day on the Firth, other comforts. . . .

Someone knocked at the cottage door. She suppressed the urge to gasp and began hiding things, as she always did when they came. *Just a while,* she thought, *they will trouble me for just a while and then they will tire and go away.* She smiled slightly at the thought of the disappearance of the visitors she had not even seen yet, suppressed the smile as well, and unlatched the battered door. Julia took a breath and opened the door.

Priests. Oh, how pleasant.

She did her best to seem unperturbed. "Top of the evening," she smiled, and looked the priests directly in the eyes. It was a habit her father had taught her (". . . And lass, when you meet a man, look 'im straight i' the eyes. And he'll know your strength. No matter what you don't have and they do, look straight at them and never look away.") So she had done just this for her entire life and had managed to scare away every male she had ever met. Well, *almost* every male. And so now, with the priests, she sent the same message as always, immediately. *All right, get to it. Do not waste my time and I will not waste yours.* And she did this chiefly by that small but significant habit of looking directly into people's —

Eyes. Strange. No other word for it, she decided, realizing that she knew neither of these men of the cloth and that they had very unusual eyes. It was not the eyes which seemed utterly strange, though they were indeed unusual, but it was vaguely strange to be seeing them there, staring at her. The two priests wore the garments of the church in its complete simplistic regalia. One was a bit taller than the other, but both were largish of body, judging by the way their heavy cloaks lay over their lumpy shoulders and backs. Both looked like they had been living in a cave, or at least inside a monastery, judging by their pallor.

"Good evening," smiled the taller priest, who, despite his gray hair and big back, had a very youthful, gaunt face. "I am Father Kincraig, and this," he nodded toward his older colleague, "is Father Perth."

Nice voice. *Young priest with a nice voice,* she smirked inwardly, *the monastic life must be positively hellish on you. Go ahead. Say something I can respond to and get it over with.*

The tall one looked at his partner in embarrassment. Perth was an inch or so shorter, similar but lighter gray hair, and retaining much of the youthfulness of his colleague. He had a somewhat broader face, though not remotely fat. *Don't they overfeed you anymore?* she thought. Less charm, more study, she could tell. Perth, in a gravelly voice, spoke for his momentarily lost companion:

"We are friends of the Oban Parish priest. We have suit with you. May we come in?" he queried, indicating with his hand as if she had no notion what "in" was.

No. "Yes," she said simply, opening the door and ushering the two into the room. The sun was going down, she noticed, and she sat them in her two mismatched chairs and busied herself lighting a lamp. She leaned against the table and looked at them. Rather than ask them to go on, she simply stared at them, hoping they would get around to whatever it was, though she knew what it was, and *weren't those eyes strange?* Both their eyes seemed dull in the whites, as if white ink had been layered upon them. She could not get a good look at the pupils. They both seemed to have gray eyes, but they reflected so much in the centers that now, in the candle light, she could not make the colors out.

"We have come to ask," he grated, "if you are raising a child here."

That was not wasting time. "A . . ." She cocked her head in mock confusion.

"Child . . . ?" Kincraig said helpfully. "Four or five years old, black hair, like yours —" *Thanks for noticing.* "The parish seems to think that you are raising a child on your own."

"I spend my day catching fish and my night cleaning them. I have no time for a child." *Your eyes, the center of them . . .*

"But if you do have a child, you realize . . ."

"That," said Perth, "it would not be in the best interest of the child to be —"

"There is no child here," she said firmly, staring into their eyes to indicate her truthfulness and to get a better look. *Oh. Damn, I should have known . . .* She stood up and slowly moved around to the opposite side of the table, toward the cupboard. *Your eyes reflect like mad, don't they? Like light going through a block of crystal. Just like his did. Just like . . .*

"You are, of course, being difficult. The folk say that on some days you do not fish, and some have seen you near your cottage with a child."

My cottage, which is a good hour's walk from town? She looked out at the moon and back at those eyes and down into her cellar (*shouldn't have done that*) and said, "It is late. I have no interest in the mad rantings of spying neighbors who cannot imagine that I could live alone, much less with a child, who does not exist."

"I think," smiled the smooth, younger one, "that —"

"I think that you should go," she said, indicating the door with her hand to illustrate the obvious, or, she thought, *I shall probably have to kill you, and no priest in Oban will know, will he?* She wondered if she could, for a moment, if she had to, wondered if she could reach the sword in the cupboard in time, if she could survive. *But you don't want to fight, do you? You have what you need, don't you, Fathers Smallfish?*

The Fathers looked at one another for a moment and seemed to make a decision. Perth moved toward the door and opened it himself. "Very well then, sister, but realize that we only come in the interest of the Lord's children." The younger looked her in the eye on his way out, directly behind Gravel-throat. *We know.*

Julia shut the door behind them and looked back at the cellar. It was obvious, wasn't it? She had dug it in the floor herself and built the door which looked like floorboards, but they knew, didn't they? She dismissed it: They would have known either way. They were sent, she knew, to learn and do no more. They had been practically flawless, even their embarrassment had been well-contrived. But they did not have to be perfect. It had been a game, for her benefit. And if they had had suspicions, now they knew. She cursed herself silently. She had known that her time would run out, that coming home had been a mistake, that no alias would hold long, that he would have found them eventually, no matter what the Sisters had done to keep him at bay.

Julia opened the the cellar to cast light upon one of the items she had so hastily hidden. After a moment her eyes adjusted. In the dark she could make out the shining, crystal eyes of her son. She called to him and embraced him, and lied that the danger had passed.

In the night, two Darklings flitted their way to the Erl-King. They had good news.

CHAPTER 3

Oberon stood at the edge of the rocky cave and watched the waters dancing along Glen Etive, two thousand feet below. As soon as he had been called, he had come to Buachaille Etive Mor, the hulking, hunched mountain called the Great Shepherd. Travel was not the burdensome thing for him it was for MacDuff. Queen Titania had been annoyed that Oberon should want to leave, when so many dances were being held and planned, so he had allowed her to remain with the others. She would be joining him soon with the bulk of his subjects. Oberon was trying to see what he could. The Great Shepherd lay silent and saw all. Not thirty miles away, Malcolm, king of Scotland, was beginning to panic.

A first glimpse of Oberon would lead one to believe he were viewing a small human child. A closer look would suggest a miniature man. In the history of human art, early sculptors would create "children" by sculpting perfectly proportioned, scaled down counterparts to the bulging adults they accompanied, and this was the best way of describing Oberon, king of the Syth. Oberon could easily have been sliced out of the *Laocoon* and given a crown.

Oberon tapped pensively at the bowl of his long, thin pipe and lit it with one of his pocketed sparkers. Men would not discover the contemplative value of smoke for centuries. Oberon's people had figured the process out rather quickly, and the taste suited him. He drew on the stem and watched the polished bowl glow in the morning light. A sensuous stream of smoke curled through the air. Like his thoughts, they began at a fire in the center and moved outward. Oberon liked his pipe.

His people were revellers by nature. They lived a simple, joy-filled existence of honey eating and dancing in ritual *lays*, celebrating all with which they had been blessed. The humans knew of them as they did the Sisters: they never truly understood, were usually only able to define the Syth in terms of relation to humankind. But then, the humans were silly, so Oberon and Titania could dismiss them easily. The Syth shared the witches' fondness for the occasional merriment derived from dealings with men. More often than not, if they were involved, they came down on the side of the humans because they had no particular enmity for them. Usually.

They liked their ground, for instance, and their territory was liberally defined. Not a small number of humans had made the painful mistake of plowing over the hallowed sites of their midnight *lays*. Borders must be respected. For their part, they had done their share of stealing a babe or two to put to work as a henchman in Oberon's service, but only very occasionally. A human raised by Oberon would live an extremely long time.

The humans generally regarded the Syth with a simplicity that was actually more apt than Oberon cared to admit. As king he felt a need to be slightly more serious than most of his subjects, but even he could usually only carry it so far. If the witches considered themselves guardians and slaves of order, Oberon's people were simply lovers of it. The way things were was wonderful, and his people prospered and stretched across the globe, indeed had taken new kings in some lands, as need and distance prompted them. In their constant effort to better understand things through the process of labeling, the humans had named them, over and over again. In England, they were the *Pixies*, as ridiculous and fitting a term as human languages could devise. In Ireland, from which Oberon had been called only a night before, they were the *Aes Sidhe*. And in Scotland, where humans had a warier look about them and the best road was usually the shortest, they were the Syth.

The Syth who had told his king about the wall had been right. It was, indeed, growing taller by the day. Now, as the sun rose in the east, it stood nearly three feet tall. No human could miss it now, and he had a fine idea what was going to begin when they noticed that a blockade had appeared overnight. He wrinkled his brow. His subjects in Scotland had seen the wall for several days and had failed to get around to telling him until it had apparently struck them that, once it was high enough, even the magicals would have no way out. Oberon knew, as he stood there, that he was allowing himself to be walled in, knew that when those in the British Isles whom he had been able to contact arrived — if they arrived on time as he had ordered — they, too, would be trapped. But though dancing *lays* was important, this could not be ignored. There would be time for *lays* later, he had to hope. War between the races had not happened in a very long time, and Oberon prayed this one would be short and that he would lose as few as possible.

The meeting would be tomorrow at dawn. He had come early to see what could be seen and view the

progress of the wall, even to check the veracity of the local
Syth's report. It had been true, and the message to hold
the meeting in the Syth cave in the brow of the Great
Shepherd had gone out in the early morning hours. The
delay on the meeting was intentional, though not at all
necessary for the Syth who, though they could not fly,
could run like the wind. The delay was for the benefit of
the human.

The First Sister, whom Oberon knew well enough but
from whom he retained the commonly understood distance of magicals, had come to him when he had first
arrived the previous night. She met him as he had skipped
up to the top of the Buachaille Etive Mor and looked for
the Erl-King's blockade.

"I can't say I like the idea of bringing all of my people
here and then not being able to leave," he had said.

Susan had laid a hand on his shoulder as she stood
behind him. Graymalkin studied him closely, sniffing at
him, trying to decide whether or not he was human or
other. By the smell, distinctly other — inedible. "If you do
not," she said, "you will face him alone once he has destroyed this land and moved to the next."

"We could all go, you know. We could leave the humans
to the Erl-King and go somewhere far away. He may very
well stop with the humans. We've never crossed him
before." He tapped at his pipe and puffed on it.

"Neither have the humans. He simply wants them.
Make no mistake, Oberon — he has no respect for us,
either. He will take this world and take us with it if we do
not move against him now."

The King of the Syth was silent for many moments, as
he looked out over the marshy land, at this small, tense
land of tired, short-lived humans who had so little to offer.
But Susan was right. He had no real choice. "And you
believe it is absolutely crucial that we fight alongside the
humans."

"Be sensible, Oberon. The dark elves are man-sized, twice the height of your tallest warriors. They are magical, true, and so are we, and we can do a great deal, but fighting the Darklings will involve as much physical combat as it will magical. Along with the wood elves, the humans will balance the scales."

"The wood elves. Humph! I'd very much like to see Golanlandaliay move against his cousin."

"He may."

"He may not."

"Then we fight without him. The humans should be enough, I suppose, when you figure in our powers."

"Is that all we have to go on?" he asked, watching the white speckles of light bounce along the trickling glen. "My Syth, your powers which, we must admit, are limited, and the brute force of homo sapiens? The Erl-King controls all things chaotic if he wants to, he —"

"No. There is another hope."

"Oh, of course, your celebrated Thane —"

"No. MacDuff is necessary, but he is not all." She was remembering the wall, flowing alive with the souls the Erl-King had trapped and used to build it. "We may have the powers of the Erl-King himself."

"Don't be overhopeful about getting him to turn over a new leaf."

"I won't. I was rather thinking of his son," she said flatly, and Oberon missed the importance of this.

"Which one? There are a thousand of the bastards."

"Aye. Elves like himself, and converted souls of humans. But only one human child."

Oberon caught her eye and understood. "You mean he *literally* has a human child? How did —"

"One. And it is my suspicion that the child will be able to help us as much as the humans can, if we can properly communicate the notion to him."

"If we can get him," said Oberon, blowing out a long

stream of smoke. It curled up and bounced off the roof of the cave, flowing in circles.

"Aye. If his father does not get him first," she said. A cold wind blew up the mountain and into the cave. Oberon sucked on his pipe and shivered slightly.

A Scot named Seyton held his cloak tightly around himself and grimaced against the wet air. He nodded at the helmsman of the small boat and the helmsman turned his head away to look out to sea. The waves were choppy but at least marginally negotiable. They were rounding the Black Isle and moving into the Moray Firth, and Seyton looked back through the fog to catch a glimpse of the Highlands as they steadily, slowly shrank in his sight. He was leaving Inverness.

Inverness had been his post for his entire adult life: Seyton had gone there as a gawky, curly-haired child to serve a soldier he had much respected and of whom he expected great things. He had been a boy then and, as boys do, he had wanted to be there when great things happened. The Chinese, he had no way of knowing, have a curse: May you live in interesting times. Seyton had seen interesting times.

He had gradually worked his way through the ranks of the guard at Glamis, had taken his place as their chief in the castle at Inverness, had served his master diligently, had never turned, never doubted his master's wisdom. MacBeth had taken him and trusted him, made him all that he was. Seyton was a peasant, and in MacBeth's court he had found his place. And then his master had gone mad.

What does one do when the person he has worshipped for decades inexplicably goes insane? Seyton had done what he regarded as the only decent thing to be done: he stayed. He knew, of course, that it was not completely true. Madness was no true excuse, then or ever, for the sacrifice of every value a man has ever believed in. A man faces choices: he can go this way or that, he can see what he wants and earn it, he can take it, or he can hope for it. He can destroy others in his path to get that which he desires, but in doing so he will have betrayed what he stands for, unless all he ever stood for was naked ambition. When it happens to an enemy, you expect it and call it evil. When it happens to a friend, you call it madness.

But Seyton had stayed, when all the others left, when there remained only a handful of loyal guards. He had seen the few new guards trickle in, those impure scallions stricken with the same disease that tortured his master. But he had stayed as the last truly loyal one, who had made a promise and was keeping it because he knew no other way. And in the end, the peasant-cum-soldier Seyton had been left alone, his master dead, his profession ended. He had returned from Dunsinane to Inverness, far in the Highlands, and had stayed there until the ghosts of his former happiness and rushing, great-eyed exuberance had finally driven him to leave.

He did not know where he would go, this Highlander. Seyton had found a young, adventurous boy, one James, to steer the boat and told him that, if the lad wanted interesting times, they would most assuredly find them wherever they ended up. So they had launched on the Moray and headed out for the North Sea, perhaps for Norway, perhaps around to England, as the mood hit him, or so Seyton had told the boy. Though he could not really tell his servant this, he did not expect to live through it. But he was reasonably certain that the boy would survive. As boys do.

"Ho!" cried the lad, bringing Seyton to reality. He thrust his bony hand out into the air and pointed farther into the sea. "My Lord! Look!"

Seyton looked — *what could it possibly be*, he muttered to himself, *a blasted fish jumping?* He envied the boy's youth again and *what in Hell is that?*

It was floating, he could make out through the thin fog. Something that looked like a four-foot-wide plank of black oak was floating on the water. Four feet wide and may-as-well-have-been a thousand miles long. The boat reeled violently as the boy yanked the rudder and pulled the boat around alongside it, short by about ten feet. Painfully cold water splashed onto Seyton's cloak and all warmth was lost. The Scot failed to notice: he was staring at the mono-lithic object. It was black. Jet black. Seyton stared at the underside of it. Yes, he had been right, it was floating. He could see that it did not actually go under the water. If it had, though, he may have been relieved, because what it did he did not understand: it adapted to the waves. With each lick and rise of the sea it warped and flowed, seem-ing liquefied and yet hard enough to bounce back the waves that struck at its higher reaches. It was a wall on the water.

And now, very faintly, he noticed that it produced a noise. Rather, it sang, moaning, so softly that he could barely hear it, and yet the moan was so *there* that it was almost painful. The side of the singing wall seemed to flow and fluctuate, like the top of a calm pool of water, with little knobs of water poking outward here and there, bumping, shifting, pushing against its own turgid wall-shape. Like a horde of faces.

He gasped as the boy did the same, seeing the faces pushing at the wall, trying to get out, moaning long and low on the water, trapped. Trapped.

As we are trapped, Seyton realized, crossing himself, feeling the numbing cold again. *All of us*.

In the coastal town of Burghead, on the northernmost tip of Caithness, not fifteen miles from the Sisters' heath, a man named Abel Galloway was trying to take his son out of a home that had suddenly fallen into chaos.

A neighbor named Barney had seen the wall as he had

gone out that morning, and had run back to the town to alert the people. Barney was imaginative, and his embellishments of the "Devil's Blockade" were, if unnecessary, effective. Someone had walled them in overnight, he said. Realizing such a wall could only mean a threat to the country, hundreds of people who would never have thought of leaving Burghead had panicked. Panic, in any town, usually meant most of the townsfolk believing they would be safer somewhere else, and the rest seeing their fellow citizens as the enemy in disguise. The obvious had followed. Fights were breaking out in shops; people were stealing food from farmers and marketplaces.

Abel had risen that morning to find his own neighbor pilfering sacks of oats on his land. Abel had rushed the man and had nearly put the full force of his massive, two-hundred-and-fifty pound farmer's frame into striking him a blow he'd not be wont to forget, when Abel had seen something in his neighbor's eyes and knew the man was not completely sane: a quick trip on horseback into town had confirmed his suspicions. People were running through the streets, trampling one another and going nowhere in particular. Abel tried to grasp what was happening, but none of the shrieked warnings made any sense. "Wall. Enemies. Devil . . ."

Abel had made his decision and was ashamed to think that it was the same decision most others were making. He had to leave. But he would go southward, across his own farm at first, before meeting the road into the next town. Avoiding the crowds seemed prudent.

It would be merciful to say that the panic was the cause of the imagination, that the people were in no immediate danger, that there was no reason to panic or fear yet. But this would be a lie. As the townsfolk ran screaming about an object that really held no immediate threat, they completely missed that which did, as it passed, undisturbed and unnoticed, creeping through Burghead.

Abel held the four-year-old Jess in his lap with one arm and the reins in the other. He had loaded what he could into a satchel and tied it to the meager saddle. He felt fortunate that the horse was his most prized possession that could be moved. He was taking little else. No matter; Abel had seen panic strike towns before, he knew the signs of plague and death and what they could do, and now was the time to put distance between himself and the destruction. Whatever drove the people, whatever meant their mad stammerings about walls, of which he had seen none, or devils, or whatever frightened them, he neither knew nor cared to learn.

The steed pounded through the oat field. Abel watched the fingers of grain part as the gargantuan body of the draft horse plunged through them, separated like waves under a ship's prow. He could go to Elgin, he thought, or Forres. Yes, Forres. It was farther but larger, and somehow he felt right about directing his course southwest.

Jess was visibly upset. He was confused, and as his small body bounced violently, kept from flying away only by the protective, massive arms of his father, he tried to understand exactly what was happening. Since Abel did not entirely know, he made no attempt to explain. To the child, some explaining would have been everything, would have put his mind at ease. Instead he stared at the ghostly, parting sea of grain and exercised faith that Father knew what he was doing, and that God knew what Father was doing.

And then someone called to him. It was after the horse took them down a short grade and Jess was thrown hard against Abel's forearm that suddenly, above the deafening, rhythmic pounding of hooves against the ground, a male voice spoke his name: *Jess.*

It reminded him of the priests who had come, that day in his short memory, to take away Mother and put her in the ground where he could not see her. Could *not*, Father insisted, *never*, though he knew despite his immense belief in Father that he really could, if he tried hard and severely wanted to. This voice reminded him of the men that had come that day, who wore sweet robes and spoke hushed, and treated him gently. Could Father hear the voice?

No. He cannot hear, Jess. It is just you and I. Come with me.

Jess looked up at his father, who seemed lost in the parting rows of grain. *What?*

Come with me, Jess. I love you.

Jess stared at Father again, silently imploring him to help to understand.

Do not look at him. He is not listening to us. Come with me and we will play games. Many games.

Games . . .

I will give you presents to play with, pretty things that you enjoy, that your father does not understand.

Presents . . .

That your father could not give to you if he wanted. I love you. We will play, you and I, and you will have many brothers and sisters to join you, who will love you and care for you . . .

"Father," said Jess, aloud, but so quietly that Abel could not hear. *Father cares for me. Father!*

And it is so hard, Jess, so hard, isn't it? He is big but tired, your mother is gone and your father works so hard to keep you and it is so taxing upon him. The voice was in the grain, emanating in hypnotic waves from each waving, amber tendril. *Come with me, Jess. I love you. Your father loves you but there is a better life, for him and for you. Your place is at my side.*

Was it true? His mind raced in its minuscule, four-year-old arcs, trying to see, to pass the cloud that always seemed to keep him from grasping things when he had so many *questions*. This voice was sweet, and he knew that sweet voices came from sweetness, like that of Mother, and that the voice would not lie, but *Father! Can I leave Father?*

The horse dropped down another three feet or so and stormed along. Abel Galloway tore his eyes from the hypnotic, swiftly flying grain and looked at his son. The boy felt hot against his naked arm and had gone white as a sheet. *Sick. No, God, no.*

Jess was lost in his own mind in conference with the voice. *A better life, Jess, where you will always have plenty to eat.*

Eat . . .

And so will he; Father is big, isn't he? And he needs so much food, and if he is alone he will do so much better.

Father! Jess wanted to cry, not really calling for help anymore, but calling, not noticing the violent bounce of the horse, not hearing the rhythm of the hooves. *Father.* He had made what would be the closest to an independent decision he would ever accomplish. *Good-bye.*

Somewhere in the roar of the hooves Abel heard a tiny cry and sickening gasp of air. *No!* He jabbed the horses flanks and whipped the reins violently. *There must be time, have to get to a road, have to get somewhere,* and now he felt the ducts in his eyes open and blind him as the waves of grain opened, and he and the horse and the boy poured out into an open road. Abel Galloway yanked the reins and halted, not wanting to look down again.

His son was dead.

CHAPTER 4

It was storming on the lonely hill where two figures moved steadily upward. The storyteller was leading Mac-Duff up the hill to be shorn. MacDuff was moving along to the best of his ability on all fours and bleating at the top of his lungs.

"Move along, Thane of Sheep!" cried the storyteller, and he waved his shepherd's staff ceremoniously along the wet and muddy ground toward the setting sun. His one good eye gleamed in the dusk and the clouds seemed to gather around him, circling his frame in the sky, swirling in creeping blackness, attracted to the seductive energy emanating from the staff the shepherd held high.

MacDuff pushed his sturdy frame clumsily on all fours and felt himself slipping as the ground sloped. The moist ground slid under his naked — *My God, I'm naked!* — feet and he tried to pull himself in the direction the tale-bearer led him. Where were they going?

"Come along, Sheep!" the talebearer appeared over the

Thane's bare shoulder and knelt down behind his ear. He whispered in a hoarse, sensual rasp. They kept moving slowly upward, MacDuff slipping every inch or so. "Time to go, lad. Time to lose your skin. Ye've been mucking us up too long, ye've slipped out. Time to move along and get it over with."

"What is going to happen to me?" MacDuff cried, and though forty-five years of experience kept his voice from choking, he felt the cold against his bare skin and suddenly wanted his mother. His feet were buried in mud and losing hold whenever he thought he had found it. He dug in with his hands and the grass gave way to more mud, which splattered in his eyes as he fell and shot out a grunt of air. He gasped and turned to the old man, who still knelt beside him as he struggled. This always comes. The teller tells the story, then he tells the end. The talebearer was about to tell the end.

A blue-gray lock flew past the talebearer's patch. With his left hand the old man mopped it off his forehead and he appeared to be squinting through the rain and wind. "Ah, lad. I wish I could explain. What is going to happen is what happens to all of us. Slaughter is a cold word for the most natural thing in the world. Call it the shearing. The cutting down. Ye've slipped past, but I've got to bring you to where you need to be. D'ye understand?"

MacDuff swallowed and felt a handful of earth slide down his throat. He tried to see through the mud and water caked in his hair and flowing past his eyes. He knew there had to have been a mistake in having lasted this long. This confirmed everything. "Aye," he said, and he felt like he was responding to orders long overdue.

"Good then, little sheep. Time to go to the shearing place."

"Where?"

The old man did not answer, but only looked along the hill. There, shrouded in torrent and disguised by its own blackness, stood a shape MacDuff could not completely make out. He knew only that it was a structure, that it was magnificent and dark, and that he would go there to be shorn. *We are all of us sheep, MacDuff.*

I knew it. I knew it all this time. Something went wrong and I've lasted too long. The wind howled past MacDuff's ears as he tried to see through the dark and water to the black structure. He was overdue there. MacDuff dug his feet into the mud and did his best to stand. The rain and mud spattered across his naked breast as he heaved his last breath of fear and decided to move forward. *We are all of us sheep. But I go with dignity. I am led, but I know it is right and I am led with pride.* The skin and mud stretched across the bone and tissue of the Thane of Fife and began to move it all towards the end. The swirling clouds above broke apart as a blinding flash of lightning clapped at the Scot's ears. MacDuff screamed but did not lose his footing. He merely, and instantly, awoke.

The steady pounding on MacDuff's eyelids kept him from needing to open them. There was no fire. The fire would have gone out hours ago. MacDuff half shuddered but was too used to awakening in the rain to be surprised by the chill. His tunic and bedroll were soaked. They would dry. A thousand tiny thoughts raced through his mind and skipped off in their own directions; he watched them spin away and did not chase them, but waited for his mind to clear. Realizing he would have to move in the morning (he knew instinctively that it was not yet dawn), the Thane thanked God that he had a penchant for long riding, because it seemed to be all he was doing. *Yes*, he thought, feeling the chilling rain trickle over his face and seep through the thick hair on his beard and chest, *tomorrow I will have to move. I am led. We are all of us sheep.*

Sheep . . . that he had to go to the Great Shepherd did not take a Thane to discern. MacDuff wondered in the rhythmic drizzle whether or not the Great Shepherd would tell him to go get shorn. Even so, that was where he must go, he knew, even if he did not know exactly why. And as the Thane of Fife lay in the Scottish rain, the clouds swirled in his mind and urged him back to a sounder sleep. And he would have pulled a blanket past his face to cover it, but he wanted to feel the rain drumming at his eyes.

"You said it would be safe."

"I know," Ruthe said.

Paddock fluttered his wings and shifted his weight. He sat on a wooden post, against which Julia had always tied her fishing dinghy. Julia took a piece of fish from a pail beside the cottage door and fed it to him. She ran her hand down the fowl's sturdy frame and changed the subject.

"I see Paddock remains well-fed."

Ruthe shrugged slightly. She listened a moment to the massive bird's heartbeat. It was pumping regularly. Any owl was an efficiently built natural machine, but this one, being *other*, was bound to live an extraordinarily long life. She turned her gaze on Julia's frame. The woman's heartbeat was slower than most, Ruthe noticed. It, too, pumped a great deal of blood through its host. At Julia's age, the unreliable pump with which humans are cursed should have long since sped past a healthy pace, but a vigorous life had kept the fisher fit. Julia had the heart of a girl half her years. A few joints would give, in time, and the whole body would eventually wear out, especially at the pace she was going. But the heart would last. Ruthe winced inside and suppressed her tendency to guess the life expectancy of the humans she encountered. She did not want to know when her friend would die.

Douglas came ambling up to the stoop where his mother sat and proudly produced a toad. His hair was caked in whatever dirt he had chosen to roll around in. "Look!"

"Wonderful," Julia smiled. *How revolting*. His propensity for filthiness confounded her, but she tried to hide it. "But I think Aunt Ruthe should like to feed that to Paddock, so you should probably take it somewhere else."

She poked him in the stomach and the pale boy skipped away again, unsure of his mother's verity but not taking chances. He got four yards from the stoop and eyed the owl for a second. *No*, he was sure, *Paddock does not want my toad*. A closer look showed him the owl was in fact eating the fish only out of politeness, and the boy labelled the feeding a game. He dismissed his mother's game and ran on. Mother had said they would be leaving soon, and he wanted to play more.

"He's grown beautifully," Ruthe smiled, sitting down by Julia on the stoop. She propped herself against the doorframe and lay her head on her right hand.

Julia scowled. "God knows he should, the way he eats." The scowl gave way to a smile as she watched her son. Douglas was busy trying to convince the toad to do backflips. She glanced back at Ruthe and lay against the door herself. "He'll be quite a man, I suppose." She closed her eyes a moment. She remembered in a second the entire ordeal. The Sisters had helped her, then, had taken her away and seen the birth of the child in all of its incredible pain. *God, no one ever tells you about that*. They had helped her slip back to Oban and into her life. Only Ruthe had visited on occasion since; Susan and Joly had chosen, perhaps wisely, to keep their distance.

Ruthe had taken her own share of warnings about enjoying a friendship with a mortal. She had never done so before, but she knew it would end in hurt. Any magical could see that the span of one human's life would seem, in the hundreds of years she would view after her friend's demise, like a breath. Gone. Barely remembered. Emotion of this sort was dangerous, it was why the Sisters chiefly stuck to either amusement harassing the humans or a simple, contemplative distance. The cycle would continue as always. One human was nothing. And when she had made a friend of a nothing, she had set herself up for unnecessary pain. And in a vague way, the seeming lack of necessity had made Ruthe love her friend all the more. The pain shackled her as it exquisitely shackled all mortals to their lives. Julia would go, someday. For once Ruthe had allowed herself to see as humans: now was a very valuable now, when one ignored the cycle.

"How much can you see?" asked Julia.

"Not enough."

"He will not take my child," Julia pronounced flatly.

"Not if we can help it," Ruthe answered, honestly. There was no need to lie. "We will need him on our side."

Julia sat up and rummaged through her sack of goods. She needed very little. She felt a moment's elation and agony as she reminded herself that she had sold her dinghy to buy a horse. Her bridges were burned. She slipped Paddock another sliver of fish and he snapped it up good-naturedly.

"I'm not certain he understands completely," said Ruthe.

Julia laughed almost bitterly, but the laugh was tender. "I'm sure Douglas will understand enough when the time comes. He may understand too well." She stood up and ran her fingers through her thick, black hair. "I suppose we're through here."

Ruthe unfolded herself beside Julia. The fisher slung the sack over her shoulder and walked to the horse, which she had hitched to the fence that surrounded her cottage. Ruthe followed. Julia ran a firm hand over the length of the animal's side and felt the lull before the storm passing. "Where?"

"The far side of the Great Shepherd," said Ruthe, behind her. "Julia." She touched her friend on the arm and Julia turned to meet her eyes. "I promise —"

"Don't. I know you can't. We'll do the best we are able. My son is strong." She turned toward Douglas and the toad, which the boy had already succeeded in training. Douglas looked up and saw his mother motioning for him to come along. "And the Erl-King is out of order."

"As always," Ruthe said. Douglas came running up and she mussed his hair. Julia was already on the horse. Ruthe deftly picked up the boy and placed him in front of Julia. He winked a crystal eye and Aunt Ruthe winked back.

"Aye," Julia said, taking the reins in hand to begin the forty-mile trek. "As always." She sighed and looked past her friend at the rolling form of the Great Shepherd in the distance. She saw the shrinking silhouette of Paddock, already well on his way.

"He lived," Donner said. He clutched slightly at his chest, constantly aware of the mellow ache that came from the long cut along his breast. It was not deep, it merely stung, and he felt uncomfortable wearing the bandage that surrounded his torso underneath his tunic. It was obvious and it hurt his pride. Donner waited for the king to answer. He wondered what to expect. He had rather expected a burst of kingly wrath in punishment for a failed mission. *Fine*, he thought, *if you wanted the old man killed, you should have sent Dukane. Dukane would have quite literally bitten his head off.* He doubted even this, though; he doubted there was anyone who could have beaten the soldier he had been told to attack. He had known it was impossible because everyone knew it. But the king said differently; he was king, ergo he was correct. But Malcolm had not been correct, and now Donner's target was alive and his friend was dead and his career was ruined for certain and his chest hurt like Hell. Welcome to Scotland. The king simply sat there, looking tired. Donner had waited half a day to make his report.

Messengers had been scurrying in and out of the king's chambers at a constant and rapid clip.

"Lived," King Malcolm repeated. Ah. Well. So Mac-Duff lives. "And the . . . other?"

"Dead, my liege."

Malcolm blinked and understood, absently staring at the bulge in Donner's tunic that he felt sure was a very large swath of bandages. It was just a focal point; he did not care. "How unfortunate."

Donner accepted this and filed the thoughts of his partner away. "He said . . ." Donner began and shut up.

Too late. "What."

"Nothing, my King."

"What?"

"He said . . . you should leave him alone. Sir."

"I was rather hoping to kill him."

"We failed."

"Yes." Malcolm looked the young soldier over and thought of the Thane . . . the Earl of Fife. *MacDuff's out there. And judging by all accounts, he must still be in Scotland. Has to be.* His mind threatened to begin a review of the day's mountain of reports on how the kingdom was falling apart under siege. He had wanted to kill MacDuff two days before when things looked stable. Now it didn't seem so important that he die. A tiny voice told him it might even be important that MacDuff be alive; he ignored this.

The king sighed and rubbed his head. He needed to send an army to the Northern Coast to settle the rioting before he could send one to the south. And the west. And the east. And he had to prepare for the attack that was bound to come with the siege. And he had to meet with the collected clan leaders. And he had to wonder whether an enemy that could put an unbreachable wall around an entire country could be beaten. He had to rest. He suddenly remembered the soldier was still standing there and wondered if he looked as disjointed as he felt. "Ah. You may go."

Donner blinked. He felt justified in being resentful. *You don't care? I lose a man you called a "dire enemy" of Scotland and lose a friend in the process and you don't care?* But he was not ignorant of the situation. He simply felt a moment's sadness that what had been important to Scotland when he was asked to risk his life about it had lost its importance and been replaced by something else. He felt annoyed, as much as any believer was capable of, that his kind seemed destined to perpetually fall between the cracks. He felt sad that he could never stay on top. Malcolm was feeling something very similar.

"I said that will be all, soldier."

Titania had arrived at dawn with a great following and her usual pomp. She and her retinue of Syth had travelled by night across the plane toward the Buachaille Etive Mor. The impression Oberon had as he watched her approach was that of a queen in a coach. They skimmed across the land, she in the middle, as four guards spun revolutions around her. He watched her approach, as if in slow motion, the central point in a blurred wheel of bodies flung around her and keeping time as she ran towards the Shepherd. If she slowed, they slowed their forward momentum and maintained their revolving speed. It was a headache to learn, Oberon knew, and he tried to imagine why in the world he had allowed the custom to spawn, so many years ago. Incredible. He had seen the soldiers train and knew that only the most agile became the bodyguards of the queen. That spin-shield they created was as much for show as it was a real defense, but royalty is royalty, and tradition is tradition. The young cadets fought over the right to flank the queen, and they worked hard to get over the nausea the maneuver created.

They spun their way up the hill to the edge of the cave

and halted at Titania's command. Suddenly a blur became four Syth standing square around their queen.

"Darling." Oberon smiled, as a curl of smoke punctuated his greeting.

"Oberon," she said. "I think you would be naked without that thing hanging out of your mouth. Someday I shall have to share with you a few theories I have about oral fixations." She stepped out of the square and embraced her husband warmly. Titania was somewhat shorter than Oberon but just as sturdily built, just as proportionately small, just as much like a refuge from the *Laocoon*. Her hair was white and curled, with a few strands of red here and there, like licks of fire in the snow. No wrinkles surrounded her green eyes, nor flanked her thinnish mouth. That would take centuries. And, of course, she had centuries.

"Now," she said, as she slid out of her cape and handed it to the young Syth at her side, "just what brings us to this neck of the woods?" Titania smiled. The war had not started yet and for a moment it was gone.

The Thane of Fife reached the western face of the Great Shepherd by mid-morning. He felt dazed and listless. He was tired of travelling on hunches. MacDuff scanned the hillside for a moment, before his eyes came to rest on the obvious trace of a cave entrance. The green silk that carpeted the Shepherd had been punctured half a mile up. *Well. I imagine that's it.*

MacDuff sighed and slid off his horse. He winced slightly. So much riding had chafed his thighs and the leather of his pants slid viciously over the welts. There had been a time, he knew, when he did so much riding so regularly, that he had callouses there to afford enough protection for any trip. But since the campaign wherein Malcolm gained the throne, he had had little to do but watch the government stumble around. He winced again and smiled, and began to slowly climb the grade. Limping was useless. The callouses on his thighs would come back. A few more days like this, he was beginning to think, and he would be able to crack walnuts between them.

Something flew past him on the right at an incredible speed. MacDuff felt a slight wind and looked to catch a fleeting blur, but no more. He shrugged. Just then he felt another one a yard or so to his left. He heard an odd sound as it passed. He remembered a particular battle on a day that seemed to be a hundred years ago, when the Thane of Cawdor had turned traitor. In the course of things some fool rebel had actually thrown a sword at him. As the blade flipped past his head he had heard the distinct *swish* of splitting air. Just now two more objects flew past. *Swish.* He stopped now to wonder if the noises — and the blurs — had just started, or if he had perhaps simply not noticed them until he got off his horse. Whatever they were, they seemed to be avoiding collision with him.

MacDuff turned and continued to climb the hill and listen to his screaming thighs. Another blur flew by after a moment. By now he took it for granted. At one point he watched a rapid succession of twenty of the things fly past. He was curious, but he reflected that he was climbing a mountain seventy miles from home because some witches told him to, and he knew that curiosity had its particular limits. He swallowed the urge to trip one as well.

By the time the human MacDuff had reached the cave entrance, at least two hundred Syth had passed him within a radius of fifteen feet.

He heard noise past the entrance, which was about seven or eight feet high and some twenty yards across. He could hear people talking — throngs of people — but the noise was far back, and he could see nothing past the entrance hall.

"Welcome, Thane of Fife," said a woman's voice.

MacDuff turned slowly to see a beautiful, auburn-haired woman where he was certain none had been before. As if he would have missed her. The Thane bowed slightly. "You have me at something of a disadvantage."

"Hm. You may call me Susan." The strange woman raised a slender, bloused arm to flick a patch of hair from her eye. It was a humanizing effect, but not enough of one. She smiled only slightly, then stared at MacDuff for a few moments, as if waiting for another question. "Well," she became animated suddenly, "come along, then. The others are waiting." She turned and began to march down the hallway.

"Others?"

She kept walking. "We called you to a meeting, Thane. It should start soon and, under the circumstances, I imagine you should find a place off to the side somewhere."

MacDuff walked briskly to her side and matched her stride. "You called . . . Christ!" He stopped and grabbed her arm. She spun around, looked him in the eye. "You're a damned witch, aren't you?"

"I might argue the epithet, but the spirit is dead on." She shrugged loose and continued her walk. She spoke over a shoulder. "Look, I've played enough games. The meeting will start soon. You'll know everything there."

"And how am I supposed to trust you?"

"Oh, do come along," she shouted, as she turned the corner ahead of him. "I can't see that you really have any choice."

A young Syth named Kreen stepped into the newly renovated meeting hall at the Buachaille Etive Mor and stopped dead in his tracks. The room that the Syth had tunneled out for the meeting was huge, and at this particular moment it was filled to capacity. Everyone who could get to the meeting had arrived, and there was the usual hubbub with which Syth meetings were associated, only strangely altered. In the air was a mixture of many feelings. Seeing so many of his people at once first struck a jubilant chord in Kreen's mind: this was a *lay*, obviously, and what a grand *lay* it was, when nearly every Syth in the world had come here. But Kreen knew this was more than a *lay*. He could see Syth darting back and forth across the room, excited as he to see their brethren, some they had not seen in years, but a pervasively dark mood held back the fullest extent of their joy. He could watch their faces and see that half of them were greeting one another and saying the one phrase which all sentient beings seem to learn by rote and never fully swallow: wonderful to see you, sorry it couldn't be under better circumstances.

That a meeting had been called did not surprise him; it was time for the fall meeting in any year. But that was not the complete explanation. Strange things were afoot and he rather hoped that the king would waste little time in explaining. Kreen's chief had led them from Ireland. Skipping across the water was easy, but they had all been quite surprised to have to climb a thirty-foot wall when they got to Scotland. They had been told of a barricade in vague whispers; they had expected the six foot wall, but apparently it had grown faster than their informant Syth had expected. They had had to find land it crossed and use ropes to haul one another over: Without speed on their side, they could not stay above water. What had surprised Kreen most was the thinness of the wall: it was little more than a half-inch in width, despite its imperviousness to the Syth's most cutting blades.

Kreen leaned against the back wall and tried counting Syth that he recognized to pass time before the meeting got started. He had reached sixty faces or so before he quit counting.

Humans. At least, he thought so. In the north corner of the hall he saw Oberon and Titania seated and speaking with a group of four human-sized figures, all female. No, five; one had a child. How odd. Three of them looked vaguely familiar to him, as if he knew them without having met them before. Limited as he was, he tried to reach out and feel them. Clearly they were connected, sisters, he would guess. Ah. Of course. The Sisters. And despite appearances they were too obviously *other* to be human. The woman with them was human and gave off an aura of strength he was shocked to find coming from a female. The child was . . . the child was impossible to understand. And loud. He had an aura like a brightly burning book in a different language. Kreen couldn't miss it, but he also couldn't read it.

Conversing among themselves near the king and queen and his guests Kreen saw three more human-sized figures. By their long, muscular bodies and amber complexions he could make them out to be wood elves, though he, like most Syth, had not actually seen the elf tribes. *Aha. A delegation from Golanlandaliay. What is this?*

Then, Kreen slowly moved his eyes to a large stone in the south corner of the room. Atop it sat a figure, cross-legged, hands drawn together as if in prayer, chin perched on the ends of his thumbs. The figure seemed to be studying the entire crowd. It was a man, obviously, and a large one. Black, gray-streaked hair flowed back from a high forehead. A well-trimmed beard did nothing to hide the thinness in his cheeks, but Kreen could tell that this specimen was quite healthy, even if tired. From two hundred yards away Kreen could see the man's eyes burn. His aura was fully human, but . . . hard. Dark. Just a little bit *other*. And very closed. Where the boy's otherness seemed a part of him and burned brightly and seemed to invite deeper investigation, this man's aura greeted deeper investigation with naked hostility. Despite his apparent serenity and detachment, he emanated quiet rage, and Kreen made a note not to get too comfortable around him.

The man on the rock suddenly peered out past Kreen to the horizon. The light was dimming, Kreen noticed.

The short days were coming early. He glanced across the hall at King Oberon. Oberon was also eyeing the horizon and Kreen saw the king nod a few words to the Sisters and turn to the crowd. Apparently it was time to start the meeting.

The king rose and three thousand Syth fell instantly silent. It was the first time Kreen had ever actually seen him.

CHAPTER 5

"This is not an ordinary meeting," Oberon said. He stuck his pipe in his mouth and looked over at Titania. A thin stream of smoke rose high and bounced off the rock ceiling in repeating curls. "I thank you for answering our summons as quickly as you have. Many of you have travelled from Ireland, as I and our Queen have. Many of you have come from even farther." This was an exaggeration. Few Syth had arrived from beyond the British Isles. It was, nevertheless, perhaps the largest gathering of his people the king had ever seen. "What I tell you now I cannot say comfortably. Those of you who are now in Scotland," he chewed on the words a second, "will not be able to leave."

Hubbub. Whispers. Silence.

"The Erl-King has begun to gather his forces to attack the humans in Scotland. We have reason to believe he fully intends to destroy them all and then move on to all others. Do not ask why. It seems to be his way." Oberon glanced around him to look at the non-Syth. "We are here to fight him.

"You will notice that at this meeting we have some guests. To my left are three individuals whom you may know by fable. These are the Sisters. It is due to them that we are made aware of the danger at hand. I will pass the meeting now to the First Sister."

Susan stepped up to the natural platform and nodded her thanks to the Syth king. She looked out at the crowd for a moment. Her eyes swept the room and saw four thousand miniature humans staring at her. They feared her, it was plain. But the king had said listen, so they were listening. Good crowd. She reached up to move the same unruly lock of hair from her left eye; it fell and she let it go. In the corner of her eye she could see Ruthe gently bouncing Douglas on her lap. Douglas was watching Susan and petting Graymalkin at once and could not seem to decide which was the more important. For a moment Susan wondered the same. She clasped her hands firmly in front of her. The dancing light of a hundred torches lit her face and made it glow.

"You have all seen the wall," she began, "and so have the humans of Scotland. It seems to be constructing itself at a steady geometric rate." She stopped for a moment and looked slightly distracted by the notion. She returned to her speech. "Right now the towns of the country are falling apart. The people know they are under siege and are in a panicked state. The Erl-King has taken this first advantage to begin his attack with his usual habit. He and his children are making siblings by the thousand. Those souls he takes by force, he is using to build his wall and, we presume, his fortification, wherever he should choose to locate it. When he feels ready, he will attack the humans."

"And what the hell do you care?" said a thick, Scottish voice from the back. The Thane glided into a standing position. Many Syth turned their heads in surprise at the lack of etiquette shown by whoever spoke. "It seems very unusual that you would trouble yourself with what happens to us. So tell me, Sister, do all of us die, or just a few? Do you get a good view of it? Will you feed on our carcasses when we are all dead?"

Julia stood. "You're out of line. The Sisters do not oppose us."

"The bloody hell they do not, woman; I have seen their handy work. Go on, Sister, though you look little like you did when I beheld you last. I've had enough. I was told to come here, so I came. I was told to keep quiet. Now I'm talking and I want answers. What is the future of the humans, and what do you care?"

Susan glared and glanced back at Joly. "We cannot tell you that."

"Why not?"

"Because we cannot see it, MacDuff," Joly shouted. Her small form ran to Susan's side. "It's black. All black. We don't know if you live or die, don't you see, that's the problem! God, you're so damned mortal!" She stopped and threw a look to Ruthe. "To tell the truth, we don't care, MacDuff, as you mean it."

Susan tried to restore the calm. "But we cannot let all of the humans be killed outright."

"Even if we knew that for certain, though," Joly went on, "we would not be so concerned. We have no outright love for you any more than we have for the rest of the universe. It all comes and goes. But we can't see what is going to happen."

"And what does that mean?" MacDuff demanded.

"It means that we are in danger as well. Our future is enmeshed with yours and is equally uncertain. All magicals are in a precarious position. The fact that we cannot see the future means that the Erl-King just might win, and by that I do not mean that he will simply wipe the earth clean of living humans."

MacDuff jumped from the rock and walked swiftly through the waist-high crowd to the platform. He stared up at Susan. "Is that it?"

"Yes."

"You are threatened as well?"

"All of us."

"Ah." He stared. "And these . . . men . . ."

"Syth," said Oberon.

"Are to be your army? And what of the humans? Do you wait until we are all dead so this enemy you speak of can be tired enough for an attack?"

"If you would please give me time, Thane of Fife, you would hear what I am trying to say. We propose an alliance. We cannot fight the Erl-King alone. We need the help of the humans."

"The Erl-King I know of is one of legend," MacDuff said, but he wasted no time chewing on this. Legend was being redefined. "He has an army?"

"His children."

"I have not seen the wall you speak of. He has surrounded the entire country?"

"Yes. Will you help us?"

"Not a chance."

"Why?"

"The land is splintered enough, no thanks to you, without the added problem of siege fever. Our king is weak. I know him. I made him. He cannot lead them."

"You will lead them."

MacDuff sighed. "That's why I'm here, isn't it?"

"For all intents and purposes, yes."

"And here I was planning to go to England."

"You wouldn't like it."

"I know, I've been there."

"We need your help."

"All works out, doesn't it? You toy with us when you like, but when you need us, you wish us to be partners."

"Yes."

At least you're honest. MacDuff was beginning to like this auburn-haired Sister. "Well. The Scottish army and these creatures. I presume there are things about them to be of use. How do the children of the Erl-King travel?"

"Lightly," said Julia. MacDuff raised an eyebrow at the human woman. He had forgotten her. "They fly," she explained.

MacDuff turned and looked out at the Syth. "So that's it."

"Not entirely," said Susan. "The Erl-King and his Dark elves are blessed with cousins who do not agree with them."

"Cousins?" MacDuff now surveyed the three amber-colored creatures near the king. "These?"

Susan nodded. "Delegates sent by Golanlandaliay, the king of the wood elves."

"Ah." *And why not?* "Well, lads. Along for the ride?"

"Not exactly," said the front one. He fell silent. The others simply stared.

"And where is this . . ." he paused to avoid tongue-tying on the name, "Golanlandaliay?"

"Brooding in his tent," said Oberon. "It seems that elf blood, even split along philosophical lines, is rather thick."

"My king has sent me to tell you," said the front wood elf. "That he has considered the matter thoroughly."

"And?" said MacDuff.

"And at this time he sees no reason to interfere with the movements of his cousin, who at this time does not threaten him, nor can he be proved to pose any threat to any magical creature."

"And the wall?"

"Is for the humans to deal with."

MacDuff walked to where stood the front delegate. Oberon cringed but remained calm. The Thane of Fife addressed the amber man. "What was your name?"

The amber man paused. "Jan."

"Jan." He looked the man over. "And are you a soldier, Jan?"

"Aye."

"Ever fought a war?"

"I . . . no."

"The Erl-King. Do you know what he is?"

Oberon tapped on his pipe. "This is really unnecessary, my good man."

"No." Jan turned to Oberon. His amber face was drawn and serious. He was neither young nor old. "It's all right. I am representing Golanlandaliay. I will answer the questions of even the lowest orders." He turned back to MacDuff with a smile. "The Erl-King . . . is the cousin of our king."

"And he will not attack your king? Ever?"

"No."

"You are certain he wouldn't be that . . . disrespectful?"

Jan cocked his head toward MacDuff and sighed. "Scotsman," he said, "it is my view that the Erl-King would not be that foolish."

"And what if the rest of us all die?"

"The Syth will be mourned, as will the Sisters."

"And the humans?"

"The humans are mortal," came the instant answer. "They will die either way. I think you are right, Oberon, this is unnecessary. If there is nothing further . . ."

"And you are prepared to let them die this way, the way of the Erl-King?"

"Rather than go to war with the Erl-King on hearsay grounds? Gladly. Your sense of self-importance is typical for a human," said Jan, a second before the back of MacDuff's open hand flattened his face. Jan whipped the upper half of his body back with the blow and righted himself as the other two delegates flew around MacDuff and held him. Oberon shouted for order and MacDuff nodded assent. He had made his point and even felt slightly better. He threw off the arms that held him but did not move his feet from their place. Jan kept his distance and regained his composure. He raised a hand to his cheek. Slight bruise. A showpiece gesture.

Susan blushed and felt obliged to speak. *Wonderful. Perhaps a prior meeting would have been in order, where MacDuff could have gotten all of this fish-out-of-water nonsense done with.* The Iron Thane was surrounded by things he had never encountered before. She was not surprised by any of this. Susan was only chagrined that she had not taken more precautions to make it easier.

"I feel I should speak for the Thane of Fife. He has acted imprudently, but so has our friend from Golanlandaliay's camp. If we are to act together we are going to have to disregard our particular prejudices." MacDuff looked as if he were about to speak. "Oh, do be quiet. We all sympathize with you. Don't make it worse."

"If we are to plan, I want these traitors gone."

"I'm afraid," she said, glancing at Oberon for approval, "that in this case I must agree. Our call has been made and refused. Under the circumstances, I'm sure that Golanlandaliay — his delegation, that is . . . Jan . . . will understand."

Jan strode to Susan and took her hand. He bowed his long, amber body and kissed her ring. The amber man nodded to the other two silent delegates and began his exit, walking through the crowd of Syth as they cleared the way for the three.

The Syth were restless, they were asked to do little and standing around listening to speeches, even frightening speeches, was beginning to grate on such a large gathering.

The larger meeting ended quickly with a few choice, jingoistic words from Oberon and Titania. Susan and Oberon were eager to gather privately with Julia, MacDuff, Ruthe, and Joly in the back. Adjournment was welcomed by all: the larger conglomerate of Syth were eager to relax; most had only arrived in time to see the start of the meeting. Now there were reacquaintances to make and makeshift *lays* to dance and, according to tradition, a coming war to put out of one's head for the moment.

As the Syth began to mingle amongst themselves Mac-Duff looked out again at the dark horizon. Dark. *Dark already?*

Wait a moment. MacDuff felt strangely ill at ease and tried to place the feeling . . . was it really that early? He leaned against the wall and stared at the sky outside the cave as the human fisherwoman walked by, on her way into the back meeting chamber.

"Finally noticed it, did you?" Julia said.

"Noticed? Aye. I can hardly believe I missed it."

"Believe it, my Thane. If I were at home, I would still be on the water. With a few hours to fish. And you a few to ride."

"A geometric rate . . . the wall . . ."

"We were wrong. It is not just a wall," Julia said. "Are you familiar with the brochs that you see scattered about?"

MacDuff nodded. "Mounds of stone, usually, long since abandoned. No one knows who built them. Like castles, but small, completely impenetrable once you've dug in. With a small opening in the top for light."

Julia shook her head in disbelief. "Isn't that just what he's done with Scotland? Built a fortress and trapped us inside." *Damn you*, she thought, aiming her curse far across the land. *Damn you now and forever.* "He's closed us in like rabbits under a bowl."

In a place where he felt wonderfully ancient and at home, the Erl-King stood at his tower window and listened to the crying of the walls. Just as haunted as the broch that covered Scotland was the fortress that the Erl-King built, lithe and long, like the body and voice of its architect. It was black and alive with the souls of his adopted children. The Erl-King slid a tendril-like finger along the edge of the window and sighed.

"And how are my pretty children today?" he whispered. A ripple in the water trembled as it followed the bone-white hand. He listened to the house as the walls sang out, a legion of souls lodged and flowing through every inch of the structure here and across the land.

Please, father, can we come out today? Let us play.

No.

We will be good.

No. Perhaps later. We will play then.

The Erl-King chuckled to himself, and his eyes crackled wildly with delight. He gazed upon the world he was creating. Yes. This was an excellent place to start. He knew that Belial would be destroying Forres now. *How excellent*, he thought. *How positively marvelous.*

The little bit of light by which he could see the land disturbed him slightly. He did need to see by some light, of course, and thus he had left a hole in the top of the bowl, but the light it allowed in was natural; it was the light attributed to the deity of the mortals, and he felt loath to allow them this last comfort. And then a perverse notion struck him and he smiled again to the point of emitting the slightest malignant giggle. He held up his hand and felt for the section of the wall that formed the window in the top. He toyed with the soulstuff there, thinning it, stretching it, bubbling it around and over the last light in a translucent film. And now, for the complete effect, color. He twisted his hand and squeezed his fist and felt the soulstuff rupture and squeal, and he watched the film over the last natural light in Scotland run crimson. And now the Erl-King congratulated himself again, for he had placed his own, blood-red star in the sky. And as the shimmering red light bathed the dark and gray land, he saw that it was good.

Dukane's garrison of some one hundred and fifty soldiers began marching for Forres at midmorning on the same day the Syth met at the Great Shepherd. It was more or less dusky after several hours riding. When the light was gone, Dukane stopped his men to talk to them. They had Forres in sight — that was where the fires were — and Dukane knew it could wait another twenty minutes.

Dukane leaned back in his saddle and surveyed the land. There was some light, somehow, and it gave the near-colorless land an eery, reddish tint. The right hand of the king turned in his saddle and his chest clanked with the metal strewn across it. Dukane was known well by those in the kingdom for his appearance. He wore his hair long, and whatever exotic barbarian blood invaded him made it thick and curled, so that it tumbled over his shoulders magnificently. His jaw was firm and squared, his face swarthy. Every medal won, every keepsake he valued, dangled from thin chains around his neck. The hairless chest that heaved through his leather coat bore the story of his life: the scars and the flesh were a stage for the pieces of his past that clanked and jingled every time he moved. Below a long, thin scar along his forehead burned dark, obsessive eyes. Dukane was well known, indeed, for his violence in war and his unnatural yearning for it in peace, for his quickness and wit and eagerness for the clash of words or metal. Dukane was notorious and misunderstood and totally, completely built for war. For some men, war is an occasion for which there may not be time. For Dukane, it was always time.

"Men!" he barked. "I assume you notice it is dark this afternoon."

He smiled thinly, relishing the lack of ease he felt. Cherishing the fear. "The enemy has done this, whatever it is, whoever he is. That is not presently of our concern. The town you see before you is Forres. It is on fire because the people of our land have panicked and have been less than careful. Our king, in his wisdom, has sent us to go into Forres and try to restore order. The king assures me that we should meet with no real difficulty." This Dukane almost winced to say. Malcolm commanded little respect in and of himself; Dukane's respect tended to be that of men rather than office, and his vow to serve this king had rubbed his sensibilities raw. But Malcolm was king. Neither Malcolm nor Dukane had the slightest idea what lay in Forres, but there seemed little else to do but go in and find out. "Do not let the lack of light trouble you. The intention of the enemy is to provoke and confuse us. We will carry on as if his little trick were not there. Come."

In ten minutes the garrison reached the town and was hit by smoke and noise. Like most towns, Forres was chiefly built on one central thoroughfare. The road ran only about a mile long, with small tendrils moving off of it. But the houses, the shops, the taverns, and the fires were concentrated along this central line. Dukane rode along the cobblestones and squinted against the soot. *My God, what sort of people do this to themselves?* He saw no enemy, only men and women running in the streets to find one another. The enemy seen by the people was covering the sky, and confusion sent them in circles. Off to his left Dukane spotted a man running out of a shop with three saddles thrown over his shoulders. "You!"

The round man turned and stared at the dark soldier. His eyes were those of a trapped rat. He opened his mouth but did not respond.

"What are you doing?"

The man jerked his head at his load and back at Dukane. "Ss — saddles . . ."

"Do you need three?"

"Uh . . ." The saddles would fetch a handsome price, borne by the absent shopkeeper, whom Dukane had already decided this man was not.

"Are they yours?"

"Uh . . ."

"Put them back or die." Soot was turning Dukane's dark hair gray.

"But . . ."

"Fine," snapped Dukane, turning to the soldier at his side. "Kill him."

"No!" the man shouted. His bald pate was smeared with ash and sweat. The soldier moved around towards him with a drawn blade. "I need one for my horse. Please." He dropped two.

"Put the other two back then. I will not have looting in this city."

The man ran to the door of the shop and pitched the other two saddles through. "There."

"Good. Now go. Try to put out these fires if you can. Stay out of our way."

"Are we under attack?"

Dukane thought for a second, then reared back on his horse. His chest rang out furiously. He kicked the horse's flanks and shouted as he and the garrison moved onward. "Not yet."

MacHenry's tavern, on the main street of Forres, was not on fire. Even if it were, of course, the only person in the place would hardly have noticed. Seated alone at a rude table, a giant of a grief-stricken man named Abel Galloway was growing progressively more inebriated and, at this point, he couldn't have cared less if the roof had fallen in.

An empty tavern with a sturdy collection of barrels had finally distracted Abel from his trek through the town he

thought might offer a brighter hope than the ruins of
Burghead. Instead, it had offered only a more populous
version of the latter. He had a horse — inside the tavern
with him, no less. He did not have Jess. He wanted nothing more than to get drunk: The people running through
the streets grated on his ears, but he challenged them all
by whooping out whatever tavern songs he could think of
in a bellowing voice that gurgled with wassail.

Abel's hair flopped in his eyes. The liquor reminded
him of grain which reminded him of whatever took Jess,
so he did not think about the process and downed another
cup. Across the table lay his weapon. It was not a gentleman's blade this, not a respectable weapon. It was a
weapon made to be swung by a massive arm in a mighty
arc, and he had seldom had a real chance to use it. It was
Abel's axe, a double-bladed piece of cast-iron hell. Abel
stood up and went to tap the open barrel again.

Dukane had separated his men into units of twenty or
so to try to douse the fires. The inferno had started at an
inn on the northern edge of the street and had spread
from there. Others had cropped up. The main difficulty
appeared to be getting people out of the way of the fire-
fighting efforts and keeping them from looting. All the
buildings were small and most could not be saved.
Dukane was riding near the inn and shouting orders when
he noticed the whiteness in the sky.

It was just a flicker at first, a faint sparkle of light in the
southeastern sky. The soot in the air made it harder to see.
But the flicker was growing larger, and by the time it was a
mile off Dukane could see it clearly. "It" was in fact many
sparkling shapes of white. Dukane threw back his hair and
wiped the grime from his eyes. He could not believe it.
He was seeing soldiers in the sky. They looked like men,
but from their backs he saw the crowlike wings that pro-
pelled them. They looked like an army of birds of prey

heading for a feast of worms. Dukane could just begin to make out the shimmering reflection cast by the ebon blades.

Dukane spat an oath. *Wonderful.* "Angus! Come out here!" Dukane's second-in-command came out of the inn as it belched smoke.

Angus was carrying a bucket he had been using. Other soldiers were carrying similar vessels full of water from wherever it could be found. Angus dropped his. "What is it?"

"Look!"

He did. "Christ."

Dukane jangled as he whipped around. "Recall the men as quickly as you can." Dukane turned and galloped down the street. "Forres is under attack! Stand and fight!"

He was suddenly thrown back as a white figure swooped down and drove a blade toward him. The black blade caught in his hair and sliced out a lock. Dukane fell, unhurt. He turned to look down the street. The soldiers in the garrison had come out into the street, swords drawn. Many simply stood, mouths agape, unable to comprehend what they were seeing. Dukane watched as another Darkling swooped and Angus lost his head. *Good Lord, how do we fight that?* The soldiers were reduced to alternately crouching and rising to swing their swords up at their attackers, as the white creatures picked them off one by one. An eerie crackling sound mingled with the screams of the men as black wings beat rhythmically.

Dukane saw one or two take to fighting on the ground — hovering, apparently, was impossible. If that first attack were missed or parried, the Darklings had to opt for hand-to-hand combat. Dukane mounted once more and rode into the thick. Another one swooped at him. Dukane threw out his wooden shield and deflected the blade as his right arm swung his own blade across. The blade met that of the Darkling and skirted off. The Darkling had now alighted and Dukane was above him. He slashed at the elf and tore a gash in an ivory shoulder before his sword was thrown back by the elf's shield. For a moment Dukane was shocked by the crystal eyes of his opponent, the crackling aura that surrounded him. This did not distract him from swinging again. Suddenly his horse fell from under him. The Darkling, smiling, pulled his blade out of its side. Dukane threw his shield in front of his as he toppled over toward the elf. The elf fell under him, too close to use the sword effectively. Dukane had his legs wrapped around the ivory waist and grabbed the elf's throat in his left hand. He felt the blade of the elf slice into his side, but Dukane had control. The feathered wings beat frantically on the ground underneath their owner as Dukane dropped his sword and pulled his dagger from his belt. He slashed the elf's throat and watched black blood pour past the razor-sharp teeth. Dukane stowed his dagger and picked up his sword. Something made him drop it again and take the Darkling's blade instead.

On the ground, Dukane began to see how effectively the Erl-King's attack was faring. Another soldier came riding. The warrior dismounted and crouched by Dukane, first looking quizzically at the wounds. He reached toward the bleeding side.

"Never mind that," said Dukane. "It's a flesh wound. How many are left?"

"I can't tell, sir. We've lost at least a hundred." The bodies in the road above which fought the Darkling army and the speedily diminishing garrison gave testimony to this.

"Damn it all. We've got to . . ." A long, bellowing shout distracted him. Dukane rolled over to see a tavern door ajar. The building's front had finally caught, and the doorway was in flames. Standing in the blazing frame, silhouetted by fire, was the biggest man Dukane had ever seen.

"Good Lord."

There was no specific reason for Abel to assume that the flitting white things were somehow connected with that which killed his son. Perhaps it was the people running through Burghead shouting about imagined devils, maybe it was the intense battle that had finally taken his attention from his drink, but Abel looked at the swooping army of Darklings and screamed out with every burning fiber of his body. A giant, speckled draft horse came out the flaming door of the tavern and Abel threw himself in the saddle. The elves looked like they had come from whatever Hell already tormented him: this merited attack.

Another Darkling swooped through the smoke upon Dukane and his fellow. Dukane was throwing up his shield as the bellowing Abel came pounding by. The two were mesmerized by the round, gray flash of cast iron as the axe spun around and took off the Darkling's head in midflight.

Dukane shouted to the giant man. "Who are you?" He jumped up as two more Darklings came in. The soldier at Dukane's side caught a blade in his collarbone and fell. Dukane slashed at this one as it flew past and missed. He saw it double back, like some white, leather eagle, soaring up and over and back towards him.

Abel swung his axe and shattered the elf's shield. Another swing cut off an arm and his opponent fled without it. "Abel Galloway," he said, remembering the question.

Dukane was busy. He managed to deflect another blow. This time, according to form, the Darkling took to the ground. The Darkling swung and blade met blade. Dukane brought the point of his sword to the hilt of the other and twisted his wrist, pulling back his arm with lightning speed. The elf lost his grip. "Yours," rasped Dukane.

"Right," said Abel, as he finished the job by removing the elven head. Abel looked down the road. "Are these your men?" It was an instinctive question, and a good one, considering how much alcohol Abel was shrugging off.

"Yes."

"You seem to be losing," said Abel, and he sped off towards what was left of the battle of Forres. Dukane could hear him bellowing as he tore into the ranks of the attacking army.

"Thank you for noticing," snarled Dukane. He mounted a dead Scot's horse and followed. Thirty yards north, where lay the greatest number, Dukane could see, counting Abel, about twenty men left. Abel's sheer belligerence was an aid to him, he met aggression with aggression. But by the time he downed one more elf, it was all over. Whoever was in charge of the attack decided they had done enough. The point was made. Five hundred massive sets of wings suddenly turned and sped homeward, leaving only blood and fire and soot.

Abel and Dukane looked around them. Forres was in ruins. And now they could see the townsfolk, crouching along the roadside, slowly coming out of their hiding places. The eerie red light from the sky filtered through the soot and cast bizarre shadows with the bodies of the garrison.

Dukane sniffed. "We have to get back to Dunsinane. This will happen again." Abel, who had nowhere else to go, nodded. It was going to be dark for a long time.

Titania ran her hand down the carved rock wall in the ersatz meeting room. She smiled in bemusement at the collection of stone "chairs" in the center of the room: this is making do. Out of the meeting, out of the pomp, it was time to talk business. The Syth queen slid her cape off one shoulder and folded it over the back of a chair. After busying herself with it for a moment she turned her eyes to the stream of smoke emanating from Oberon's pipe.

"It will be all right, you know," said Oberon.

She nodded and sighed, and took a seat as Oberon came around behind her and stroked her hair. One hand fell to her shoulder and she clasped it lightly, playing at the palm with her fingers. "All those Syth. I hope so, Oberon. I really do."

The light from the torches along the walls made little fires in her hair. Oberon was silent for a moment, then asked the honest question. "Titania, am I doing the right thing?"

Titania looked up, not far enough to see his face, but far enough to see the stream of smoke bouncing along the rock ceiling. It curled and made unreadable shapes. It was his mark. He was here, and he was asking for help.

"Husband," she said, "I know it is hard for you. I know you have no great love for mankind. This makes your wisdom harder to evaluate but, yes, you are doing the right thing. You know the Erl-King. We all serve our purpose, husband, but this is not his purpose. The circle is broken. The truth is, you have no choice but to react. And though I mourn for our people I know this war is right, and we can only hope for the best. You are right. We will be fine."

And that is why Oberon had a queen.

"Don't get too comfortable," came Susan's voice. She strode in at the kind of pace MacDuff appreciated and went to lean on the back of a chair. Susan had a habit of looking as if she were beginning a homily whenever she had something on her mind. "We'll be moving on soon."

Oberon and Titania were pulled from one another's spell to see Susan, Ruthe and Joly entering. Ruthe, as usual, had little Douglas by the hand.

"Susan is the name, Sister?" the Thane of Fife spoke as he entered and leaned back against the doorway, his arms folded.

"I told you that."

"Aye," said the Iron Thane, glancing around to be sure

that all were listening. "Now let me tell you something. I want one thing, Sister Susan."

"Susan will do. Speak," she said. She tried not to sound annoyed or impatient or even amused. Not to sound like she admired his gall.

MacDuff walked to the table and placed his hands on it, leaning towards her. "No more tricks."

"I don't follow you."

"I think you do. You knew my land was threatened. You needed my help. Did you come to me and ask graciously? Tell me the facts first off? No. You manipulated my emotions, tried to scare me. You used images and information calculated to hurt me. Is this how you treat your allies, Sister, or just the human ones?"

She blinked and pushed the lock away from her eye. "We have never allied with humans before."

"I expect not. You must be in real danger then, Susan." MacDuff took a breath. "From here on out I want honesty between us. I do not appreciate petty manipulation. I will not be treated as a puppet."

"And how do you know, Fife-Thane, that you are not a puppet?"

"Because you, witch, are desperate. Too desperate to try to control me, if you could, and my thinking is that there are limits to your ability to control one man, let alone an entire army."

"MacDuff," she shook her head, "you could not understand how grave the situation is; we had to ensure that you would be open to suggestion."

"You miscalculated. Do not do it again." Their faces were inches apart and he could hear her breathing, angry but controlled. She understood. "No tricks. No illusions. Hurt me and I hurt you back; I leave and I take the Scots with me to leave you alone to wait for the Erl-King to come for you. And something tells me you don't want that."

Susan looked into the burning gray eyes of MacDuff and tried to read them. This was necessary. "No," she said. "We don't want that."

MacDuff sat cordially in one of the stone chairs. "Then you have yourself an alliance."

"Good." She turned to the others. Over her shoulder they could not see the grim smile on MacDuff's face.

CHAPTER 6

The halls of a castle of timber make strange echoes. Plunged into a permanent night, lit by candles and torches which made precarious shadows on the walls, the echoes that came now from the king's chamber were stranger than normal, as the most influential men who could be mustered to Dunsinane shouted and hushed one another into the night. At the head of the massive table sat Malcolm, all nerves and red hair, trying to keep a reign on a conversation that was steadily running away from him. The darkened room was lit by heavy torches along the walls. The table was a dim bath of the dull metal settings and the reflections on dark faces. Their voices echoed in the chamber, excited, tense and argumentative.

"What I want to know is," said MacDonwald, "how will we defend ourselves from this enemy?" The leader of the MacDonwald clan slammed down his goblet and filled it with a fresh helping of the king's ale.

"Who is the enemy, for that matter?" said the highlander

chieftain of the Campbells, shouting down the rest of the seven men seated at the table. His pale beard was outlined by the reflection of his goblet in the dim light. All of the men present spoke at once again, and then Malcolm cleared his throat. "We do not know who the enemy is. We do not know that there, in fact, is an enemy at all."

The Earl of Moray spoke. "No enemy? Have you been sleeping, king?"

"Aye," grumbled MacDonwald. "In England, probably."

"The fact is, MacDonwald," said Moray, "there may be no England. Why can none of our vessels get half a mile off shore? Why is there a wall as big as Scotland cutting us off?"

Armstrong, who led the clans of Borders, nodded. "Aye, it even cuts clear across the Cheviots . . ."

Campbell interrupted, "The towns in the north are in complete disarray. Burghead, Forres, Elgin . . . rioting. Burning. The people want to know who has done this."

"They want to know who took the damned sun away," said MacDonwald.

"Aye," murmured all, suddenly quiet.

Campbell continued, "And who hung a red star in the sky. Who caused the earth to turn gray. Who is stealing the infant souls of children in more and more frequent numbers. Who turned our world upside down. Malcolm, my clans have fought many a battle. They know the life we lead and they know the dangers, but we do not like the rules being so swiftly changed. Malcolm, you are king. Do you know? Who is it?"

Malcolm felt a moment's sadness at not being able to answer the man's questions. He struggled for a response.

"I have another question," said Moray. "One of conspicuous absence. Where is the Thane of Fife? Where is MacDuff?"

"In other words, could he be at the bottom of all of

this?" asked King Malcolm. Twelve eyes glared at him for a moment. No one wanted to consider it. MacDuff was not necessarily the easiest man to get along with, since the troubles, but he had been much respected. The old leaders knew where MacDuff stood. "I am not discounting it, for one," said the young king, clearing his throat. *Good. Go with this.* "He is certainly not here, is he? The truth is I have no idea where MacDuff is at the moment. He has apparently left the kingdom. In his place, I might add, I have appointed a new Earl of Fife."

The Earl of Fife, who had been silent up to now, sat at the far corner of the table trying not to draw attention. His head nodded. He remained obscured and seemed to make no effort to show himself anymore. He was obviously a spare man, with a wisp of thin hair cut short. He looked like a mouse in a hole.

Campbell scanned the new Fife for a moment, then looked back at the king. "Appointed? You appointed a new Th . . . Earl? How in God's name do you have the right to do that? The title is traditionally that of the leader of a clan. Is this man related to MacDuff?"

"I . . . uh," said the articulate Earl.

"Distant cousin," said Malcolm, matter-of-factly. "MacDuff has been stripped of his title."

"So have we all," muttered MacDonwald. The earlships were not going over well. "I have a different notion. I think you've done something with him. I think MacDuff has been taken away by you."

Malcolm glared. "Watch your tongue, man. You speak to your king." No one came to MacDonwald's aid. Malcolm, at least here, was right. To challenge the king outright was treasonous. At such a tenuous time as this, it was important for all to maintain protocol. As well-known as MacDuff was for his prolonged arguments with the king, no others wished to threaten the fabric of the recently upheaved society.

"My apologies, my liege," said MacDonwald. "I forget myself in these difficult times." He lifted his goblet. Ale sloshed over the rim. "God bless the king and his divine rule."

"Aye," said all, goblets raised. Droplets of ale flashed to the table.

"Aye," said Campbell, who licked his lips and peered down the table at the new Fife for a moment, then into his ale. "But I say this. MacDuff could not have anything to do with our present troubles. And I think we are that much more vulnerable without him."

"Aye," said all again.

"I have been to the wall," said another, previously unheard voice. A middle-aged man with sad eyes and black hair leaned forward. The other men had noticed him before but had largely dismissed him. All, however, knew well who Seyton was.

"I was trying to leave this country." He looked at Malcolm for a second, and the thoughts of his late master slithered back for a moment. This was Dunsinane. This was where they killed him. "I do not blame MacDuff if he tried to do the same. But I lack your respect for him, my friends."

Campbell watched Seyton's black eyes as the torches danced within them. It was no secret that Seyton had been MacBeth's right hand man. His distaste for MacDuff was personally motivated, even if misguided. His dislike for Malcolm was similar. Campbell wondered what kind of threat could prompt Seyton to sit at a table with the brat that overthrew his king. Now that MacDuff and Malcolm seemed to be on opposing factions, Seyton's misgivings were doubly troublesome. He cared for no regime offered, nor for the one replaced.

Seyton continued. "MacDuff, however, is not our problem. I came within an arm's length of the wall and I saw, well . . ."

"What?" said Campbell. "What is it made of?"

"That I cannot tell. But that wall is the most horrifying thing I have seen in my days. It screams and wails as if in desperate pain. It. I say 'it' but I have a terrible feeling that it is more like a they. I swore I saw a multitude of faces in that wall. They are trapped, whoever they are. And the wall traps us."

"Hell and damnation," said Armstrong. "Who is doing this?" The door to the chamber swung open and a tall shadow was cast upon the table. A flurry of wind blew at the torches as a low voice delivered an answer.

"His name is the Erl-King," said the voice. "You all know him." They knew the man in the door as well. It was the Thane of Fife.

The big tree was a world, and within its branches and below its roots lay a kingdom. The amber-colored creatures that lived in the wood and made their capital at the big tree were as much legend as the Syth and the Darklings. Like them, of course, the children of the wood were never truly understood by men nor correctly described in tale-telling. The red-colored men were the magicals known to men as the wood elves. Whereas the children of the Erl-King were absent light, the wood elves were rich with color and fertility. They flew like the Darklings, but lacked their cousins' alabaster, crackling skin and black wing color. They tended to remain in the trees and the ground. They were, arguably, to be the last hope of the allies of the Thane of Fife.

Below the big tree began a series of tunnels. Deep beneath the ground, protected by not a few guards and a number of tempting wrong turns, was the throne room of Golanlandaliay. A small group from the Inner Council were meeting with the much-distracted king of the wood elves.

Golanlandaliay sat on his throne, chin on fist. Glowing

firelight danced across his face and threw the shadows of
his company on the wood-carved walls. The walls were
magnificent, being, of course, of fine oak. Artisans of the
wood elves had carved renditions of numerous stories on
the far east for posterity: battles, births, notable deaths
and successions of kings. The way of life. There were legends there that Golanlandaliay himself could not be
certain of, but one who accepts legend for its value need
not question its verity. That the first wood elf was born
beneath the Buachaille Etive Mor and told to find his
place he held as sacred truth, as he himself remembered
the alliance, so long ago, between the first ruler of the
woods and the Erl-King against the first wave of the hairless apes to reach what they would call Scotland. He
remembered the hundreds of years that passed and the
gradual acceptance by the Woods of the men, and the lack
thereof on the part of the Erl-King. He remembered the
peace and the hatred; the final, tenuous, grudging silence.
And now, the action.

Tether, the chief of the inner council, began with the
obvious. "Sire, will the Darklings destroy the humans?"

"The Darklings will do what the Erl-King orders them to
do," sighed Golanlandaliay. The words came smoothly, as if
he were thinking of a hundred things at once. Which, in this
instance, he was. "But the Sisters do not see it for certain."

"What does he want?"

"You all know what he wants." The king looked away
from the wall at each of the five councilmen. "I am absolutely certain that the Sisters are correct in assessing that
our cousin wishes to destroy each and every one of the
humans. It is a very old wish of his. But, remember, the
Sisters are involved in a sort of a philosophical quibble
with the Erl-King. All this talk about order: it's his excesses that frighten the alliance of magicals."

"That he'll move on to other targets," said another
councilman. "Will he?"

The king's eyes closed for a second before opening with an answer. "No. No, I don't see that happening. He is, arguably, evil. But he is not stupid."

"And so we let the war go on?"

"We let it go on. See here, the humans are wonderful, but they are not worth war upon an enemy that I believe bears no malice against any but a particular foe. If he chooses to make war, let him make his war. If third parties wish to get involved because they fear his excesses — of which I am not completely convinced — let them. I will not be dragged into this. The elves have peacefully coexisted since time immemorial, which is more sympathetic commentary than I can extend to Oberon and the Sisters. The alliance is mad and impassioned. The Sisters are creating a panic which may prove as dangerous as they predict if they stir up the nest enough. We will not enter this war."

Tether's eyes narrowed. "Without sufficient reason. Of course."

"Quite so. Without sufficient reason."

Tether sighed. He would be the one to pass the message along. He glanced at the other four, all of whom seemed to be calculating getting out the word on the state of affairs. They would have to steer clear of trouble areas.

"Humph. As you like it, sire. Oh —" he looked again at the king. "How's the face?"

Golanlandaliay shrugged in humored annoyance and a bit of reflection as he rubbed his cheek. "Just a bruise. Caught me by surprise, really. MacDuff delivers quite a blow."

High thing.

Flashing across the red-gray sky at full wing, Paddock the owl ascended towards the voices of the stolen children. Round, luminous eyes absorbed the available light and surveyed the blackness of the blanket laid out by the

Erl-King. He could not see where it was, exactly. But when he felt the space closing in, he knew. Paddock tried to see the ceiling, black-in-black; he knew it was close and he was flying towards it and hadn't found it yet and then it was *there*.

High thing hard to see until you hit it. The owl lurched and soared back and down a few bird-lengths. *High thing that frightens my mistress.* Paddock shivered and felt the wind fly through his feathers. His senses were unusually difficult to gauge — the winds were not right for the time of year, the rains were coming and going with no predictable regularity. Whether or not the owl could surmise that if one put a tent over an entire island-country one necessarily disrupted the weather, Paddock knew this to be the case by instinct. Erl-King did this. Paddock flew in a circle for a few moments, watching the blanket.

It moved. Paddock's left eye registered movement and pulled his head three-quarters around the left as his brain shrieked *mice* — or at least this was the instinctive answer. The bird zipped to the black ripple and lashed out with his claws and watched them dig in and right through the blackness. Nothing stuck. The bony claw tore through black water — Paddock suddenly thought of the blanket as being made of water — without resistance or effect. But water left drops and no drops were left. When foolish young owls clawed at their own reflections in the water, to get at a second mouse, for instance, the same thing always happened. Splash. Nothing. Here was *nothing* nothing. The black stuff parted around Paddock's claws with barely a ripple.

Paddock buried his beak in his breast and dipped, flying straight down a hundred wing-spans. The whistle of the air brought more sense to the world so that he could think. He twirled over and back out a few spans, surveying the land far below him. In the gloom he could make out his mistress' party, moving on horseback eastward from the Big Mouse toward the land called Dunsinane. He focused more deliberately and magnified the forms until he saw the flash of straw that marked his mistress' head. Ruthe. Ruthe was always easy to see, what with that rodent's nest on her head. Beside her, Mistress Susan's auburn hair bounced like little mice on her shoulders.

Behind Mistress Ruthe sat a little mouse — sorry, little man — with coal black hair like Mistress Julia-Man's. Little Douglas-Man. Paddock opened his beak and cooed. He rather liked little Douglas.

Movement above again. The owl flew up to the black ceiling to see the rippling mice. What the Phoenix was that sound? A constant humming, almost singing sound like men might make when . . .

Now he squinted and looked closer at the thin blanket over the running mice and trained himself to quit seeing mice and he realized that they looked not at all like mice but like the lumps and crevices of the faces of men. Inky faces poking through, or trying to, the black sheet.

Erl-King did this. In the beginning, Paddock knew, Phoenix made all. She took thousands of mice and threw them very high in the air. She scattered most and clustered some to make her nest. She told stories with pictures formed by the white mice in the sky. They were there for eternity.

Crazy fool elf. Erl-King was an elf, wasn't he? Everyone called him that . . . Paddock's head spun around to look a thousand wing-spans eastward to the red mouse the Erl-King hung in the sky. *Blasphemer Erl-King. May he lose his wings.* The Erl-King had hung a blanket and hidden the Heavens and put a red mouse in the sky but Paddock needed only take one look and see that *that was not real.* It filtered in Phoenix's light and made it look like the Erl-King's own, like a false, red eye in a false, black face.

Paddock shrieked at the indignity and flew at it. At the last second, when he reached it, he extended his talons to rip it open. The talons sunk in and came out with the same result. *Phoenix*. He screeched and flipped over and dove, down and down, feeling the air whistle past him as he dipped within a hundred spans of the land, then whipped around again. He extended his wings to full span and whipped them back in a great passionate throw, extending his talons straight back and stretching himself into a sleek, feathered missile, screeching up towards the eye. His head swiveled to look at it. It was a hundred and fifty spans away. He screeched to Phoenix and cursed the Erl-King.

Seventy-five spans. The red eye grew larger as he flew at it. Break through. Break *through*.

Twenty spans. The souls in the blanket were singing again, the little mice were squirming and rippling and he knew that they urged him to end this blasphemy.

Phoenix! The nine-pound body slammed against the red film and it warped back as his head dug into it. For a moment Paddock saw inside it. A red and black sea flowed past his eyes and sang to him and then it threw him back. The owl screeched again and he absorbed his own momentum and flew for the earth as his brain exploded with the painful song of a thousand lost souls. The whole world had gone *badmice*.

Phoenix! Paddock cried, trying to focus on the figures coming up fast. *Ruthe! Badmicebadmicebadmicebadmice* . . .

MacDuff did not stop speaking as he entered, followed by no less than what appeared to be four women and a small child. Susan and Joly took seats at the far end near the door. Ruthe, who carried a long T-shaped stick, and Julia each took Douglas by the hand and found three chairs together. The owl Paddock, who had created quite a stir when he caught up to the pilgrims from the Great Shepherd on the ground, now silently flitted in and perched beside Ruthe. No one saw Graymalkin slink past MacDuff's feet and under the table.

"You have seen him in your dreams and heard the stories a million times over. He steals children from their parents and makes them his own. He thrives on your fear," said the Thane of Fife. For Thane he still was. Thane he would always be.

MacDonwald looked away. "Real . . . ?"

"Aye. As real as Hell." Several of those gathered made as if to speak but MacDuff silenced them with a hand. "He has placed this dome, tent, broch, whatever you wish to call it, over Scotland. I do not know how far it goes, north or south." His eyes darted around the table. Armstrong of the Borders was here, good, thus they are inside. There was no Thorfinn. This displeased MacDuff but did not surprise him. Thorfinn ruled the Orkney Islands to the north; he was a king of his own lands. Either the Orkneys were outside the dome or Thorfinn was too busy to come all the way to Dunsinane or Thorfinn simply did not care. Vikings, MacDuff mused, could be like that. "Canmore?"

Malcolm raised his eyes.

"How goes the war, boy? I trust you didn't send the rest of your army to have me killed."

Malcolm frowned. "I don't know what you are talking about, MacDuff."

Not with the rest here, MacDuff thought. *Fine. Now we can keep an eye on one another.*

The king continued. "I have sent a garrison to Forres, to begin with. There are riots on all the coastal towns. Dukane leads them."

"Have there been any entanglements with the Erl-King as yet?"

Life has a way of handing out cues. Malcolm was moving his lips to answer "no" when a sudden ruckus of footsteps and voices came from the hallway. The clanking of thin chains became audible and MacDuff turned to the door in time to see none other than Dukane drag himself in. He stopped and leaned against a wall, breathing hard and bleeding from his side. Behind him by three steps came a huge blonde who, after having to step under the doorway, followed Dukane and stood to his right. He still held the massive double-bladed axe, smeared with black blood.

MacDuff looked the two men over. "I take this as a sign of an entanglement. Dukane. How pleasant to see a familiar face."

Dukane ignored the dubious cordiality. "My men were attacked at Forres, King."

"How many . . ." said the king.

"Lost? One hundred and thirty all told. A massacre."

"Auspicious," said MacDuff. He looked at the silent blonde. "I do not know you."

"Abel Galloway."

"A fine weapon, Abel."

Dukane nodded. "An able one as well. This man is a farmer and a remarkable warrior." He paused, biting his lip, and said it anyway. "He saved my life."

Abel's eyes smiled slightly. "I was in a useful place."

"May I see that axe?" asked MacDuff. He took it gingerly from the giant and hefted it in his hands, playing at the weight. He held it up to torchlight for a moment and peered at the black blood. He held out a finger and dipped some onto the tip. "Hullo. Susan, what do you make of this?"

"Elf-blood," she said. She raised an eyebrow at the giant farmer. "It looks as though you got one."

Dukane's proud eyes gleamed. "Got several, in fact."

MacDuff raised an eyebrow. "Black blood. Interesting but incidental. What do they look like?"

Susan began to speak but Dukane cut her off. "As white as a bleached bone, they are, Fife. With wings like crows. They flew down and picked us off one by one."

Campbell swore. "Wings? Fife, what the devil . . ."

"Believe him," said Julia, who was tired of her silence.

"I'm sorry," said Campbell. "But who are you?"

MacDuff cleared his throat. "This . . . ah, gentlemen." He brought a hand to his chin. Well. Introductions. The oddity of his crew had rather slipped his mind. "We lack the time to grapple with the problems you may have believing all this. Let it be. Suffice it to say the Erl-King's activities have drawn the interests of several . . . powers, as it were, who have decided to form an alliance against him." He extended a long hand toward each.

"This is Susan. She and these two, Ruthe and Joly, are . . . er . . ."

"Sisters," prompted Susan.

"Sisters. Aye."

"And what of it," said Campbell, smirking, "What use are they to us?"

MacDuff leaned across the table. "I don't think you quite comprehend: *Sisters*." Everyone understood: everyone knew who the Sisters were. "They will help us. Believe me, I have every reason to distrust them, and if they play the kind of games they're accustomed to playing with me," and he nearly said *again*, being still remotely angry over the rather harsh vision of his family, that being their way or not, "I'll destroy them or die trying. But I believe they are sincere, and that is all we have to go on." MacDuff threw a glance at the slumped, exhausted Dukane and Abel. "For goodness' sake, sit down, Dukane. Do you need help?"

"No." Dukane sat. Abel followed, finding a seat across from the woman named . . .

" . . . Julia; she seems to be a former concu —" MacDuff looked at the boy and thought better of it. "She has important knowledge of the Erl-King.

"We also have enlisted the aid of the king of a large army of warriors know as the Syth — yes, those Syth, Armstrong, how many do you imagine there are? — Oberon is his name. He is making camp now."

Malcolm spoke. "Well, MacDuff, as long as you brought these, why not bring the faerie king as well?"

"Are you mocking me, Canmore? Because when this island is destroyed you will not laugh. Your name has two meanings: 'great chief' and 'big head.' Which do you wish to be remembered for?" MacDuff's ice-cold eyes were still and the humor burned.

Moray cut the silence. "And the lad?"

MacDuff looked at Julia.

"My son's name is Douglas," she said. "I cannot say he fully understands all of this." The boy threw her a don't-be-silly-mother look, which she ignored.

"The Erl-King is his father." Julia's voice was steady but the eyes gave the sorrow away. They held still, purposeful and strong. No tears. "I have no doubt that we can be of immense use to you. Seeing the Erl-King defeated would be worth whatever price I must pay. My son has power. It is the one thing his father gave him."

"But in a war . . ." started the Thane of Fife.

Julia continued. "He can communicate with . . . animals, some of them."

MacDuff nodded. "I imagine his father would be more adept at it."

"With some. The more chaotic creatures, aye. Rats. Wolverines. Serpents. Nasty, messy creatures with limited will. But those creatures driven by a more independent spirit, the noble ones, they are more susceptible to Douglas."

"Wolves . . ." murmured the Fife-Thane, flame glistening in his eyes.

"Aye. The wolves are his."

"Aye," said a small voice. Douglas sat straight and his crystal eyes glowed and crackled. "The wolves are mine."

MacDuff looked concerned. "Does the Erl-King know this?"

Julia nodded. So that was a danger, MacDuff knew.

The father will want that boy. Has he tried to take him before?

"Good lad," said Abel, without thinking. He had been watching the boy intently, lost in thought, and Julia had not failed to notice. Unstretched muscles and unkempt hair. Abel had almost said *Good lad, Jess*.

Julia smiled slightly. The giant smiled back.

Susan cleared her throat. "Well. It may be hard for the rest of you to tell, but it is well past midnight and it would do no good to have our warriors exhausted already. I suggest everyone retire and we resume later." Later. She had almost said *in the morning*.

MacDuff nodded and looked at the rest. "Aye. We must be ready at a moment's notice, but we all need sleep. I know I do, and I imagine you all . . . Abel, Dukane . . . need rest. Seyton?"

Seyton looked up. He had avoided MacDuff's gaze throughout.

"Seyton, you . . . you know this castle best. Malcolm has only been here a few months; I am sure he would agree with me. We'll leave it to you to find places for everyone."

Seyton had no idea how to respond, so he simply answered the request. "Aye. I suppose the Sisters and the woman should be near one another. The east hall has a number of rooms that should serve."

Douglas whispered something to Aunt Ruthe, who spoke. "Douglas needs a room near a . . . some sort of stable."

Seyton thought. "Stable. Malcolm, your horses are in the east? Ah. Well, there is the small west stable. Julia and the boy can stay in a room above it. I'm sure I can find places for you all." He looked at MacDuff. "And MacDuff? You should have MacBeth's chamber, I think. It is on the north wing and should provide a good view of the surrounding land."

MacDuff peered at Seyton and tried to cut through the

layers. *Fine. Rub it with salt, Seyton.* But he did not object. "That should suit," he said. He turned back and surveyed the room for a second. "I have one more thing to add: Now is not the time for squabbling. Our country is very much unrested already. If we are going to conduct a war under these conditions we must set aside our differences." He looked at Malcolm and Dukane, knowing he was reminding himself as much as telling everyone else. He turned and walked, and that was that.

It took a moment for everyone to disperse. MacDuff surveyed the group and mused over the last few days. He had to be careful, he noted, about undermining Malcolm's authority. He was making a bad habit of that and he hadn't yet decided exactly what could be done about it. Malcolm, after all, was king, and there was only so much rope he was certain the clansmen were willing to give MacDuff. But MacDuff had paid attention in there, had seen how they looked to him, and he knew that with or without a legitimate title he was carrying a great deal of authority. As long as he had the answers, of course, he might be sure of that.

There were a myriad of personalities here — a number of whom had taken leave of their own territories at desperate times to meet with the king, and it would take effort to keep them together. MacDuff noted that he needed to find out how many men were actually on hand at Dunsinane. Not enough, he feared. He strode out of the chamber and walked down the torch-lit halls to find MacBeth's chamber. He knew the way. Disappearing down the corridor he could hear Seyton leading the group. How would they come together?

CHAPTER 7

Abel Galloway bent slightly as he walked down the hall-way. His head ached and his muscles seemed to be one large lump of pain, but it was all better than he might have expected. The nobleman had been right; he was exhausted. He thanked God for his life. He followed Seyton, who walked ahead appointing rooms. He was tired of thinking. He was now in the habit of following, he noticed, anyone who troubled to lead. He thought again of Jess.

"You've been to Hell and back, I see," said Julia from behind.

"Aye," he said. Seyton had stopped by a door.

"Julia? You and Douglas are here; the stable is below the window."

"Thank you," she said.

Seyton bowed slightly. You can take the man out of ser-vitude . . . He turned to walk and noticed Abel lingering. "Sir."

"Eh? Oh."

Abel peered. "Which is it?"

"The next one there."

"Fine. I shall retire shortly."

"Yes," smiled Seyton. He bent and rubbed the unkempt head of Douglas, who silently wrapped himself around his mother's legs. The boy had strange eyes and strange skin, but right then Seyton knew he would survive all this. As boys do. "Well, I shall be on my way. Until the morning, Abel Galloway and Julia of Oban. Until the morning, Douglas, and don't think I don't know what your name means. Until the morning." He turned and walked, and then, just before he turned a corner, he looked back and said, "There will be one, you know."

Abel looked around at the heavy wood hallways and the torches. He did not like it. He wanted his hut.

Julia looked at him. "You will get used to it," she said, lying through her teeth.

"I'm sure." He looked at the boy and seemed lost for a moment. "About the Erl-King . . ."

She was holding Douglas' hand and squeezed it a little. "Look, I am tired and so is my son . . ."

"He takes souls, correct?"

"Aye," she said, staring at her huge door.

"What does he do with them?" he asked, and something in his voice cared too much for her to want to answer. She shook her head. In his eyes it was clear as a bell, clear as grief can ever be.

"Tell me," he said.

"He enslaves them."

"Oh," he said. He did not want to think about it. There was another thought, but . . . no. Change the subject. "What did Seyton mean? About the boy's name."

Julia tossed back her black hair and relaxed her hand, putting it on the lad's shoulder. "It means Dark Child. That is the one that fits. Or Dweller by the Dark Water.

But what Seyton meant," she smiled, "I have not a clue."

"And if we beat this Erl-King," said Abel, axe in hand, "if we finish him, can we set them free?"

Julia winced. She knew who *they* were. *Oh, you poor man.* "We . . . yes. Yes, we can free them."

"And the souls. They will be restored . . ." Abel did not want to ask it but had to, she knew.

"To life?" she finished. She looked at him and wanted desperately to say yes, to say anything that would take this gentle giant's pain away.

"No," she said, and her own tears finally came again for a moment. Then she stopped them, choking them down, defeating them. "They can never . . . be restored . . . to life."

Abel stood still. It was stupid to hope, but he could not help being crushed all over again.

"I am sorry," she said. She opened her door and looked in, then bent down and patted the lad, urging him in. "I am so sorry, Abel. But this war will not return those who are already lost. We are humans, Abel. We always will be small, fragile things in this world. Good night." The door shut before Abel could answer.

Abel Galloway turned and walked alone to his room with its ugly wooden door and squared off walls. Alone, he went to sleep, but not before crying for hours and praying for intervention. Alone he slept and dreamt of Jess.

From experience the Thane of Fife knew where lay the chamber of the late MacBeth, Thane of Glamis, Thane of Cawdor, King of Scotland. His boots clacked against the hard wood as he found his way past the torches. One misplaced torch, he mused . . . funeral pyre. Here and there he noted a fissure, a water mark, or a bit of mildew. A small puddle up on the left betrayed a leak. He heard a rat scamper in the distance. Ah, yes. Castle life.

He took another turn and finally stopped at a door with

no outside bolt. It was dusty but sturdier than most. Mac-
Beth slept here. MacDuff shoved at the door and it slid
open, creaking only slightly. His eyes adjusted to the com-
parative dark of the room and saw nothing unusual. He
took a torch off the wall and carried it inside.

Lady MacBeth, with her usual flare for the dramatic,
had thrown a massive, flowing bearskin on the floor.
Standing by the doorway, MacDuff saw that the head
turned away from him and toward the bed. The bed was
large, built for a large lord and a reasonably sized lady, and
a tasteful canopy covered the whole affair. The room was
tidy.

The flames cast dancing shadows in the bear's fur. Mac-
Duff ran a quick scan of the room. Was the room left this
way? No. Cleaned, it had to have been; any fool could see
that. No personal effects; no displayed axes and shields
and swords. Everything but Lady MacBeth's charming
rug had been taken away — purged, as it were, along with
the Thanes.

MacDuff slid the torch into a holder by the doorway
and shut the door. No, this won't be so bad.

He sat on the edge of the bed. The toes of his boots
pointed at the bear's head, which stared up at the Thane
of Fife with its polished-stone eyes.

MacDuff smiled. Forgot to get rid of you, didn't they?
He bent to unbuckle his boots and slid them off, wincing
at the soreness in his feet and the frightful, familiar shock
of cold, bare feet on a hardwood floor. He was used to it.
Liking it was something else. MacDuff rather loved hating
it.

He slid off his vest and tunic (*Lord, how long have I
been wearing that?*) and his pants. It felt good to be naked
against the cold air. And somehow, even though MacDuff
knew he was in MacBeth's chamber, he was strangely at
peace, not vulnerable.

He lay on his back on the bed and turned on his side to

look at Lady MacBeth's bear again, mouth open and growling forever. MacDuff's eyes twinkled. *You don't fit.*

It didn't. It was coarse and old and looked like something a warrior's wife and a vicious, highland hussy like Lady MacBeth would find attractive. It did not fit in Malcolm's castle or kingdom at all. It reeked of the *ancien régime.*

Ah, MacBeth. MacDuff lay back and rested forty-five years of head on his hands and stared at the shadows cast on the ceiling. He knew what he was thinking and he was ashamed of it but he stubbornly embraced it as the truth. *MacBeth, you were an evil son of a bitch. But you were one of us.*

But I killed your loved ones, said the bear of the *ancien régime.* For all that you miss me?

Miss you, yes. Yes, indeed.

Forgive me?

Not in a million years. You were corrupted. But I fear you were the last truly Caledonian ruler we shall ever have. From here on out it will be Malcolm and his kind.

Why, Fife-Thane, I think you are coming to terms with me.

Don't be maudlin. If you were here I'd behead you all over again.

The Thane of Fife, the last, lone Thane, laughed aloud, bitterly, and felt the slightest tear develop in his eye. He was tired. But there would be no war tonight. The enemy had had a victory today and would probably savor it.

Where was the enemy, for that matter? How could he find them? There were three witches here: was he right to trust them? Oberon and his little warriors were outside somewhere. Malcolm was here. Seyton was here. Dukane, annoying but talented, was here. The Abel boy was here — and big. And good with an axe, Dukane said. Dukane would not lie. And the boy Douglas. And a whole slew of clan leaders.

MacDuff was drifting. And for the first time in months, alone with a bearskin rug in the private chamber of the man he had hated most, MacDuff fell asleep, and slept peacefully. He had a war to organize and a tide to turn. He felt right at home.

As Julia shut the door behind her Ruthe simply materialized there. Julia did not start and Douglas paid her no mind as he dutifully stripped for bed, climbing into a huge nightshirt his mother had packed into his satchel for him. Ruthe smiled at the doorway.

"My, but he's an interesting one, isn't he?" Ruthe's blue eyes sparkled through her blond bangs. Getting an idea — even a random, relatively unimportant idea, had put her in a gay mood.

Julia turned to her and raised an incredulous eyebrow. She did not answer, but turned to Douglas. "Get ready for bed now, but don't go to sleep, darling, we still need you," and Douglas nodded drowsily. She rubbed her own stiff neck. "What are you getting at, Ruthe?"

"Nothing, dearest. Silly old Aunt Ruthe is matchmaking again."

"Your eyes have a very charming sparkle when you act juvenile, Miss Eternal Force of Nature whatever," said the fisherwoman. She looked at her son and softened. "I suppose you're not at fault for the worst of them."

"I'd look into it."

"Fine."

"He's alone, you know."

"Would you please *stop*." She shook her head, laughing again. "We have more important matters to attend to, Ruthe, as Susan would put it."

"And Susan would put it exactly that way, too, that was very good."

Julia cocked her head toward Douglas and Ruthe suppressed her smile. She stepped to the window and looked out, and down to the empty stable below. "Good. Douglas, you know what to do."

Douglas' weary voice answered. "Yes, Aunt Ruthe." The boy sat at the foot of the bed. Going to the window would not be necessary for him; there was nothing to actually see right now, anyway. He turned his chalk-white face toward Ruthe but looked straight through her, out into the gray night without stars.

Douglas' crystal eyes crackled in the torchlight, emanating power, more power than the child could possibly understand, but much of which he could already use. And suddenly, in the sparkling of his eyes, in a voice distant, unattached and unheard, he began his call. It went out in a language unknown to men, skipping across brook and heath, searching the glades and lochs until it found its target, deep in the woods, brooding and snarling.

Wolves. The eyes sparkled. Somewhere, a pair of canine eyes met his far-flung gaze, followed by another and another. *Masters of the hunt. Lovers of the moon. Hear me.*

More eyes found his. Bodies rose and tensed. Fur bristled in expectation and fear. One wolf licked his lips. *Who calls*, this one said.

The master of the dark stream, said the boy's crackling eyes. *I have need of you.*

Ah, came the answer of the one, *but do we need you?*

You know that you do. We are all of us threatened. We are all of us sheep.

We are not sheep, it chuckled, and the canine head tilted slightly. *Threatened, by whom?*

By he who has stolen the moon.

Douglas felt the hot breath blow against him as it thought for its subjects.

You fight this one?

We do, said Douglas.

Call me by my name and I will call you Master.

Come to me, General Belin of the Wolves. Duty calls.

The canine eyes flared in the darkness and saliva dripped from Belin's lips. At last. Belin suddenly could not recall if the master was the master he had always followed or simply had only waited to follow, but he had no choice or preference. Had the voice come always from within, and now from without? Or always without? He shook his muzzle at the unclear thought. The dark child said come. Belin would follow. His wolves would follow him.

Douglas looked up at his mother and then at Ruthe, and rubbed his eyes. How much of what he had just done that was truly, in a cognizant sense, understood, remained a mystery. Mostly it was instinct. He knew what to do, what to say. What he was. "Don't worry," said the boy who had called himself, for the first time, the master of the dark stream. "My wolves will be here."

In the inky distance, howls rang out and were answered, skipping and flying across the grassy land. General Belin reached the stable within the hour, as Ruthe watched from the window above. Julia and Douglas were long since asleep.

"My loyal subjects," said the king of the Syth, "every good man has his weapon."

Oberon took a puff from his pipe and blew a ring, watched it for a second, then handed the pipe to Titania. "Darling," he said, at a level everyone near could hear, "would you be so good as to hand me that hook?"

Titania was holding a box the length of a Syth's forearm, all silver and purple velvet. She opened it and presented to Oberon a silver hook half a foot long, with a ring handle. Oberon hefted it admiringly just as MacDuff was doing at that very moment with Abel's axe and smiled. He turned to his left and looked out forty yards, where stood a false man — a Syth-sized scarecrow, for want of a better word. The young Syth that had built it had even gone so far as to give it rude cloth wings.

Oberon threw the hook into the air and caught it, then spun it a few times by the ring. "War is a cumbersome thing. It is not our vocation; the Lay is. But sometimes war is necessary. Our ally MacDuff lacks faith in us, my servants, but do not blame him. He is a simple human too easily fooled by what he sees." And with that, the king of the Syth disappeared. When the throat of the scarecrow exploded in flying grass, a blur was seen, and then he was back by his queen again, nimbly spinning the hook in his royal hand. A gesture to Titania brought the pipe again, and he took a refreshing draw. He tapped it for a second with the hook.

"MacDuff does not see our power. But he will."

The castle that Malcolm III more or less inherited from MacBeth when Birnam Wood came to Dunsinane was not the sort of ominous hulk with which the modern Scottish countryside is so associated. Those castles may lie in impressive ruin, but even they had not yet reached the status of gleam-in-the-royal-architect's-eye in 1057. Before the Norman Invasion, the medieval castle known to the Scots was strikingly similar to what Americans would recognize from their own frontier, with variations. On a great mound of earth, a palisade of upright logs, each sharpened on one end, surrounded the entire grounds, which could be quite large indeed. About the palisade and surrounding the mound was a motte of sufficient width to preclude an easy approach on the wall. A drawbridge provided the entrance. The castle within might be very expansive, of two or three, and sometimes four stories, focused on one tower which housed the presiding lord. But it would, as already noted, be made of timber. The fact that none can be toured today is the constant legacy of the flammable kingdom. But there were trees to burn, and posterity is a tenuous enough thing that men did not often stop to consider what other men nine hundred years down the line would think of their house. *C'est la vie.*

❖   ❖   ❖

Breakfast at Malcolm's was a hurried but ornate affair. Since time immemorial the most efficient way to learn a person's true nature is to be around for breakfast, and the crew of characters assembled in the dining hall had the opportunity to learn a great deal. Over a typical offering of thick, fat milk and tough bread, sweets, and what passed for coffee, the crew met the day without the benefit of a sunrise. For all practical purposes it remained as dark as before, with only a bit more light. The cocks still crowed, and that was the cue.

Everyone was down early. Abel looked decidedly like hell and was greeted by many eager to tell him so. Julia and Ruthe brought down Douglas, who ate nearly enough to feed a large man, though Abel was in no danger of being overtaken. Susan and Joly sipped at coffee but declined to eat, and Susan fed an occasional piece of pork to Graymalkin. Ruthe poked at food, more for want of something to do than real hunger, which overtook the Sisters only seldom.

MacDuff had come down early and sat in the dark dining hall drinking coffee and thinking. When Oberon finally came indoors MacDuff caught the Syth's attention and asked him, "Can you spare a man for a mission?"

Oberon ran his silver hair back with some water he dipped out of a pail and sat on a wooden bench beside the Thane of Fife. From the table he drew a candle and used it to light his pipe. "What do you have in mind?"

MacDuff rubbed his hands together by the flame, then doubled them under his chin. He looked in the early morning the same as he looked late at night. Together. Iron. "I am curious about the extent of this broch. How far north do you imagine it goes?" Susan had found her way to the table and sat across from MacDuff.

"The man Seyton saw it out in the Moray Firth fifteen miles," she said.

"Aye," said MacDuff. "But the farmer said the men in Burghead saw it right off the coast. So sometimes it rides the coast and sometimes it cuts across the water. Apparently where it is convenient, as odd as that may sound. Perhaps it is arbitrary. Moray says the wall in the south is at the Cheviots, so Northumberland and England are out. But I want to know if it only encloses the mainland, or if it holds the islands in the north."

"Why?" asked Susan.

Oberon sighed. "I see. You want me to send a scout to the Orkneys to see if they are there or not."

Susan frowned. "What is the point?"

MacDuff sipped his coffee. "Just a thought, really. As long as we're going into combat we should know how large the field is. I also would like to pass a message to Thorfinn, if I can."

"If he's inside," said Oberon. He blew a ring of smoke. It hovered a second and drifted upward. The Syth had long risen in the field to the east on which they lay in their tents. They were wandering the countryside hunting food for their own breakfast.

Susan looked puzzled. "Thorfinn?"

MacDuff nodded and took another sip of coffee. "He rules the Orkney Islands off the coast of Scotland in the north. He is not one of us, as you might say it." He gestured vaguely toward the table where sat the king with the visiting Earls and clansmen. "Thorfinn is one of the Viking horde that chased the Picts southward to clash with the Scots, so that they finally formed what are now, for convenience, called the Scots. This land was once a conglomerate of many peoples; largely due to the coming of the Norse, we are now by and large one. Or two. The Scots, and them — the Vikings. But they are there, and I would like Thorfinn's thoughts on the situation. If he is surrounded with us, then I'm sure he has some. If he's outside . . ."

"Merry Christmas, as you say," said Oberon.

"Aye. The trip to Orkney, to the main island, would be nearly two hundred miles. One of your Syth could cover that in, what?"

Oberon puffed a moment. "A day, normally. But, with occasional rest, stopping for information, the unknown terrain in the dark, being careful not to trip or hit anything at maximum speed, and given that the wall of the broch may offer a few surprises, etc., etc., as much as three and a half to five."

Kreen was slinging the pack on his shoulder and trying to listen to the constant orders coming at him. The king had asked for volunteers for this mission and his family had encouraged him to stand up, and so here he was, going off alone and the king was standing there with a human and talking to him as if Kreen knew what he were doing.

. . . here is a map of Caledonia you will find out how far north the wall goes if the Orkneys are enclosed you will find the Earl of the Orkneys and you will pass a message to him which is in the pouch on your back you will report back as soon as you can you are not to engage the enemy use whatever means of information gathering are at your disposal . . .

And on and on until he was quite sure that he understood as much as he could remember and Kreen the young Syth was off with a pack, a quiver of arrows and a message for a human king he might not even find. He was exhilarated and frightened and suddenly keenly aware of his own youth and mortality. He loved it. He was patted on the back by every Syth he had ever met and a few he still had not and he was off before he had even seen much of Malcolm's field. For this, he was lucky. He had no notion how lucky he was.

❖   ❖   ❖

There were, all in all, three thousand Syth at Dunsinane under Oberon's command. The human count was not as extensive, considering that they were the ones under threat. Dukane had dispatched requests for able-bodied men to come to the aid of their king, and many had responded, but calling up an army was a tremendous difficulty under the circumstances. The dark uncertainty led many Scots to man the sword or pike at their own door, in fear of a direct attack on their own cottage from roving bandits as much as from any threat supernatural. Dukane had dredged up eight thousand for the moment. These were scattered around Dunsinane, many sleeping in tents — notably separated from those of the Syth — in the bowling fields within the Palisade, most across the moat in the open on Dunsinane Hill. Of those, the majority were pikemen. Some had their own swords and axes, if they had been in battle before, and the armorer was busily fashioning as many swords as he could pour into moulds for the best and brightest. Cavalry was limited. Clan leaders like Armstrong and Moray and fortunates like Abel and Dukane had their own steeds, but these numbered at the most two hundred present.

"I don't know," said MacDuff, as he stood on the east wall of the castle watching the army mill around.

Dukane watched Seyton, far below, instructing a unit of pikemen in battle tactics. A sword was a gentleman's weapon. But Seyton had survived the pike and could teach it well. "Eight thousand will have to do for now," Dukane said. "How many does the Erl-King have?"

Malcolm spoke. He knew this one. "One thousand."

"No," said MacDuff. "A thousand. The Erl-King, it is said, has *a* thousand children. It is, of course, a simplification."

Malcolm nodded. "Ah, yes. The extrapolation of peasants who cannot count. 'He has many children,' then, I imagine would be the translation."

"Which still tells us nothing," said Dukane. "We may assume he has a large number greater than our present roster."

Susan had been listening from the ground below and came gliding up the wall. She leapt over the waist-high partition at the top on which leaned the three. "But a limited one, at best," she said. "Remember, the souls of the children are not included in his army. The Darklings are his real children, and they, like the Syth, are born, and there is a limit to them."

MacDuff looked across the hazy field. At least it wasn't raining. "Can he run out of men before we do?"

Susan surveyed the eight thousand. "At this rate, if this is it . . ."

"But it's not," said the king. "This is but a fraction of the men we could muster. The army gathers periodically for exercises in the south, and numbers in the tens of thousands."

The Thane of Fife chewed on this. How to get them out of their homes . . . "The men are frightened and confused. In unusual circumstances they are remaining to guard their homes. Which I . . ." He was lost in thought, now. This hurt. ". . . I respect. But it is plain we will need the full might of the Caledonian army. And I do not know how to gather them."

A voice came from below. Seyton was waving a pike. "MacDuff!"

MacDuff started. "What?" He expected an army of giant bats to come rolling over the plains. *Watch it, Fife-Thane, don't get jumpy.*

"Your turn," Seyton yelled. "I thought you might speak to the men and show them some sword work."

MacDuff nodded. Good. Seyton was willing to sacrifice his pride to build the confidence of the men. Good man. By Seyton's side stood a fellow with a pike taller than he, a strapping youth named James, who MacDuff heard Seyton had dragged clear out into the middle of the Moray Firth before they hit the wall. The boy was obviously loyal. MacDuff stopped a moment to wonder why men are most loyal to those who get them out of the most danger, even if they put them there in the first place, and then he let it go. He took his leave of the king, Dukane, and the lovely wall-walker, and took a ladder down, himself. Despite the ubiquitous soreness in his legs, he preferred the ladder in this over taking the stairs inside and coming through the door. The ladder made better drama. Had one been handy, for the men, he would have slid down a rope.

CHAPTER 8

When the attack on Dunsinane came, it came without warning. Malcolm's army lay ignobly asleep in their tents, scattered across the hill. MacDuff stood on the east wall of the castle looking out when he first heard the call of the sentry at the west. "Thane! I think I saw something," he cried. Malcolm peered into the night. It was James, Seyton's man, who could not have been more specific had he tried. MacDuff peered westward, encumbered by the lack of any real horizon. Just then he saw the figure of an owl soar into view and down to a window in the wall. It was Paddock, shrieking hysterically.

A flitting shape seemed to dance across the black wall that passed for a sky, slightly illuminated by the red glow from the orb, partially self-lit. It was fairly glowing in the distance. MacDuff ran to James's side and tried to get a better look. The shapes hovered some half-mile from the wall on which the Thane of Fife stood. What time was it? How long had the men been sleeping?

"MacDuff!" Susan came flying up the wall from her window. "Get your army in order, MacDuff! This is it!" She ran to the small bell on the wall and began to sound it as rapidly and loudly as she could manage.

MacDuff slammed his fist against the wall. "Boy! Go! Ring the alarum bell! We are being attacked!" And now this truth became apparent, as the glow of the Darklings blended with the red light in the sky and grew more and more bright. Far in the distance the Thane of Fife could hear shouting. Belial and his army were flying at full wing. MacDuff turned towards the castle. "Malcolm!"

James was scurrying down the ladder into the courtyard and screaming his head off to whoever might listen. He made it to the bell tower in a matter of seconds. The sexton slept until James kicked him and jumped on the great bell rope. He came down and yanked hard on it as the first mighty peal sang out. Men in the courtyard were already beginning to shout.

The Syth were naturally quicker to ready themselves, speeding out from their tents by the hundreds. The clanging of the bell was deafening. Scots roused one another as two thousand hands reached for their weapons.

Belial the Darkling looked down from the red-gray sky and smiled. *Unprepared.* He picked a tent in which he saw no movement and swooped down upon it. He grabbed the cloth with his long-nailed right hand and ripped it away, revealing two particularly groggy Scots. They sprang up just in time to see the sword that removed their heads.

For a moment the sky was filled with wood elves. Four thousand eyes crackled in the night and then set themselves on the ground. Belial floated above them for a moment and called out to them all. "Take them!"

In a bedroom in the east wing of the castle Julia awoke to the sound of a great gasp from her son. She pulled her eyes open to see Douglas bolt upright. It was then that she

heard the bells ringing and the shouting of men below.
She sprang out of bed and threw on a cape. "Douglas.
Darling, we need your wolves."

"My father is here. I feel him near."

"Call your friends. Call them out of the den and into
battle. Please."

Just then she heard footsteps running down the hall
and Ruthe tore into the doorway. "Julia!"

"We're still here, Ruthe."

"Good, did you ask Doug to . . ."

"Please!" snapped the five-year-old. "Let me do this."
The small body slid off the bed. Douglas rubbed his eyes
wearily as he walked to the window. He pulled a stool over
to it and climbed up so that he could see out. Below was
the den where he had led the wolves. He had made sure
his mother got him a room above them for this reason
exactly. For a second he allowed himself the perverse admiration of the gray-and-red sky, even the crackling
whiteness of the coming enemy. He felt a moment's kinship but dismissed it. Douglas levelled his sparkling gaze
on General Belin of the wolves, who already stood and
growled at the gate, waiting for some sort of command.
The other wolves were awake in anticipation.

A mental howl flew down the wall to the noble creatures below. "General Belin! I need you! Fight those that
crackle and fly!"

Belin turned around and snapped his pointed head up
toward the window. He could see the sparkling eyes in the
dark window above. He howled, a long, vicious howl in
recognition of an order from his master. He whipped back
to his army and snarled. "The master calls. Catch them
and tear them to pieces and then eat the pieces!" Then
the den was flying hay and blurred fur as an army of
wolves poured onto the field.

Abel Galloway reared back on his horse. He swung his
axe around in a great arc once to feel its natural rhythm in

the air. He kicked the steed's flanks and galloped into the fray. He came up on a Darkling exchanging swipes with a pikeman. He had no time to think. Just as he saw the Scot fall under a fatal wound to the collar bone, the draft horse thundered up beside the glowing figure. The massive arm yanked the axe out and up the Darkling's back. A wide cavern opened between the elf's shoulders and his wings fell. The edge of the axe slid out of the base of the elf's skull as the night-child shrieked. The axe spun around in Abel's grasp as he galloped on.

Abel looked up in time to see another Darkling flying towards him. The Darkling held his sword horizontally to get a swipe at his head. *What have you learned, Abel?* Abel saw the fanged grin as he let his axe slip down and felt the leather strap wrap around the back of his hand. He dropped his head a little at the last moment, waiting until the screeching demon drew close and then swung the axe like a mace. The blade flew up and slid clean through the Darkling's head, slicing off the tops of the elf's ears as it did the top of his head. The flying figure slammed to the ground as the black sword dropped.

The field was ablaze with the crackling light of the Darklings. The din of metal and voice filled the air.

Oberon sped across the field with his hook gripped firmly in hand, looking for targets. He spied a Darkling exchanging blows with a Scot and ran towards the elf's legs. *That's it. Keep him distracted.* The elf was swinging his sword and winning in combat with the young soldier, but Oberon could see the boy was holding him off. The Syth king ran past the elf but slowed long enough to catch his hook in the thin cords of sinew behind the Darkling's knee. He heard cloth and flesh rip and the familiar snap of the elf's hamstring. The Scot took off the elven head as the agonized Darkling fell in horror.

Perth the Darkling turned to see the galloping Seyton moving towards him. He sprang into the air with his

sword. Seyton blocked the black blade but felt himself
thrown back off his horse. He lost his breath as he fell
hard on his back. He was quick to upright himself. Perth
stood on the ground and swung, and his blade sparked as
it met Seyton's and bounced away, around, and up again.
Seyton blocked his blow again and again, trying to get a
swipe at the Darkling's body. Suddenly Perth's eyes grew
wide. Seyton allowed himself the dangerous luxury of
looking down to see what had caused the shriek. He
expected one of Oberon's hamstringers. He was wrong. A
mammoth gray wolf had latched onto Perth's ankle. The
wolf growled and Perth could see the saliva of the animal
mixing with his own black blood. As Seyton swung his
blade at Perth's white neck the Darkling whipped his
wings and took flight. He screamed in pain as he felt his
right foot tear away. The wolf dropped the souvenir and
moved on, licking his chops.

All in all the allies were making the best of an incredibly bad situation. MacDuff cursed himself again for
allowing Malcolm to run — and destroy — the show. The
Scots were fighting but disorganized. They had no plan of
defense and Belial knew it. Now MacDuff caught sight of
Malcolm on horseback. Malcolm was at the top of a
smooth grade a half-mile from the castle. He sat on his
horse, eyes and mouth wide, betraying his dumbfounded-
ness. The boy looked as if he had never seen a battle
before. This was not the case: he had simply never been
attacked before.

MacDuff pounded across the outside of the field
towards the king. As he rode, the Thane tried to get a view
of how they were faring. He saw more humans lying dead
than Syth or Darklings combined. Blood covered the
field. At areas he could see running soldiers splashing
through where it gathered in puddles. And the Darklings!
God, what horrors! Those wings of ebon, body coverings
of glittering black cloth, arms and faces of chalk white, all

splashed with the red blood of the fighting Scots as they swooped in and sliced away at his men!

Malcolm stirred slightly when MacDuff rode up beside him and yanked the reins.

"Fife," said Malcolm.

MacDuff's horse was nervous; it pitched under him as he steadied it and looked the king over. "My liege," said the Thane of Fife, "Malcolm, we are undermanned, underprepared and under attack. I was afraid this would happen and now it has. It's your country, Canmore. What do you do?"

There was a strange glint in the eyes of Malcolm III. From his side, opposite MacDuff, Malcolm's arm flew back and out from under the king's robes to reveal the glint of a sword, a fine one held out by a strong, young hand. It flashed as he cocked his head toward the fray. "What I do is surprise even you, Thane." His red hair flew back as he whipped the reins and prepared to burst onto the field. MacDuff's thick arm grabbed his shoulder and stopped him.

"Wait," said the older man. "Look at Dukane. Do you see him?"

The king squinted. In the distance, illuminated by the faint red glow and the iridescent crackling of the Darklings, Dukane was visible on the field, hacking away at his opponents. Yes, that had to be him, with his long hair matted with black elf blood, flying like a sling with his every turn.

When Malcolm nodded, MacDuff continued. "Dukane told us something of how they fight. Remember it. Watch . . . see that? They swoop down and try to get a hit in. If you can block them then, they tend to alight, especially if they're caught up in protecting themselves. That is all we know. We don't know how many there are, nor who the leader is on the field. Parry them on that first swoop and you have a chance. Watch your back. Ignore the bodies."

Malcolm surveyed the field, *his* field, which was rapidly filling with slaughtered men and far fewer allies. What would Duncan do? Exactly this, Malcolm decided. Before plunging into the melee, Malcolm looked back at Mac-Duff. "Are we going to lose?"

MacDuff was gone already but he shouted back over the noise. "Just keep yourself alive."

Belial finished off the ridiculous human armed with a piece of wood and took to the air. He flew toward the castle. Good. His army was doing well; the Erl-King would be pleased. He whipped his wings to ease off, then noticed a pile of three or four glistening winged bodies, and atop them, their destroyer, a human, swathed in black blood and unmounted. The human was busy with another of Belial's men.

The lifeless body of Dukane's horse lay nearby. Dukane grinned as the Darkling he fought became exhausted yet again by treading air and took to the ground. Dukane destroyed him almost instantly, driving the black sword deep into the creature's chest. He looked up and lost his grin.

Dukane hit the ground when he saw Belial flying in low. Belial flew past as Dukane got to all fours. The Scot noticed a wolf pass his nose and ignore him. The wolf had a white hand in its mouth. Belial was coming around again. Dukane stood with his sword ready. In his periphery Dukane barely registered another glint of reflected light before Belial was suddenly knocked viciously sideways, losing his sword. Belial spun in the air, one wing dragged under him and around. He hit the ground laying on his right wing.

Ach! Bewildered, Belial looked up and knew what had happened. Standing over him, a blur became a Syth, standing still, holding his small weapon. The little beast had jumped and hooked his wing. Belial winced when he became aware of the pain where the wing had been torn through by the silver hook. He took to the air, cursing the Sons of Oberon.

Douglas stood on a stool at the window, next to his mother. He was trying to keep track of the wolves, but Belin had brought so many. Their losses weighed heavily upon him as he followed their paths and called orders to General Belin. In many ways, he knew, it was best to leave the real, on-field decisions to the wolf leader. Douglas could only watch and throw in the occasional situational advice. He wanted to shout out each time a wolf was injured; he thought he felt the pain shoot through his small body and rack it as it did the wolf in question. In each case he was repeatedly surprised to live through the feeling, before reaching out to another one.

MacDuff had taken to riding to the aid of the pikemen engaged in ground combat with the Darklings. Man after man fell beneath the superior ebon swords and elven quickness. The Darklings swooped on and on, in waves, seemingly endless in number. MacDuff cursed as he maneuvered his horse among the broken tents and bodies. The wind had grown deafening, so that the shouts of the men were incomprehensible. MacDuff looked into the air and saw the figure of Ruthe silhouetted against the reddish sky. She seemed to be directing. *Yes, of course. She is controlling the winds.* That was at least one advantage.

Seyton was visible across the field and MacDuff broke loose and rode towards him. Seyton drew his sword out of the felled opponent in front of him and seemed to have difficulty standing straight. The man was tired, that was obvious. When MacDuff shouted out to him Seyton looked, then looked directly past MacDuff. MacDuff turned his horse around and looked toward the castle.

"My God," muttered Seyton.

"Someone is on the wall," said MacDuff. A Darkling was barely visible, standing on the wall. The figure had taken a torch from the gate and now stood on the battlements, swinging the torch, as if giving a signal.

Belial whipped the torch in his hand in a wide arc and called out to his Darklings. His gray mane flew back in the wind as he tilted back his head and cried:

"Take the castle!" He did not care if the words would be heard. His brethren would get the idea.

So did MacDuff. The Thane of Fife looked away from Dunsinane to Seyton. "The rest . . ."

Seyton was already riding for the castle. One after another he could see the Darklings disengaging and turning their attention toward the wooden fortress, leaving their bewildered combatants to scurry after them.

Belial flapped his wings and tossed the torch into a hay-lined stable. A crackle of flame licked out and began to roar, exploding and spreading throughout the stable and onto the wall of the castle.

Joly sat on a cushion. The images were coming, but slowly. She could get a glimpse of the future here and there, but she knew she fought a losing battle. She could only try to read what she could of the present, get a glimpse of the Darklings' present thoughts or intentions. She only saw the fire, however, when Belial lit it. She merely shrugged at the thought of losing a lot of wood before she remembered that Douglas and Julia — Julia, at least, for certain — were mortal. They could die this way, she recognized with a sense of annoyed remembrance. She got up and began to run for Julia's chamber. She could not turn off the barrage of angry thoughts that flooded her mind. Joly shuddered as she ran when she suddenly knew that death was not what Belial had planned for the two.

In the many little things that Belial wanted to do in this

little battle, there was one thing he was required to do. The rest would be more or less unimportant. He turned a corner and flew down through the courtyard to the giant doorway. It was bolted. Belial shrugged inwardly and flew higher. *Fine. A window will do nicely.* He looked back before going in. Four or five Darklings followed.

At another window, Douglas gasped. Julia looked out. "What?"

Douglas spoke and thought as fast as he could control it all. "Father wants us." He sensed that Belial had flown in through a window and was inside. A great wave of Darklings now circled the castle as they stayed in the air, immune to all of the humans but the handful of archers who had trouble hitting any but the lowest of Darklings. Then they began to pour into the castle the way Belial had gone.

"Get away from the window," said Julia. "They might see you." She bit her lip angrily. The courtyard below was a mess of metal and gore. *Some protection,* she thought. *We should have already gone.*

"Too late," Douglas said calmly. "They are inside already." He turned his mind toward the field. "Belin. Help us."

Belin led the pack through the stable, the only way into the castle he could reach. He threatened to reel when the strong odor of burning hay flooded his nostrils but kept moving. Flaming wood fell in chunks about him and he ignored the piece that fell and grazed his shoulder viciously. A second slower in moving sideways and it would have broken his back, but he had not been a second slower, and Belin did not think of such things.

Behind him followed the gray army diligently. Belin could hear the pups breathing heavily. They were too young for combat, but they had come, and Belin had not stopped them. This was the way.

Abel was a full hundred yards from the castle when he

saw the elves streaming into the structure. The skins were about to burst. Red flame was spreading viciously across the base of the castle and up the west wall. How long? Abel whipped the reins and directed the horse toward the courtyard. The door would not be open, he knew. A flurry of gray fur caught his eye and he followed the wolves to the stable. Once there, surrounded by burnt hay and a flaming entrance, he lost sight of the wolves.

Julia heard footsteps outside her chamber. She listened by the door; the sound seemed to disappear down the hall. She placed her hand on her son's head for a moment, then drew her sword. Her calloused hand lifted it as easily as she would a basket of fish. Silently she drew the bolt, grasped the handle with her free hand, and slowly swung the door open.

The hall was silent and the only sound came from far away, where she could hear incomprehensible shouts. The sounds of running and shouting men and elves were faint echoes, in another world. To her left the hall continued before turning off. Julia stepped through the corridor, sword in hand. She signalled for Douglas to follow her. She took a deep breath and waited for Douglas to take her hand again when she noticed a strange reflection. In the light of the wall torches, she could see a path of red liquid trailing down the hallway and stopping . . . she looked down the hall in the other direction to be sure . . . *here.*

"Douglas," she said, "get back inside . . ."

A drop of blood hit Julia's sword hand. She looked up to see the bloody end of a familiar style of black sword, held by a shadow of a creature she could not make out. She did not have to. It swung down, aimed at her throat. She dropped to the ground and scurried back into the room, grabbing hastily for the door. The figure was unfolding, lowering into the hallway . . .

Douglas stood at the end of his bed and saw his mother

pushing on the door. Soon the superior strength of the hidden creature won out and the door swung wide. A slinky figure in sparkling black clothing, with crackling white skin and gray hair, stepped through. When Julia raised her sword to him, Belial seemed to ignore her, keeping his distance from her and his eyes on the boy.

The gray hair sparked with internal electricity that was evident in his eyes. "Hello, Douglas," the creature said. Belial grinned, exhibiting a row of magnificent, sharp teeth. Good for tearing, like those of a rat. *What manner of man is this?* thought Douglas. He knew. He could feel the blood of this man drumming through his veins. Yet somehow, for all the recognition he felt, he knew there was a difference. His mother was right.

"Your father would very much like to see you."

Julia got in front of Douglas and held her sword in front of her in both hands. "In Hell, Belial."

"Julie, how droll. You don't come around enough, really; it isn't Hell at all. Though that could be arranged."

"My son is not going anywhere."

Belial winked a crackling eye. "So charming. I've missed you. You'll be coming along with us, of course."

"I'm afraid I can't oblige," she said, as she swung the sword at the Darkling's neck. He stepped back and parried with his own sword.

Douglas spoke. "Mother?"

"I have no wish to harm you, Julia." He expertly deflected the woman's next swing. He seemed content to stand there and fend her off as long as she wanted. "Julia?"

Douglas turned and looked out the window. "Mother?"

Julia swung again and felt the sword getting heavier. She breathed heavily, annoyed by Belial's newfound passivity and proficiency with his own blood-soaked blade. "What?"

Belial looked over Julia's shoulder and raised an eyebrow. "Behind you, Julie."

"Do you think I'm damned stupid, Belial?"

"Mother!" Douglas shouted as three winged figures came flitting, one by one, to the ledge and through the window. Julia looked back to see them, all white and crackling, all armed. All like young, smooth *dopplegangers* of the Erl-King.

Belial spoke again. "You may as well drop your weapon now, Julie." Rapid footsteps now sounded from the corridor and toward the door. "You are coming with us."

"No!" she cried, taking a great swing with the sword. Belial swung his blade with incredible speed to meet hers at the pommel. Julia watched the black, supernatural blade meet her father's old, battered sword and break it just above the hilt. The useless piece of metal fell to the wooden floor. She reached back for Douglas and felt four arms take her by the shoulders and arms. Douglas shouted as one of the elves picked him up.

Julia thrashed against her captors and watched her son squirming in the arms of the Darkling that held him. The creature thew a sack over the boy's head.

"Julia!" came a woman's voice from the hallway. Joly was running for Julia's door and could hear the screaming. Ruthe's favorite was in danger.

The Darkling flew out the window with Douglas in hand. "Joly," Julia screamed, when she recognized the witch's voice. Her hands were being tied behind her back. She screamed as the black cloth fell over her eyes. She felt two hands grab her under the arms as the Darklings prepared to lift her out.

Joly made it to the door and tore inside, only to stop in her tracks at the sight of seven armed Darklings and the captive Julia. Belial gave a signal and turned to Joly as the woman was whisked by two of them out the window and into the night. "I assure you, Fraulein, we mean her no harm." He turned and walked to the window and looked out. The castle was on fire in over a hundred places. He knew his soldiers even now were flying through, dropping torches on the wooden floors. Smoke was coming up through the floors. Silly wooden traps.

"Come along, gentlemen," he said. "Oh, and Jacob." He looked at one of the elves. "Kill that one," he said, gesturing vaguely toward the Third Sister.

The witch fell. As she lay on the ground she saw a piece of her throat beside her, torn and steaming as warm ichor hit the Scottish air.

General Belin snarled at his wolves: bad things were happening. The voice of the dark child had suddenly, completely disappeared. As he padded along the wooden floor, looking for more Darklings, he reached out and tried to hear Douglas, but the leader seemed to be too far away already. Had they been abandoned? Belin sniffed. Smoke. This place was burning; why was he following this leader anyway?

The smell of blood mixed with smoke and Belin looked down to see the trail of blood leading down the hallway. The blood was beginning to give off steam as the boards grew hot. He followed the trail to a doorway and looked in. He cursed and looked back at his followers. "Nothing here but a dead human." He turned back. "Let's go. This place is falling apart."

The wolves disappeared down the hall, looking for the first exit they could find.

The last things Belin saw in the castle were the tight leather boots of a huge blond human running in the opposite direction, before he stopped where he knew the door was and saw that it was barred shut. There was nowhere else to go.

Susan sat on the back of MacDuff's horse and looked at the castle. She had seen the screaming, hooded Julia fly overhead in captivity. The Darklings were moving off and following. All that remained was to watch Dunsinane burn. Soon the last of the Darklings flew out of different exits in the castle and disappeared in the distance, leaving only the allies, their corpses, and their burning headquarters.

"Well," said MacDuff. "Good-bye, MacBeth." Dukane and Malcolm rode up beside him.

MacDuff looked at the grim Dukane. "About your garrison. I no longer hold you responsible, Dukane. These are going to be hard opponents to beat."

The fire in the young king's eyes conveyed their own message, but Malcolm did not say a word. MacDuff answered him likewise.

Susan suddenly gasped. "Oh, no."

MacDuff looked at her, confused. "What else is wrong?"

"One of us . . ." She looked around at the heavy, barred door of the castle. She saw that the boards atop the frame had given slightly under the weight of the collapsing structure and now lapped over the top of the door. It was, in effect, barred on both sides. The flames were licking at the castle, devouring it as Susan watched and knew that something was very wrong.

"Ruthe! Joly!" she cried.

In a second Ruthe came flying over the battlements from the other side of the castle. "Susan, I'm fine, but I fear that . . ."

Something slammed against the giant door and made it bow out. The boards hanging over the top held it stuck in place as the lower halves of the doors strained to open. The boards settled back before another slam bent them out again and the frame boards began to give. Smoke belched through the cracks in the boards. Someone or something was trying to get out of a jammed doorway. All at once a great slam was heard over the roaring fire, and the boards bowed and cracked one last time. The hinges

in the doorway gave and tore out of the posts. The unco-
operative boards blocking the top of the doorway waited
another blow to break and fall as the giant doors flew
open, belching smoke. Countless wolves poured out of
the castle past the lone figure that slowly stepped out of
the groaning castle.

"Joly!" whispered Susan. Her Sister lay nestled in the
arms of Abel Galloway, who cradled her as he might a
baby, his blond hair steaming where it had been singed,
his right shoulder a bloody pulp where he had repeatedly
pounded it against the door. He stepped forward several
paces and fell to his knees with Joly still in his arms as the
main structure of the castle at Dunsinane gave a great
heave and collapsed.

"Lay on, MacDuff, and
Damned be he who first cries 'Hold,
    Enough!'"

— Shakespeare

PART II

CHAPTER 9

Singing.

Douglas awoke and blinked. The room was dark, but the light from his eyes gave off a faint glow with which he could see. He lay on a pallet of good skins. The floor flowed into the walls seamlessly; there seemed to be no door available for use. As Douglas leaned back on his palms he realized there lay no course for escape from his little cell.

Where am I? he asked, but he had lived with his mother too long to be afraid of the unknown. It was a simple question for which he had no immediate answer. *And what is that singing?* It was very faint, and yet he could have sworn it to be loud enough to have awoken him at so early — or late; what time was it? It seemed to be coming from everywhere, a distant, homogeneous, high-pitched hum. No answer now. He turned his mind back to the question of where he was.

Douglas ran his tiny hand through his jet-black hair and tried to remember how he had gotten here. A sparkling white winged man had taken him. He knew they existed; his mother had told him of the Darklings. He had been sufficiently convinced of their reality to use his influence with the wolves against them. But he had never actually seen one before. Fascinating. Then it was all real. *Here I am, brought by my brothers to be a guest of my father.*

It is impossible to accurately describe how Douglas felt about the Erl-King. How does one feel about one's estranged father when one's mother has told him that the fellow is a liar, a killer and, for all that, a several-millennia-old elf of the evil persuasion? One deals with it, frankly. Douglas, for being chalk-white with sparkling eyes, for having always to pretend that he didn't exist and hiding from the neighbors, for having a mother who had always treated him with a clever mix of deference to his intelligence and patience with his ignorance, for living a life that seemed at once safe and incredibly tenuous, Douglas was perhaps the most serene five-year old humanoid ever born to the Scottish hills, or any, for that matter.

Douglas was . . . how could he put it, how had he tried to explain it to his mother, once when it finally dawned on him what was different about him, aside from the eyes and all those accidentals? . . . circular. Yes. His mother was linear, like a table edge; she thought and lived that way, logically driving herself along the plane from one edge to the other. No going back. Douglas, who could respect a good logical argument like any decent intellect, nevertheless felt obliged to always find a way back to the beginning. "Circular logic" did not bother him as much as it did his mother, because he could see past it to what it represented, a continual beginning, a continual end. A never-ending present. By the growth in his bones he knew that he was aging as his mother was, for now, at least, but he had no idea if it would stop. This, however, was not important to the circular nature of his soul and of, as he knew it, the world. And he knew — and this was what he felt more than anything else the first time he saw Aunt Ruthe, and the first time he saw the Darklings — that these were people who thought like him. Whatever this fundamental difference was, however it may be understood, it kept him generally at ease and prepared.

Circular nature of all things notwithstanding, there were things that should be and things that should not, and Douglas knew that he should definitely not be here. He gathered from the meeting that his father was out to kill the humans entirely; he decided he was probably being held as some sort of bait for the humans to come after. He hoped, as desperately as he was capable of hoping, that his mother was safe. But Mother could take care of herself, and he knew that she was alive.

Singing. Douglas looked around him again, got up, and walked to the door . . . or at least, he felt, where the door would be, if there were one. Looking down, he noticed that his clothes had been exchanged for the sparkling material worn by the Erl-King's sons. Absently he laid his hand on the wall to lean against it and gasped.

A thousand swirling souls were screaming in his brain, singing out in unison. Help us. *Free us. Father, please.* Douglas was among them, swimming in an ocean of souls, lost in the inky blackness of his father's creation, bent by his will, led by his pleasure. Hating and loving the hatred. And somewhere, within each and every soul was a portion that was growing louder by the day in its search for release. *Please.*

The dark child tore his hand away from the wall. The screams fell to a faint hum, a singing observable only to the attentive. Douglas concentrated for a moment and could hear it all again, less intense this time. He could hear it without being *in* it. It was now that he noticed the peculiar rippling of the walls themselves, like inky black liquid stone. And then it suddenly dawned on him that he could see faces in the wall.

Douglas sat down on his furs and looked at the floor, which, like the ceiling and the walls, was soulstuff. The architect — his father, he presumed — had organized every ounce correctly: the ceiling and floors were more solid than the outsides of walls, everything in balance. Everything according to the father's plan. Like the red star in the sky. There was, Douglas observed, something just a bit admirable about such power.

Come, he thought, *let us talk to the walls.* Just as he placed his tiny hand against the floor a door opened where there was none before.

Douglas did not look up. "A Darkling, yes?"

"Af is my name." The light had multiplied to include the new shimmer thrown off of Af's eyes and hair.

Douglas traced a face on the floor with a tiny finger. "Do you always do my father's work for him?"

"Eh?"

"All this talk about the Erl-King and we've really seen very little of him. I'm beginning to wonder if he actually exists." Douglas looked up to see Af's smile.

"Would you like to see him?"

"Not really," said Douglas. "I would, however, like to see my mother."

"And that will happen."

"Ah," said Douglas. The boy crossed his legs. "So are you going to take me to my father? That is what you are here for, yes? I presume you did not expect to leave the decision for me."

"And why not?"

Douglas looked into the sparkling eyes. "Because I have all the time in the world. Do you?"

Pause. "No. Come with me, then."

"So you are going to force me?"

"I thought you might cooperate."

"Well, you already carried us off. As far as I know, my mother is dead." Douglas, who understood far more than his mother could realize, knew this was not the case. But he wanted his point made. "So why should I cooperate?"

"Because . . ." *My goodness*, thought Douglas, *could this elf actually be flustered?* "Your father wants to see you."

"So you are going to force me to go see him. Against my will."

"The Erl-King . . ."

"Are you always this indecisive? Good thing you're not a general, then."

"I refuse to listen to this!"

"Are you actually my brother?" *No*, Douglas thought. *More like a half-brother. You know something about me that makes you afraid. My, we are different, aren't we?* "Never mind about that, just a thought."

"Fine. Stay. And we'll see what the Erl-King has to say . . ."

"Actually, I was just thinking how hungry I was, and I imagine going to see my father might not be such a good idea at all."

"Ah."

"Ah. Yes. Take me to my father, then."

And so Af the Darkling took the young Douglas to the Lord of the Dark Elves. And he wasn't really sure if he were leading or following.

The rain set in to douse the last fires of the ruins of Dunsinane. The last house of MacBeth was a pile of charred wood, surrounded by a reddened motte that swirled with gray ash. MacDuff sat on the edge of the motte, his back turned to the house, and looked into the water.

"The war," he said, "goes badly."

"Aye," nodded Oberon, who took a seat and watched the raindrops hit the water. He pulled his hood over his head and lit his pipe. Smoke swirled out from under the hood and made him look even more mystic than he was. "Do you always sit in the rain like this?"

MacDuff looked up at the morning darkness. "Hmmm. I like the rain. Very rhythmic." He gave a slight smile. "Besides, there is no castle to go into." He looked over at the pen, still standing, in which the wolves had made their bed in the night. They, too, he observed, had suffered losses.

"This will not do," said MacDuff. "This is not the way to fight this war. I . . . we do not even have half the men that Scotland can offer; they're all home manning the sword against the unknown. We have been put on the defensive. We have your army and a host of elemental creatures, and we have not properly used them."

"How," asked Oberon, "would you . . . your king normally handle a war situation?"

"A war situation? Normally the king would contact his Thanes, who would in turn call out to the fighting men of each clan. But, as I said, the normal lines of communication are disrupted. Kingship here is a curious thing, really. It's partially a matter of who appears most able to manipulate the most men. When the whole country is under siege and fragmented at the same time . . ."

"You should be king, MacDuff."

"Curious, King Oberon, that you should say that." MacDuff tugged at his beard. "But I misrepresent kingship, I'm afraid. I speak more of the past. Now, kingship is becoming something more along the lines of an administrative position. I am not an administrator."

"Malcolm is."

"Aye," said MacDuff. "His rule is one of the future, a Scotland marked by less war and more status quo. The Thanes are now Earls, ruled by a king who is more of a big Earl, who will probably end up a vassal to an even larger Earl outside of Scotland. That is all I can predict."

"We are, however, in a war situation now. And at this

rate there will be little left for administration. MacDuff, I speak to you with utmost sincerity: I doubt Malcolm's abilities."

"I will not take his throne."

"Do you know, MacDuff, that at one time Sparta had two kings? One for, as you say, administration, the other for war?"

MacDuff watched the raindrops mix the ashes and blood. Whose blood was that? "The system of which you speak failed."

"When it was no longer needed. All systems fail, by nature of their being systems. All things must die." He gave a smile when MacDuff threw him a wry look. "Most, anyway. Even us. There are those who I knew as far back as Hellenic times, who I thought would be around forever. Who are no longer with us. Many were lost last night. Unearned luck is sometimes hard."

"Unearned luck." MacDuff looked across the motte at the hill where the Syth and human bodies were being stacked. A pyre would not burn: they would all have to be buried together. "I have made many choices which did not take into account the missiles of fortune."

"There is nowhere to go, this time, MacDuff. I make it no secret that my alliances with humans have never been enjoyed. I have never fully trusted hairless primates."

"I have never fully trusted *others*."

"Aye. But you are different. I put my trust in you because I see no other recourse, and because only you can get us out of this. But that leaves us with a condition." A puff of smoke blew out of the hood in a sheet. The wind took it and let the rain slice through it like ethereal claws. "You must take charge. The administrative world you so detest is on the other side of that wall. After this, I cannot tell you what comes, but if you do not act, there will be no after this. Perhaps for all of this. Perhaps for all of your kind."

"Malcolm must remain king."

"Everything in life, MacDuff, does not have to be official. Thane of Fife, make no mistake: I am placing the
lives of my men in your hands. They will not be wasted by
your whelp king."

MacDuff thought. "I see." He got up and began walking towards the large tent that had been pitched for the
wounded. He had people to talk to. "Then the first order
is to move the army."

"And then?" Oberon was up and following. MacDuff,
he noticed, had an admirably brisk, intent stride that was
refreshing to observe in a human.

"We put the call out to the men we do not have yet."

"How will you do that?"

"I have an idea that we can combine the two efforts."
He threw the flaps of the tent open and stepped inside.
The tent was large, made of furs and blankets pulled from
the castle. The rain made the roof and walls bow in, held
up only by the sturdy poles throughout. Torches burned
inside to reveal the casualties of the battle, laid in rows
along the ground. There were only about fifteen: Few hit
had lived. One of them, lest anyone among the allies had
actually thought she could die, was Joly.

"How is she?" MacDuff asked Ruthe, who sat on a fur
beside her Sister.

Ruthe's yellow hair was flat with rain and ash. "Her
throat was torn out. She lost a great deal of ichor."

Oberon tapped his pipe. Not often you see this kind of
injury to an immortal. "How long will it take . . ."

"To heal?" Susan came in through a flap in the tent with
Graymalkin in her arms. "I imagine that is up to Joly."

Ruthe indicated the dormant Joly's throat. She pulled
back the cloth that lay over her throat. "Look here. Nearly
an inch of the esophagus gone, jugular torn asunder, and
fused, by the way, to stop the bleeding. A hole some four
fingers in size torn in the flesh of her throat. This will take
some time, at least."

MacDuff let out a low whistle. "Incredible." Cut a human's throat, never see him again. Rip out that of a witch . . .

"Well," said Ruthe, wiping her brow. "She won't die, anyway. But I'd be surprised if she speaks for the next ten years or so." She looked at Abel, who was on the floor beside the Sister, head in hands.

Susan nodded. "We can thank Abel for not letting it get worse. Had her body been consumed, she just might have died. I don't know. None of us has ever been thrown from this sort of height before."

Ruthe looked at MacDuff. "She was in Julia's room. Susan told me that you saw her and the boy being taken away." She bit her lip. "I promised her that we could care for her. We worked very hard to get her away from him in the first place, and now."

"We will get her back," said Abel. "If I have to go alone."

"You won't," said MacDuff. "But we will get her back. Still, for now, though I hate to say it this way, the loss may have bought us some time. We must move out now, and re-organize, and be ready for whatever the Erl-King has in mind. He wanted to destroy our capital. He did that. But he didn't destroy us. Taking the woman and the boy seems to have been more important."

"Aye," said Ruthe. "I only hope he does not kill my friend in the process."

"Always a risk, Sister," said Susan.

MacDuff noted the unspoken argument. "Enough of that." He turned toward the other side of the tent, where Malcolm stood with Dukane and the Earls. "Malcolm!" The king saw him and left his group to join MacDuff. "We are moving this afternoon to another castle."

"South of Dunfermline, I take it?"

"No. My house will not do. Is the Earl of Grampian with us?"

"Aye," said the king. "On the field, beneath a pile of pikemen."

"How unfortunate," said MacDuff. Unearned luck. "Very well, then. We are going north to Grampian, to Braemar."

"Braemar?" exclaimed Malcolm. "What on earth for?"

"I quite like Braemar, don't you, my liege?"

"Yes, but only when it's time for the summer games. This is January."

"Hmm." MacDuff strode to the tent flap and pulled it back. The drizzle fell on his face as he stuck his head out. Clouds. He had wondered if the dome would hold clouds. "For all I know, in this beguiled time, it could be summer."

Malcolm shook his head. "You want to hold the annual Braemar games? Now?"

"I certainly intend to announce them. It is time we began acting like it is our country, and not theirs. It will be good to see everyone together. Besides," he looked at Oberon, who smiled lightly as he blew a spectacular smoke ring, and then pointed at Abel. "I would put money on that being the best hammer thrower in the country."

Malcolm ran a hand through his red hair. "Are you certain this is such a grand idea?"

MacDuff walked to Malcolm and put his hand on the boy's shoulder. He kept his smile but the voice became much harder, one that Malcolm recognized. "King, I specialize in grand ideas. Make the announcement. Send out the heralds. And tell everyone to get stowed, because we have thirty miles to cover."

MacDuff turned around to speak with Susan. He looked back over his shoulder. "Now, Malcolm."

The burned out shell of the wolf's den was cold. Belin the wolf snarled; his head felt groggy. He shook it, snapped at the air and shook his head again. His fur bristled as he began to pace slowly, feeling the damp stone beneath his feet. He began to question why he was in this den of humans.

Belin turned around to look over his troops. Some of them were moving around. Six or seven were scuffling over the pitiful dead lamb the men had thrown to them. Some were fighting for no reason at all, snapping with irritation at one another. Some simply sat and stared at the open wood gate, licking their wounds. Some slept.

General Belin shook his head again. He saw another pointed gray head raise itself from a sleeping pile of fur. It was Leir.

"Leir," snarled Belin. "Get up. Come here."

"Sir." Leir roused himself. His taut hind muscles ground painfully with the wounds he had received, but he found them moveable. Belin looked him over. Leir was young and would live to rule the wolves, if he could live through this nonsense.

Belin ushered Leir into the corner, away from polite earshot. "It is time to go."

"But the master said we must fight for the humans. He . . . ooh, I'm sorry, my head is pounding . . ." He shook his muzzle violently. One ear was torn and the fur beneath was matted in blood. He shook off the ache and looked Belin in the eye.

Belin surveyed the stone walls of the adopted den. "I followed him and we nearly died. I may have been a fool to follow him in the first place. At any rate, the master is gone. I have not heard his call for some time and I fear he may be dead."

"Now what?"

"Our duty is finished. We have no reason to stay to be slaughtered further. I suggest we rouse every wolf and go home before the sun comes up."

"But the sun . . ."

"I know, Leir." Belin had a bad taste in his mouth.

Leir turned to the wolves and barked. He eyed Belin for a second, hesitating, then spoke. "All hear. The General will speak."

"Aye." Belin waited for the wolves to turn to him. The pups turned instantly. Those fighting over the lamb took little time. Food was food, but one need not risk the wrath of the General. "Get yourselves in line according to rank. We are leaving. You will follow me." He raised his voice slightly. No questions. "Our business here is done."

A voiced hissed out from atop a slender, smouldering post. "Wrong!"

All wolven eyes flew to the darkness whence came the hiss. A young one yelled, "Cat! Cat!" and was joined by the others as all legs rose taut and all fur bristled.

A cat who spoke Wolf, no less. A cat like no other, of unspeakable power and unknown origin. Belin snarled at the figure, six feet below the hiding shadow. "You are not welcome here, feline."

"You will not leave, Belin, you or your massive canine brethren. You agreed to stay and shall do so." A black figure sprang to a more visible position near the gate.

"That gate is open. We are free to go."

"You are free to go because you agreed to stay."

"The master who commanded us is gone! The battle you fight is lost!"

Graymalkin hissed and his eyes glowed bright, absorbing every particle of light the Erl-King's dim orb provided. He had had enough of vacillation among the allies. What he could fix, he would. He knew his role. "Where will you go, General?"

Belin snapped at the cat on the gate as the other wolves stood back, ready for command. "We will go where I wish, cat."

"And you and your children will all be destroyed."

"Don't be so certain! We are wolves! There is room enough for us in the plan of your enemy!"

"Traitor!" hissed Graymalkin. "Traitor! Fool and traitor! Join the Erl-King and he will use you in his battle until he tires of you and then you will die like the rest of us. Do you want him, Belin, to do to your children what he does with those of the humans? To take their spirits and warp them into his own slaves?"

"We serve no one! You talk rubbish! I fear not the Erl-King!"

"Then why do you leave, coward?"

Belin screamed and snapped viciously at the cat. Graymalkin leapt to another ledge. Belin breathed thickly through his bared fangs. "I leave you because you ally yourself with the enemies of one with whom I have no quarrel."

"Think again," screamed Graymalkin as he sprang off the ledge. He turned in mid-air and landed square on General Belin's back. He sunk his claws into the wolf's neck and shoulders. Belin howled and snarled, whipping his head around to meet his foe, finding no recourse. He felt the cat's claws dig deep into his shoulders and hook around slit muscle.

"Leir!" Belin screamed. Leir drew back to fly at the cat. "Tear this fluff to pieces!"

"No!" screamed Graymalkin, as he tore one paw loose and raised it high and forward. His claws were extended, hooked and bloody. "One move and I destroy him. Believe me, underling. I can."

"Do it, Leir!" Belin tore his head sideways but the claws remained firmly embedded in his shoulders.

"Are you prepared to lead them, Leir? By the time your army has torn me to pieces, if you can, I'll have done irreparable damage to you all. Leave, and the Erl-King will destroy you in the end. Stay and fight and prove your honor. Preserve your home. It's up to you now, Leir. This is a good cause. But for the General's life I offer you a very short career."

Leir stopped. His haunches burned with wound-pain. He looked at the General, who had stopped struggling. Belin's eyes were wide but strong. They were wolves. But even Leir had heard the whispers about Old Graymalkin. What he could deliver in physical pain was rumored to be nothing compared to the torment of the souls he took when he saw fit to kill. Even humans knew that, and would not sleep near a black cat, lest it indeed be Graymalkin, there to steal their soul. But the General was ready for death, and his spirit was his own. *Am I ready? Ready to have my path provided by a cat?*

"Do it!" cried Belin.

"No! Sir!" said Leir. *Damned either way.* "Not like this."

"Aughh!" snarled Belin as he flexed his shoulders with a massive snap. Graymalkin let his claws relax and he was thrown across the den. He righted himself on a smoking board. The wood was hot, but he bore it and hung there. Graymalkin shouted down to Belin.

"Now. You will stay. And when this is done you will have sewn the thread of tales your descendants will tell until the end of all of us comes. Now, you will follow *me.*"

Belin stared at the cat but made no move. "These wolves are mine. Not yours. Not the boy Douglas'. These wolves will take my orders."

"And while we fight the Erl-King?"

"We will take yours, Graymalkin. For you, my little feline friend, are a wolf if I ever saw one."

The wolves of the den relaxed a bit but stood silent. General Graymalkin, as best a cat may, smiled.

CHAPTER 10

So this, Douglas thought, *was the Erl-King*.

Incredible. It was one thing to hear about him, to have his image described by his mother, on many occasions, when she cried and told Douglas who he was and where he came from. It was an entirely different matter to see the Erl-King in person.

The Erl-King sat in a large chair of the same soulstuff as the walls. His long hands he held together below his chin, as a man holds them in prayer. His face was hard, bony white, and gnarled as a tree.

"Douglas. My son. Sit."

Douglas wanted to say, if it is all the same, I would rather stand, but when he looked to his left and saw that his mother was in the room, he changed his mind. Quibbling with Darklings was one thing. There was no telling what his father would do. Douglas took a seat and looked at his mother. Julia was leaned against a wall, her arms crossed defiantly. She nodded silently at

Douglas. *Be careful, boy. We are prisoners here. Do not forget that.*

Douglas spoke. "So this is him?"

Julia nodded again. "*He,* darling. Yes, this is the liar and thief from Hell we politely call your father."

"Tsk, tsk, Julie." The Erl-King clicked his tongue, and Douglas saw it flash black behind sharp, ivory teeth. "I'll thank you not to misrepresent me."

"With which part do you wish to disagree?"

"If I may break in here," said Douglas, raising a small hand, "don't call her Julie. She hates that."

The Erl-King nodded. "Hmm. She didn't used to."

"I would not know," said the boy. The three were silent. How nice to see a family together.

"Are you two hungry?" He sparkled his crystal eyes at Julia. "I imagine he eats a great deal, doesn't he, my dear? My side of the family has a tremendous appetite."

"I, for one, would not touch your food if the alternative were having my insides chewed out by a small rodent."

"Belial was correct." He smiled. "You do not come around nearly enough. Starve, then. Douglas?"

Douglas was hungry. "I . . ."

"Douglas!" snapped Julia.

The boy waved a hand. "Ah, no. Thank you, just the same."

The Erl-King frowned. "Later, perhaps. Julia, really, I'm not going to starve the boy. I need him."

"I'll bet you do. Too bad. You cannot have him."

"That may not be your decision. He cannot stay with you forever, you know."

"He sure as hell won't stay with you."

"He does not belong with humans, *meine Frau.*" The king of the Darklings rose and walked to a table that Douglas hadn't noticed there before. He poured himself a glass of red liquid from a crystal bottle and took a sip, then set it down. For a second he traced the brim with a long, white nail, deep in thought. "It took some time for me to find you, Julia. When you disappeared I had no idea what to think. My bride, my first human bride, had simply deserted me."

"You seduced me. I thought you were good and magical."

"Good is relative. I am magical."

"You thrive on hatred and death. You steal . . ."

"Yes, yes, yes, steal the souls of children. They make a great deal of that, the humans, don't they?"

"You love it."

"I don't deny that. I'm not one of your precious Sisters. I get more than amusement from humans; I don't play the aloof mischief-maker. There is no use in that. They lie that say immortality makes you so philosophical that you do not enjoy the pain of those upon whom you inflict it."

"Twisted, hellish demon."

"Again, relative," said the Erl-King. He took another sip. "You could have been immortal, my dear."

"I doubt that, elf. I would have died. The only reason you wanted me is that you thought you could make a human son."

"And I did. And you took him. And for five years I searched high and low before you finally cropped up at home. Good choice, though. I hadn't expected that. I thought the Sisters would have put you in Italy or some place. So many aliases, all to come home to Oban and fish like your father."

"It is a sound living."

"For a human. But you never gave Douglas a choice. That is all I really wanted to do here, you see? To let the boy choose whom he belongs with more."

"He is a little boy," she said plaintively.

"Oh, Julia, he is far more than that," he hissed, slowly. The long finger pointed at the child. "He is *unique*. He is meant to be with me. I did not create him to have him spend his days fishing and hiding in a basement."

"You did not *create* him."

"*You*," he cried, "were just a vessel. The only other children I have are like myself, the Darklings, they lack . . ." He twirled his hand around in thought, then let it go with a sigh. "The others are intangible, thus far, the souls I take because it is my right to do so. But this," he indicated the child again with a snaking white finger, "this is my son. A mediator if you will, in my final dealings with the humans. An heir to my throne. The Prince Regent of the dark elves. And that is what you took from me. That is what you took from *him*."

"Douglas would have no part . . ."

"No? Look at him. Look at him! Does he not have his father's eyes? This is his destiny, dare you keep it from him?"

"It is evil that you wish of him."

"It is a perfectly legitimate choice!" The Erl-King turned to his son. "You are not human! You are greater than that! You are a demigod. Tell me the truth, do you know that you are immortal?"

The boy sat still. "I . . . was not sure."

"Rest assured. The sentences you form, the tender, controlled gestures. You know that your intelligence far exceeds that of the ordinary human? Of course you do. You can rule, boy, rule with me."

Douglas squinted at the Erl-King, who seemed to have gotten brighter. "To what end?"

"What do you mean?"

Douglas shook his head. "At this rate I shall starve before I can tell you," he said. The boy threw an annoyed look at his mother.

Julia sighed. "Erl-King. The choice is his, you say?"

"Yes."

"And the food he eats here will not . . . influence his decision?"

The Erl-King shrugged. "Only if the boy bases his

loyalties entirely on culinary talent. It is not tainted, if that is what you mean."

"And how can I know you're not lying?"

Douglas said, "He's not." And the boy knew he was right. For some reason the Erl-King was not going to force him. Somehow, Douglas wasn't sure his father could.

Julia looked at her child. She was satisfied for the moment. "Fine."

The Erl-King looked at his son, and then at Julia. "Fine, then." He clapped his crackling hands together. "I shall have you escorted to your rooms, and food will be brought to you," he smiled at Julia, "whether or not you eat it is up to you."

He turned to the door and called out, "Af! Tap!" The Erl-King nodded in the two prisoners' directions and the two Darklings each escorted their charge to the door. "I have other matters to attend to," he said.

"Douglas," he said, already turning away, "we shall talk again soon."

After the spectacular success enjoyed at Dunsinane, Belial winged his way home without being depressed about his wound. Julia and Douglas were long gone. Belial had chosen to lag behind with the army. He felt the wind slide over the raw wing and enjoyed the feeling. Belial looked about at his brothers, all flying in formation. He had lost few. This was a good night.

On the Darklings flew, glistening in the reddish light like a flock of magical fowl. The red glow shimmered nicely on the shiny black feathers of their wings, bouncing beautifully off their fine, black suits, mixing with the crackling white light from their skin, hair and eyes.

Belial looked down. The flat land was growing into a wood. At first the trees merely dotted the landscape, then they became a thick foliage. In the dark they looked like lumps on a gray rug. The wood . . . Belial looked over his shoulder at the Darklings. Such energy should never be wasted.

Belial shouted to those nearest him as he recognized them. "Turel! Carrion! Come, brothers! Let us make mischief!"

Turel and Carrion, fine, upstanding Darklings, put out the call further, and soon all the winging army was swooping down into the woods below.

Turel flew up beside the leader, laughing in his excitement. "What do you have in mind?"

"Icing on the cake, Bruder. We showed our power to the humans tonight. Now let us give a further demonstration to those who need it more."

They dipped below the tree line and began expertly winging through the wood. Belial enjoyed flying through woods; he had always done it well and enjoyed the show of the ability. Even the youngest Darklings were trained to maneuver through the woods; it was brilliant fun and but one thing they could do at which the wood elves were less proficient. So they couldn't hover very long. Who wanted to hover?

Belial peered up ahead. "Wait!" he hissed, and the army slowed down. He could hear the familiar singing and dancing not a quarter mile away. The wood elves were pictured in his mind before he saw them. He knew they were doing their fire dance, much like the ones the Darklings performed. The wood elves would be painted for the dance and probably drunk.

"Good. They're out of the ground and the trees to dance and sing about their precious nature god," he sneered. He did not need a god. The Darklings had the Erl-King.

"Let us kill them," he grinned, then turned to his army in mock seriousness and screamed, "Attack!" Easily motivated after Dunsinane, the Darklings thought it a

wondrous idea, and plunged through the trees with unbri-
dled mirth.

Up ahead, Dennen, population two hundred and fifty, a
minute wood elf hamlet on the far edge of Birnam Wood,
was alive with its night games. The entire town was out,
flying about from tree to tree, flying in circles about the
great fire, and generally frolicking. Most of them were,
indeed, drunk. None of them were armed. This had never
happened before.

When Belial burst through the trees into the clearing
and gleefully sliced off the wings of the first amber elf he
saw, the wood elves took little notice of him. By the time
six painted heads had been removed, a few of those in
flight became aware of what was happening. When a
legion of Darklings swarmed the place, cutting everything
amber in sight, women and children included, cutting
even each other in the frenzy, the whole town barely had
time to realize it was dying. At the massacre of Dennen,
where the Darklings finished off their heady night by
drinking their fill of wood elf ale, no one escaped. Almost.

As Belial flitted home with his drunken, blood-soaked
brethren, he smiled. He knew his leader would be over-
whelmed.

Wood elf Aniel of Dennen was thinking a very similar
thing.

Alen tapped into a barrel and poured himself a glass of
stout. The tavernkeeper at Pitlochry, Alen had noticed a
slight rise in business lately, or at least a rise in company.
Most who came in stayed merely to talk and speculate.
Once the initial rioting had ceased the town had fallen into a
general drudging existence. In this, unlike the unfortunately
fated Forres, Pitlochry was not unlike most towns in this
part of the beguiled time. Those who could not spend time
gossiping in the tavern were those who felt the need to stay
home and man the broadsword against . . . whatever. Faces

in the tavern muttered in the torchlight and drank, their hollow eyes betraying confusion and resignation, and dull, barely held off, aching fear. The wheels of societal machinery, for all practical purposes, had quit turning. Alen wiped his brow with a rag and leaned on the bar. It was hotter than he was accustomed to and he blamed it on the bizarre weather experienced since the sky had disappeared. He could get used to this. A man can get used to anything, he observed.

And then, unannounced, on the day after Dunsinane — unknown to Pitlochry — was burnt to the ground, a herald of King Malcolm III came to town.

Alen looked up when he heard a horse stop outside the door. From what he could see in the perpetual night, it was obviously the mount of a nobleman or some other man of means. The figure that stepped down held a torch, and in the flickering light Alen could see a slightly familiar crest.

"Well," muttered Alen. "A king's man."

The figure stepped into the tavern. He wore a blue cloak and a shirt of decent mail with the same crest on an iron badge at his shoulder. He held his torch up and looked around for a moment.

"You can put your fire over there," Alen said, gesturing to the end of the bar. A makeshift tree of torches had been put up, with small slots in which newcomers could slide the handles of their torches. "We've got plenty of light in here."

The youth — and now Alen noticed that he was young, in fact, no older then the king himself was said to be — nodded gratefully and walked over to the torch tree. He found a notch and slid the finely carved handle into the tree. It was lined with metal and reusable. It looked jarring next to the other, simple, wooden jobs. Rank, Alen noted, had privileges.

The young man turned to the bar. "Are you the tavernkeeper?"

Alen raised a jovial eyebrow.

"I am Donner, Herald of King Malcolm Canmore."

Alen nodded in observant agreement and placed his hands on the bar. "What is your fancy?"

"My . . . oh." Donner brushed back his short, brown hair and thought a second. "The stout looks fine."

"It is," said Alen. He turned to pour another glass. "How goes the war?"

Donner started, then said warily, "What war?"

Alen turned back around. His eyes twinkled beneath his crinkled, pink brow. "It's a figure of speech, lad." He set down the stout.

"Oh," said Donner. "Of course." The herald raised a glass to his lips and looked around him. Every eye in the darkly lit room had turned to watch the visitor from the king. He set the glass down and cleared his throat self-consciously.

"Go ahead," smiled Alen.

"With what?"

Alen laughed. "You said you were a herald." The youth was obviously new. Whatever the king was up to, his best men were with him.

"Oh!" the herald exclaimed. He fished around in the bag that hung from his waist and finally produced a scroll. He turned around to face the room and unrolled it. He opened his mouth to speak, drawing back his head in a grand manner, then abruptly turned back to Alen.

"Would you consider this the center of this town, I mean, for people gathering and such?"

Alen nodded again, smiling.

"Ah." The herald turned around again and resumed his grandiloquent pose. "Hear ye, hear ye!"

Alen groaned. Donner threw him a look and continued.

"Be it known that his Majesty, King Malcolm III, Canmore, right king of Scotland, has planned and shall host the annual games of Braemar."

The people in the tavern looked at each other in disbelief and began murmuring.

"The games shall be held in three days time in Braemar field, at the Earl of Grampian's castle. Strong and good men of the separate clans are requested to attend and compete. Those wishing to prove their superiority in spear-chucking and hammer-throwing, caber-tossing and tug-of-war, will surely be eager to attend this event, so as to bring pride to their clan and their king. All those in hearing of this announcement are expected to notify those not present."

The boy stopped and looked around. One man in the back jeered, "What now?"

"Ahem," said Donner. He looked back at the scroll. "Cowards, fools, and weaklings need not attend. Signed, your king, Canmore." The boy rolled the scroll so diligently prepared by the Thane of Fife and replaced it.

Alen held out Donner's stout. The herald took it and drank a swallow, then set it down and turned to go. In a moment he was back on his horse. He had only to post a few notices in town, speak to the local sheriff about perhaps helping the townspeople make the right decision, and then he would move on to the next town. Behind him he could hear the whispers of the tavern grow to shouts.

Alen held his glass aloft. "Drink up, gentlemen. I suppose I'll be seeing you all in Braemar." Alen turned back to the barrel. *For the best*, he thought, resignedly. *All for the best*. At least it was something.

En route to Braemar, Susan was asking the Thane of Fife, "Will it work?"

"Aye, it will work. If I know these people, it will work." The wheels were starting to move again.

Not long before, an amber fist slammed down on a giant table. "What?"

Bluish blood flowed liberally from a cut across Aniel's forehead. He stepped forward into the light. "A massacre, Gol. An unprovoked, unmitigated massacre."

Golanlandaliay's lip curled. "How many?"

"The whole hamlet, my liege. Young and old. Male and female. It was the Darklings."

The king of the wood elves rose from his throne. "I cannot believe it. He has never done anything like this before."

"The Erl-King is out of control, as the Sisters said. You wanted proof. You have it."

"How could he do this? Killing humans is one thing, but to declare war on the rest . . . what could he be thinking?"

Tether stepped forward. "They warned us that the Erl-King would move on to greater targets. It seems he has."

Golanlandaliay shook his head. "We have had peace for a millennium . . ."

"Damn it, king!" shouted Aniel. "I lost my family tonight. The peace is over."

"Tether," said the king. "Bring me my armor. Fetch bows and quivers and begin manufacturing more arrows. Arouse these wood elves from their peaceful slumber. Find out where the allies are. If they lost Dunsinane, I want to know where they are going. When the time is right, we join."

The back of the amber king's shirt tore open as his feathered wings unfolded and expanded to full length. He drew a dagger and turned to the carvings on the wooden walls. Four feet from the floor was the ancient panel representing the two elf kings making peace, all that time ago. He drew back and let fly the dirk; it jabbed into the wood, separating the two clasped hands. "Out wings! Fly arrows! If the Erl-King wants war," the taut face turned back to his council, "by God, I'll give him one."

CHAPTER 11

"We must be a sight from the air," said Susan, as Paddock flew down and perched on the back of Ruthe's saddle.

"Aye," said MacDuff. He looked behind him at the caravan. A line of torches dotted the countryside where a line of pikemen and cavalry moved northward toward Braemar in the red-black night. Even the Syth, exhausted, were walking: there was no sense in getting there before the humans, anyway. After the previous night, a long walk was a rest. The announcement had been met with resignation and muttering, but they were moving. These men had actually been in the battle; he expected their spirits to be low. Still, it was a malady he hoped to cure in Braemar.

He had sent out a goodly number of heralds, after overseeing the writing of the notice. The new Earl of Fife had been good for a laugh, of course. He thought the idea silly and irrational and had said so, and MacDuff had given him the option of going home to Dunfermline or staying with the rest of the war party. The Earl's people would be needed, though, and the silly man had been convinced to stay. A part of MacDuff wished he had moved the party south, if only to have the opportunity to kick the man out of his favorite chair. But no, that was not his home anymore. He was, he realized, the last real Thane.

The rain had stopped. Up ahead, MacDuff could barely make out the splash of mud underneath the steeds of Dukane and Abel, who rode in front, silent. Now and again MacDuff caught a glint of metal. Abel was nervously spinning his axe. The chains around Dukane's neck were audible from the distance, keeping time, as agitated as their wearer. MacDuff felt a strong kinship for the both of them, now, for the loss of one and the life of the other. He laughed inwardly at this, then scolded himself for daring to be amused when so much had gone wrong. But somehow, despite the tragedy, he could not help it. He was moving. It felt good.

In a draped wagon, on the floor, covered in blankets, Joly turned in her sleep. Titania patted her brow with a damp cloth. She had not opened her eyes yet.

Old Man . . . Old Man . . . Joly was running across a lake, a lake as black as death, and in the center stood a giant man, black as the lake, and he looked at her. *Old Man . . .* Black waves splashed up at her and she was covered in the blood of souls, and every cell cried out to her for safety. The waves were in the power of the giant. She was . . . small, so very small, next to him. The giant man opened his eyes and they sparkled like jewels, but no value lay there, only destruction and malice and deep, dark emptiness. His hair flew back and dripped black rain upon her, and now she was slowing. She could not run anymore, but stood on the lake, being covered by waves of screaming blackness. Now she was sinking, and when she had sunk to her knees she heard a new scream, that of a woman.

Ruthe's favorite! She looked up at the giant man and saw his heart, and a tiny window was open in the chest of the colossal figure. Julia was there, screaming. Joly fought to pull her legs out of the mire but could not budge. The drops of black rain slapped her face and slid together to form a thousand tendrils that wrapped her body and soaked into her pores. *No!* The more she fought the more deeply she sank, until only black liquid flowed over her eyes, only black liquid filled her lungs, and every drop cried for release. And she knew that she was his, and Julia was his, all were his, and he was giant, and all darkness, and very, very old.

Old Man . . . Old Man . . . Old Man!

Titania saw Joly lurch and gurgle, trying to speak in her sleep, trying to find a voice without a throat.

Susan, who was riding silently beside MacDuff, suddenly gasped and broke free to ride back to the wagon. Ruthe was already going in the same direction. "Titania!" Susan yelled. "What is happening?"

Titania pulled back a side flap and looked out at them. "She roused a bit, Sisters. She must be dreaming, poor dear. She hasn't said a thing. Hasn't even opened her eyes." The two Sisters nodded, sullenly, and rode back to the front.

MacDuff looked at Susan as she took her place. "What was that about?"

"I thought I heard my Sister call. It was nothing. I hoped it was . . . something." Susan shook her head and rode on, staring northward. There was something in the edge of her mind, on the tip of her tongue, that she was sure that she heard.

"Ho!" cried Abel. "My lord!"

"Eh?" MacDuff cried.

Abel waved his torch eastward. "The hill!"

MacDuff looked to the east and saw what Abel was

calling to his attention. A handful of torches were topping the hill, and holding them aloft, men on horseback. As more came over the top one of them broke free. MacDuff nudged his horse to ride and meet the figure.

"Who goes there?" he cried.

"My name is Tairn, of Crief." He waved his torch back towards the cavalry behind him. Tairn was a tall fellow, with brown hair and a trimmed beard and moustache. "And we serve the king. And you?"

MacDuff laughed. "I serve the king as well," he said, and it was more or less the truth. "I am MacDuff, Thane of Fife."

"Ho, now," said Tairn. "There are no Thanes anymore."

MacDuff gave a wry smile. "Well. There is one."

Tairn looked him over and decided the man was all right. "We are going to Braemar, to take part in the games."

"Join us, then," said MacDuff. "For we are going to Braemar to start them."

"The king rides among you?"

"Aye," said the Thane.

"The self-same Canmore, who slew the tyrant Mac-Beth? Excellent!" he cried, looking around at his men. "I will be honored to join the party of such a warrior."

MacDuff nodded. "Fine. The Grampian mountains shall become more pronounced soon. A large party is always best. Bring your men alongside."

Tairn raised a hand to direct his men. "Tell me, Mac-Duff. Is the land under siege, as it is said?"

"You'll find out soon enough." MacDuff turned and rode back to join Oberon and Susan.

"Well, well," puffed Oberon.

"Aye," answered the Thane of Fife.

Susan smiled. "It appears you know your countrymen well."

MacDuff looked at her. "Did you doubt me for a second?"

"Never," she said.

Oberon raised his eyebrows and gestured grandly with his pipe. "Especially when we ride in the company of such a fine warrior as Malcolm."

"Ha!" MacDuff shook his head. "Aye, the self-same."

Douglas was asleep. He saw himself walking along a pleasant path through a pleasant wood. He looked about him and saw that everything — the trees, the grass, the flowers — were all his friends.

"Not your friends," a voice said. Douglas turned to see his father walking with him. "Your brothers and sisters."

"All of them?"

"Yes. Not so awful, now, is it?" The Erl-King was walking with his hands behind his back, as if he were taking a morning stroll. "Do you hear them?"

Douglas listened. He did. He heard voice after voice, greeting the two as they passed by. "Hello, father! Hello, brother!"

"Hello," Douglas said, to no one in particular.

"This is what I offer to them, you see." The Erl-King gestured with a long hand towards the countless trees. "A home. A far greater home than any of them ever knew before."

Douglas noticed that the stones on the path, too, greeted him. My, but there were a lot of them.

The Erl-King continued. "The poor, undernourished, emaciated children I take under my wing and give a place. I adopt any and all who will join me. I become their father. Many of them," the Erl-King said pointedly, "never had a father.

"I take the babes who have been left to die by their heartless natural parents. They, especially, are grateful for my generosity." The stones and the trees were echoing him cheerfully. Grateful. Generosity. "I feel, then, that I have been largely misunderstood. Your mother misunderstands me, that is why our discussion got nowhere with her to interject. Alone, you can see things as they are." He stopped by a stone and indicated it to Douglas, who took a seat. He ran his fingers through Douglas' fine, black hair and tousled it.

"What I offer you is a place, Douglas."

"But I have a place. With my mother."

"Your mother means well, Douglas, but she does not understand your needs. She cannot take care of you forever. She barely gets by as she is, doesn't she? It must be very hard supporting oneself and a child as a fisherwoman."

Douglas nodded.

"I realize you love your mother, and that is why what I am saying to you is very important. You are a very special child, and that makes it very hard for her, Douglas. She goes to an awful lot of trouble to keep you and watch you, when, in fact, she could not provide you with what you need even if she understood what it was." The stones and trees were still echoing him, and he spoke on. His eyes sparkled like jewels, and Douglas could not turn away from them, nor, now that he thought about it, did he want to. His voice was like no other he had ever heard, sweet and soft, serene. It was a voice to be believed.

"Life with me, as my son, will be one of joy. Such games, Douglas, I can show you, things your mother could never show you, even if she knew how, even if she could afford to. You, Douglas, are the most special child I have."

"Why?"

"Because already you are my child. You always have been. You are, in fact, more my child than that of your mother's. This is why the place you take with me will be superior to any other, because you are special, you are unique."

"Do you need me, then?" the question came from somewhere Douglas could not quite place.

A flash disrupted his father's eyes, then they grew serene once more. "Need? Why, I love you, Douglas. By virtue of loving you I could not do without you. Yes, yes, I need you." He leaned forward and took Douglas in his arms, holding the boy close and whispering in his ear. Douglas could still hear the woods singing his praises and echoing his thoughts.

"Come with me, Douglas. I know you love your mother, but it is better that you leave her. I can give you a place." Somewhere Douglas thought he heard a pebble cry *No!*

"You will be a prince and rule with me over my whole family. You will be happy, never sad again, never alone, never in hiding, never rejected or neglected . . ."

No! another stone cried, somewhere. Douglas saw his father's eyes flash once more.

". . . happy in my family, where all of us live in harmony . . ."

No! More voices.

". . . such games . . ."

No!

". . . your mother could not . . ."

Liar!

The eyes blazed furiously and the Erl-King drew back and turned to the forests and the trees. He remained calm. "Did I hear . . ."

Liar!

"But, children . . ."

"You lie, father!" cried Douglas, as he rose from the stone.

The Erl-King spun around. "How dare you speak to me this way?"

"These souls are your prisoners!"

"I gave them a home!"

"The kind of home you want to give me?"

"No," he said, his voice calming itself. "No. You are different."

Leave us, father! cried the voices. *Let us go!*

The Erl-King snapped, "You're not going anywhere."

"So," said Douglas, "they are you prisoners, after all."

"They do not actually want to leave. I have simply been busy and they are annoyed at the lesser amount of attention I have been willing to pay."

Liar!

"What happens if one of them says no?"

"That," he said, "never happens."

"But if one did? What if one . . . what if I were not willing . . ."

"Then I'll take you by force." The answer was automatic. The crackle that ran through his eyes was sparking in the deep crevices in his ivory face.

"I don't think so," said Douglas. "You need me. Why?"

"I love you."

"You *need* me. Why?" The forest was growing louder now, and Douglas saw the trees swaying, crying out for release. Then the whole picture ruptured and melted, and all was blackness, and a thousand thousand faces swam madly through the sea of emptiness, crying for release from the Erl-King's "family."

The Erl-King looked at him and bared his fangs. "You will join me, Douglas. One way or another."

Douglas sprang up in his blankets and looked around his cell. The light from his eyes showed him he was alone. Alone, save for the singing walls.

Julia writhed in her sleep and moaned.

The Erl-King was there, standing over her, as she lay on the soft furs. She had thrown off the covers and lay revealed in the sparkling light of his eyes, beads of sweat glistening on her body.

She opened her eyes, dreamily, and looked at him. He was exactly as she remembered him: tall, muscular, thin, like a magical David. His shoulders were sleek and white, and the curves along his chest flowed down with her eyes, to the taut, white, muscular abdomen. Every line of his body crackled with the same energy that came through in his eyes and hair. He was a god.

Julia . . .

He sat next to her on the furs, all lines and sinew, and drew a long hand to her shoulder. With every movement of his arm the muscles in his chest reacted; he was a great machine, pulsating with energy. She saw his face, not at all lined with furrows as she recalled, but smooth, hard and polished, like his body, like ivory. Her shoulder buzzed and crackled where he touched her; his energy was astounding. She felt caught up in his magnetic pull, just as she had been, so long ago.

He smiled once, and she saw his teeth, flat and square, housing a long, black tongue. She swallowed; she felt like her mouth was made of cotton. He bent forward and kissed her on her collarbone, than her neck, and then he took her head in his crackling hands and took her mouth against his, and she was filled with warmth and energy. His nimble tongue played against hers as she raised her arms to his ivory shoulders, sliding them across his long back.

She slid her left leg up, felt her knee crackle as it brushed his stomach, and now he was on top of her, his crackling hands gliding across her, playing at her stomach. She closed her eyes and could feel him, like so long ago, could feel the small of his back as her hands crackled against it, guiding him, as he crackled and surged. He was magic, he was powerful, and she was filled with force and power that crackled and exploded within her, and every inch of her was alive with the power that he brought. And then, she heard him give a soft chuckle and she felt the wings (No . . .) on his back where she had not felt them before and when he kissed her neck again she felt his teeth (No . . .) and then all at once she opened her eyes and screamed, "No!"

Julia looked around the room. She could see nothing in the darkness. Her sweat cooled on her body as she caught her breath. The dark could not hide him. She was alone.

The Erl-King looked out his window and dug his ivory nails into the black sill. It was going to be more difficult than he thought.

An ivory fist slammed down on the huge table. "What?"

"A massacre. You should have seen it."

The Erl-King stood from his chair and leaned on the table, his eyes flashing at Belial furiously. "Whose idea was this?" He already knew.

Belial stopped smiling. The father was not as pleased as he had anticipated. "It was mine, my liege."

The Erl-King struck the table again. "Why did you violate my orders?"

"I thought that . . ."

"You thought! You thought! I did not ask you for your thoughts, Belial!"

"But you said we would attack all the supernaturals, and I had the . . ."

"Do you have any idea what you have done?"

Belial was silent.

"Let me tell you. I have every intention of destroying the wood elves, but I had rather hoped I could wait until after the conflict in which I am already involved. After I have won over the boy and strengthened my power over the stolen souls. You have jeopardized the entire effort, Belial. Golanlandaliay will strike, if not now, soon."

"We can beat him."

"I am aware of our capabilities," snapped the Erl-King. "I am also aware of our limitations."

Belial was confused. *Limitations! Since when had they had limitations?* "What now? Do we attack the wood elves, then? Finish off the Sisters and their forces?"

The Erl-King shook his head. "No."

"We must act, father."

"Listen to me. I know what we must do and now is not the time. We have the boy. I will work with him."

"But . . ."

"Belial!" The Erl-King let his wrath subside and turned his back. He took a seat. "Leave me, Belial. Go and rest."

"My Lord . . ."

"Leave me. I shall not remain angry with you if you leave me now. There is blood on your wing. Clean that wound. There will be battle soon enough."

CHAPTER 12

MacDuff's plan was not so strange, really. Diversion is a human need, as is the assertion of one's identity. One of the plagues of the captive man is the loss of identity and sense of place. The fearful stupor of nights spent waiting in captivity turns men into rats, it takes tall men and bends them low, crawling from place to place. MacDuff wanted to remind the Scots that they were still at home. All they needed was a push.

Besides that, he needed reinforcements.

The games at Braemar lasted only a brief while, a short few days, but the men turned out, as MacDuff expected, in droves. Every town and clan sent its competitors, or rather the competitors got together and sent themselves. Highlanders and Borders came, from the best of the Camerons, Campbells, and Chisholms, to the MacKays, MacHenrys, and MacDonalds, to the Rosses, Sinclairs and Sutherlands. Though he could not know it, it was an accumulation of Scotsmen not to be seen until Robert

Bruce routed the forces of Edward II at Brannockburn in 1314. It was an accumulation of amateurs that MacDuff intended to professionalize.

And while Seyton, glad to be busy, oversaw the games and even tried to get along with Malcolm, MacDuff oversaw his own preparations. Except for the tug-of-war, MacDuff stayed out of the games and was content to observe and plan. And while Abel Galloway proved himself, indeed, the finest hammer-thrower in the land (no record could be kept of the throw, however: the lit field was too short and it sailed out of sight), MacDuff had James bring him a running tally of the best men according to their particular talents.

MacDuff fired up the kiln at Braemar and commissioned all available smiths to forge as many spears as could be managed (those tipped pikes, Susan observed, had to go) and had as many Syth as Oberon deemed sufficiently talented carve arrows and bows. Training the men to use them, he knew, might be a challenge.

The Syth, however, did come out for one event, which MacDuff deemed a worthy one to introduce the race to the humans: tug-of-war.

MacDuff looked across the torch-lit field at rapid-legged Oberon and called out, taking the rope in his hands, "Are you sure you want to do this, little man? You could be in for a long haul, and I would not want to embarrass an immortal."

"Very kind of you, Iron Thane, but I really have nothing better to do, and I expect that this should be over in a few minutes. I hope you like mud."

"I like the looks of it on alabaster kings," said the man of no woman born.

"Mark!" cried Seyton, and the rope pulled taut and MacDuff felt himself fly forward at least two feet as the lower half of the opposing team all but disappeared. Near a thousand pairs of Syth feet, with Oberon at the captain's place, began moving with the speedy power with which the gods had blessed them. And now MacDuff looked across the expanse of mud in the center of the field and felt for a moment certain that he was about to go down in the shortest tug-of-war he had ever led.

"Pull!" cried the Iron Thane, but his cry was not needed. For no sooner had the humans begun to slide forward under the tow of the swift-footed Syth but the huge and heady Scots sought to even the score with their own gifts. The fires of Hephaistos burned in the sinewy arms and chest of the Thane of Fife as he felt that first pull, and now he made his pain worse: he dug in his heels and pulled on the great rope, feeling in his hands that his men were doing likewise.

Oberon found that he could not concentrate on the game and his pipe at the same time and spat it aside. His feet moved with all the speed the gods had given his people, but he found that he was no longer moving backward.

Ramm and Jikk, two Syth of the retinue of Titania and brothers, looked down in horror as they saw, through the transparent spin of their own legs, that they in fact were moving forward. "Impossible," cried Jikk, "we are Syth and these are humans. Pull!" But it was the pull of another that made all the difference.

At the anchor of the human side, Abel decided that if there would be a time for him to move, it would not happen again in this game. Once had been enough. When he heard his captain yell, he made up his mind and set his giant legs at an angle and leaned back, and knew that only the fires of Hell would keep him from moving forward again. He gave a great heave and began to pull the rope back with those giant, god-like forearms.

On the sidelines, the King of Scotland sat on his throne and watched the game enrapt. Near him, equally caught up in the goings-on, the Sisters watched and made silent bets.

Ruthe turned to her auburn-haired sister and asked, "What was it you said to MacDuff when he took the rope?"

Graymalkin the cat batted a lock of hair away from her eye. "I said it was good and gamely of MacDuff to try, that he was dealing with immortals, so he should be sure not to be too disappointed."

Ruthe raised an eyebrow. "And what did our melancholy Thane say to that?"

"He was very gruff indeed, as usual, and said," Susan dropped her voice down in mockery of the thundering voice of the Iron Thane, "that we were dealing with the strongest mortal arms in the world, and the best of clans, and that I should step aside before I got hurt. It was very masculine, really. All this clan business really gets to the mortals."

Ruthe smiled. "Of course it does. Some say it makes them immortal, in their own way. I find it charming."

Susan nodded. It was good not to think about her healing Sister for a moment. "Oh, I know you do. You and your mortal attachments."

"Yes, well, oh doomsayer, just you watch your step." Ruthe waited for Susan to cast her a look again. "Or they'll grow on you, too."

"Oh, do shut up." Susan was watching the games again.

"Well, at least one."

"Hush. Watch the game, Sister."

Ruthe turned her attention back to the game but cast a glance back to Susan who was slightly smiling, for once. She gave Susan a wink and jerked her head back toward the field when she heard a loud cry from the captain of the Syth. In the light of the fire, she could make out the carved, massive arms of Abel pulling the rope the full length of his reach as the whole other team moved slowly forward. Every man pulled steadily, as Oberon cried out again, legs still spinning, and finally let go and sailed with the rest of his men into the mud.

MacDuff was the first to extend a hand to speed-gifted Oberon, king of the Syth, to lift him out of the muddy pit.

"Why, thank you, lad," he said.

The Fife Thane nodded curtly, when he realized that the mighty king of the Syth was pulling him into the mud. Thus the games truly began, and thus the Syth and the humans finally had their proper meeting and became allies. That is, after *all* of them were covered in mud.

Malcolm III, meanwhile, passed out prizes and acted kingly, in his own way, and stayed away from MacDuff. The king occupied the time of the men by making a number of vacuous addresses, which, provided the attendants had enough ale in them, all seemed to enjoy. The chieftains, for their part, knew to defer to MacDuff in matters of the war and to Malcolm in matters of no great import.

And on the fourth day, when he decided that enough time had been legitimately wasted, the Thane of Fife made his own address.

Malcolm — and everyone else as well — had avoided the subject, but all who were not present at the battle of Dunsinane knew that the country was at war. It hung over the festivities as obviously as the dome that hung over the land. When Malcolm introduced a speaker "of great national consequence," a hush fell over the crowd. As the tall, gaunt man with iron-gray eyes and a haunted look took the platform, looking out to the sea of faces, they knew, instinctively, that this, if not in name, was in truth a king. And when he spoke, they listened.

CHAPTER 13

"I bid you all good evening," he said. "I trust it is evening. I sometimes cannot tell anymore. I am MacDuff, Thane of Fife. I come tonight to speak to you of the obvious. We are at war.

"Men of Alba, none of this is new to us. We have seen war before. We are a strong people, hard and virile. We will survive. The blood that runs in your veins and in mine is a mixed one, with a great history. When the first Scots came here, they fought long and hard against the residing Picts, and out of these two great peoples came a greater one, the Scots we know today. Together we grew, absorbing what the hardships and blessings of our land could afford us. Our fight is legend.

"We have been walled in before. When the great empire of Rome swore it would rule the world, it stopped at Caledonia. When all other nations fell in its path, time and time again their generals came crawling home with the same news. We cannot fight the Scots. They love their land too much. There was not a Roman warrior who did not quake in fear when he faced us in battle. When we took the field on our own land, they said, something unnatural, something supernatural, happened. We fought together, as one, extending our alliance across every clan line. The din that rang from the clash of the first axe against their armor was echoed on their brains, forever. We are Scots: tread not here. We fought until we tasted our own blood, until from our bones our flesh was hacked. Still we fought, killing our foe even as we fell to the ground, for we lived on in our kinsmen, who drove the outsiders back and away. They could have their empire. But not here. Finally, defeated, they threw up a wall to keep us inside. Its ruins stand still today. The men who built it are gone; their empire fell as ignobly as did their useless constraints upon us. They are gone. We are still here. Their crumbled wall is a reminder.

"I do not know why it is Scotland that interests the outsiders so. Perhaps it is that they wish to be like us. Perhaps they have seen how strong are our men, how brave our warriors, how thick our blood. Perhaps they have noticed the beauty of our music, and how it stirs the soul as we ride into battle, how it carries us along and drives us forward as we crush all that lies in our path, all that would challenge us, all that would destroy us. This would lead them to want this land. Perhaps they see that, for us, to live is to fight; to die fighting is to live forever. To hear the din and go out to fight the enemy is our sport, and if we lack a sword we fight with a spear, and if we lack a spear we fight with rocks, and if we lack rocks we fight with our bare hands, until every limb is torn from our bodies. Perhaps the outsiders think it is this homeland that makes us so. Perhaps they are right."

MacDuff stopped. He drew in a breath and surveyed the crowd for a moment. The torches were the only movement on the dark field.

"This is a strange time. When fraternity ends and kings go mad, our land falls into darkness. We did not need a giant wall to illustrate the problems we faced. We are all capable of mistakes. I made many mistakes all at once, and once was all that was necessary. I looked away from my home and lost it. My wife. My children.

"I thought we had lifted the curse upon our land with the destruction of MacBeth, but we have not. We have lost consciousness as a people, and have been thrust into the dark. We have been faced with a challenge. And we have not answered it!

"I stand before you a man who has seen much of battle, and a man who has made mistakes. I understand how they are made, and how to learn from them. I bear upon my body the scars of my battles, and each tells me a story. I bear one trophy each and more, for untempered youth, for incompetence, for inattentiveness, for lack of preparation. But on my back I bear the scars that shame me most, those earned when I was young, and had to turn around to see who had sliced my back to ribbons. The stripes on my back I hold as testimony to fear.

"I am not, I feel, destined to see many more battles. I had thought my greatest battles behind. But I am here today, with you. Learn from me and the scars I bear.

"We are in a war the likes of which we have never seen. Our enemy is from the fires of Hell itself; his army, its winged, demonic denizens. As allies we have forces we cannot comprehend, whom, before this, I had never thought truly existent. All things impossible have become real. To that, by the eternal night you see around you, you can easily attest. We are but men, small creatures in the mix, who bud and blast away in only moments upon the eternal earth. We are in a league entirely unknown to us. But the results of this conflict may determine the fate of mankind.

"But it has always been thus for us: always have we

known we are not immortal, yet we live on in the tales and deeds of our sons; we are, in our own way, eternal. Perhaps in a greater way. The basic truth remains the same.

"The foreigners have attacked us: they will fail. They have thrown us into darkness: we demand light. They desire our home: they will not have it. They wish to destroy us: we will thrive. They have invaded our home and slaughtered our people: we demand vengeance!

"Men of Scotland, join me. Take up the sword against those who dare oppose us. This is our country! We demand that it remain so. We are not sheep, we are men! We will act as men! We will live as men! If need be, we will die as men!"

MacDuff looked out at the crowd, then up at the pale, reddish sky, and the red star in the center of the dome. Somewhere a MacLeod began piping out the haunting sound of the Ceol Mor. "I tire of the dark, lads," shouted MacDuff as his sword was held high in the air. "Let us reclaim the light!"

The men roared passionately as more pipers joined in, and the world seemed filled with the sound of the gathered army, singing the old songs. And MacDuff stood alone on the stage, content that this would surely be his last war.

"Who are you?" the voices sang.

"My name is Douglas. You cannot escape?"

"There is no . . . leaving."

Douglas thought a moment. "And he controls you, too, doesn't he? The form you have taken?"

"Yes!" they cried, but then, as quickly, "no!"

"What do you mean, 'yes' and 'no'?" There was no answer. Douglas looked at the walls of his cell and then at the floor. He envisioned the dome outside, stretching across hundreds of square miles, made up of all those souls. Somehow the Erl-King had learned to control them. Douglas wondered if he could control them, as well. "This wall, who holds it up, you, or the Erl-King?"

"There is no escape . . ."

"Come with me," he said. "Leave the wall."

"No."

"Why not? Are you trapped by the Erl-King?"

"We — he is our father. We have a place. We love our place."

"But earlier you called him a liar. You said . . ."

"No."

"You said that he lied, that he was using . . ."

"No!"

These children, thought the boy, *cannot make up their minds*. "I have heard you all, crying, all of you. I know that you are unhappy. I know you crave escape, you cannot deny it!"

"Yes! No!"

Douglas struck the floor with both fists. "Make up your minds! Either he holds you captive in the wall or he does not, and you are here because you want to be!"

"He is our father . . ."

"Do you know what I think?" asked Douglas. "I think you made a bargain you did not comprehend. I think you are contemplating escape."

"No!"

"I think the Erl-King knows this, and it is becoming increasingly difficult to hold his fortress together. I think the effort is wearing him out. I think you know this, and you could escape if you wished."

"You don't understand . . ."

Then it hit Douglas all at once. He reeled in nausea at the cruelty of the realization. They could not escape from the soulstuff. They were the soulstuff. This was the life they had chosen. To be separated from it would . . .

Douglas stared at the floor in silence, seeing deep into the soulstuff. The souls were there, silent, afraid.

"We would die, Douglas."

No other words came.

Kreen the Syth stood before Thorfinn Sigurdsson, the Viking king of the Orkney Islands. He was, indeed, within the wall.

The king scratched at his red beard. Mounds of red hair flowed past his face and over his shoulders. From the side of his sturdy throne hung a quiver, a mace and an axe. He set down a giant mug of ale after taking a drought. Liquid sloshed over the side of the wooden cup as light reflected off the bands of gold around the man's forearms. Bits of liquid remained on Thorfinn's moustache. "My men say you wish to see me. What are you?"

"I am Kreen. I serve Oberon, King of the Syth. I have a message for you."

"Either you are telling the truth, or I am drunk," he said, giving a great laugh. *A little of both,* Kreen thought. Thorfinn threw a glance at the other long-haired warriors in attendance, who laughed heartily with him. At his side, a largish woman with equally voluminous yellow locks in braids, smiled. Thorfinn said, "Thorfinn the Mighty is my name. I am king here, little man. This is my queen, Ingi-jbord."

"I was given to believe that you were Earl of Orkney, of Scotland."

"Oh!" He laughed. "You must come from Malcolm's court!" he roared, then bent forward. "Let me explain something. I am a Viking king! I rule the Nordreys, where we serve the true gods Odin and Thor, and all else serve me. I do not serve the Scots king, regardless of whatever patronizing nicknames he bestows upon me."

Kreen had heard of Vikings, of course, but had never taken any real interest in them. Strange. "Very well, King Thorfinn. I have come to tell you that the land is under attack."

Thorfinn snickered and looked at his wife, then at his attendants. The snicker echoed into another bellow. He waved a hand, and furrowed his bushy brows in mock seriousness. "No, surely you jest. You came, what, three hundred miles to tell me that?"

"You know?"

"Are you mad, little man? The damned sky's been shut up."

"Do you know who it is? Have you faced him?"

The king lifted his cup and took a drink. "No. Whatever he has been waiting for, he hasn't attacked yet."

"His name is the Erl-King. I am sure you have your corresponding name. You may find this hard to believe . . ."

"Don't be so sure," said Thorfinn. "I believe in Valhalla. Besides, I have never been visited by one of the little people before. What is more," he said, considering, "I have seen his men flying about. Very queer individuals. Does he fight well?"

"Very well. My people have faced them before. The Scots believe they will be attacked first."

"Damned insulting, that, but he may already have. There has been a lot of movement lately."

"A lot? What do you mean?"

"Thor's hammer, boy, don't you know?" asked the Viking. He stood up and moved his heft across to a great window. Drawing back the curtains and shutters, Thorfinn pointed with a banded, hairy arm at a monstrous tower to the dark southeast. "He's right here, on my own doorstep. He's on Hoy."

Kreen looked out into the dark sky. He must have passed the tower within two miles, as he skimmed across the water; in the dark he had not noticed it. The tower was a column, well over seven hundred feet high, branching out at the top into the dome that expanded in all directions.

"That . . . is all his construction?"

"No," said Thorfinn. "The first four hundred and fifty feet or so, deep in there, is the red sandstone Old Man of Hoy.

"My men are going nowhere," he muttered, completely serious. "You want to take him on, you bring your men here."

"The Old Man!" cried Susan. She slapped her forehead in a manner unbecoming of the First Sister. "I should have known! That was what I heard Joly say, that night."

Oberon shook his head. "You could not have been sure. At least now, we know."

MacDuff turned to Kreen. He had been overseeing the stepped-up preparation of the men when the scout returned. He had not slept but snatchingly in days, filling targets with arrows, training farmers and shepherds to batter dummies into oblivion with spears and swords, spending his nights poring over maps, speculating, discussing strategy with Seyton, Dukane, Oberon, the chieftains, anyone who dared stay up with him. The Thane of Fife only grew more gray, as it streaked wider by day across his head. The fires in his iron eyes revealed no fatigue. Now, finally, he had a lead. "Hoy. That was where Thorfinn said the Erl-King is?"

"Aye, sir," said Kreen. The scout, however, was showing fatigue. He turned his puffy eyes to his king. "Sir?"

Oberon tapped his pipe and looked him over. "Good work, lad. The Syth are in a camp behind the castle. Go rest."

"Thank you." The young Syth made a quick exit.

Seyton watched him go. He rolled out a map of Scotland. A dark line was drawn around the country as accurately as could be managed. With a piece of coal he finished the line, extending it around the Orkney Islands. He drew a large "X" over the island of Hoy. "That, MacDuff, is one hundred and twenty miles from here, as the crow flies."

MacDuff looked at the X. "And we do not fly as our compatriots do."

Oberon blew a smoke ring. "No. But you have the numbers, MacDuff. My men are not enough."

MacDuff nodded. "Agreed. The only option available is to move. Root him out, and destroy his new home."

"What about Thorfinn?" asked Susan.

"Well, he regards that as his territory. I should have expected that more than pride had kept him from contacting Malcolm. Under the circumstances, I am sure that he would be willing to aid us. He has done so before. I rather like Thorfinn. He fights."

Seyton squinted and brushed back his hair. "The wall is far enough out on the Moray Firth that a water route may be possible, but it will still mean covering forty-five miles by land. Then, if we had boats, we could cover the rest by water, around one hundred and thirty miles if we follow the shores."

"And land at Thorfinn's under the nose of the Erl-King?"

"Aye," said Seyton. "That's the difficult part."

"There's more," said Susan. "If that wall obeys his commands, it will be difficult getting into his castle. And he still has Julia and the boy."

MacDuff sat in a chair. "And we will get them back, I assure you. I'm not sure if it would be wise to leave the boy in his father's hands for long."

"I assure you, MacDuff," said Susan, as she took a seat across the table from him. "It would not. Ruthe, Joly and I worked very hard to remove Julia and her son from the Erl-King. He is powerful, it is true. For him, however, that boy is the ultimate weapon. He had no right to make a human child; we moved to erase that sin. It would be disastrous if Douglas joined his father's side. What is more," she said, looking at the table, "and though I do not like to discuss it, this is important: Julia is a . . ." she looked at him, and he knew what it was.

"A friend."

"Aye." She frowned at her own lack of detachment. "Of Ruthe, first, but we . . . I am really quite fond of the human. I never have approved of attachments to mortals, it . . ."

MacDuff blinked. "Yes?"

"It is problematic. But I can understand Ruthe's mistakes. Life is unpredictable, really. There are often those things we cannot see. Sometimes even immortals cannot avoid the appreciation . . ." her eyes traced the air, trying to find her words, ". . . that they may come to have for other individuals, even though they know that it is an unwise appreciation to entertain."

Susan looked at MacDuff, who remained silently attentive, and then at Oberon, who sat quietly, puffing away. She stood up. "So it is vital that we get Julia back. Do you understand? Now if you will excuse me, I must go meet my Sisters." The witch in the blue gown glided out of the room.

MacDuff understood.

CHAPTER 14

The wind lifted a few silver curls off Seyton's brow as he walked to where James stood. "How comes the net?"

"Have a look," said James. The boy was tugging at a cord that held a corner of a large net to a pole at one corner of the Braemar field.

The net had been MacDuff's idea. Given the choices of either continuing to leave his men camped on an open field, vulnerable to a slaughterous air attack, or moving them all into the woods at the southeast corner, the Iron Thane had settled on a third alternative, that of keeping the men where they were and hoisting a net over their heads. The handiwork of the coastal fishermen covered the expanse of the field.

Seyton stepped under the net, unconsciously ducking, even though at six and a half feet from the ground it provided plenty of headroom. "Well. What a headache."

James nodded. "Aye. For the enemy, especially."

"Right. A decent defense against an attack, I'd say. The

real problem is that I'm almost certain that the moment those crows see the net they'll move to cut it down and let it fall on us."

"I've thought of that," came the deep voice of the Thane of Fife. MacDuff emerged from nowhere, all shadows and torchlight, briskly walking across the damp field. "I want every man armed with a dagger; he should have one, in any case, so that when he sees those nets coming down he can slice himself out."

"There won't be much time," said Seyton. "Every second they waste cutting a hole to fight through . . ."

"Is another second to the advantage of the Erl-King, I know. But it will have to do. Let's just be ready and hope we can cause a few losses ourselves. If all goes well, the only thing to worry over will be moving out of the way as their bodies fall." MacDuff clasped Seyton's shoulder firmly and moved on.

It was getting hotter still. Not intensely, but he was now aware that it was particularly uncomfortable. And was it his imagination, or was breathing getting harder, as well?

MacDuff found Dukane busily sharpening a harpoon at a sparking stone wheel. Most of the remaining pikes had been reinforced and converted, complete with a thirty-foot line. "Good," said MacDuff.

Dukane sniffed, and his chains jingled as he turned to see the Thane. "The line of pikemen under the net will throw these at the enemy. The problem will be . . ."

"Moving out of the way of the misses. Let's hope our aim is good."

Dukane nodded. "It is my job to ensure that it will be."

"You do what you can," said MacDuff. He turned and looked out across the dimly lit field. Under the ubiquitous torchlight men were busy at all corners. A number were parrying with Abel, while at least twenty were competing amongst themselves at throwing the harpoons (sans towlines) up and through the nets. He turned back to Dukane. "If we could get daggers . . ."

"Already being issued." Dukane gave a sly smile. "For cutting through the net. I think of these things, too, you know."

"Good." MacDuff had noticed Susan leaving the castle. He took a few seconds to catch her.

"Good morning, Fife-Thane," smiled Susan. She moved fast, and MacDuff noticed that the blue material somehow avoided absorbing the fine mist that lay across the land.

"Top of the morning, Sister." MacDuff looked ahead. They were headed for the armory. "How fares Joly?"

"Still not talking, still not conscious, but she seems fine, for all that. Ruthe and Titania are like two mother hens. A common patient makes strange bedfellows."

They had reached the armory door, and MacDuff felt a sudden blast of hot air hit him as they opened the door. About thirty Syth were inside, involved in various stages of weapons-crafting. A deafening roar barely hid the noise of hammer clanging against anvil.

Near a cooling rack stood Oberon, looking over the shoulder of one of the Syth. Oberon turned and saw Susan and MacDuff, patted the Syth on the back, and stepped near to them. He signalled towards the door.

As the three stepped out, Oberon drew off his huge leather gloves and slapped them together, then slid them under his belt. The king of the Syth wiped his brow. Steam poured off his face and hands. "Here, let us walk. Damn heat." He fished his pipe and a bag of tobacco out of a pouch on his hip and began to fill the bowl. "You two are up early," he said.

Both MacDuff and Susan answered, "How can you tell?"

The three walked at their customary pace to the mess tent and seized a pot of coffee. MacDuff poured the two immortals a cup each and sat down with his own. He tugged at his beard.

"How are those bucklers coming?"

Oberon puffed at his pipe a second. "The ones with the spikes, those bucklers? Fine, you delegatory despot. I'll have you know it isn't easy to fashion a weapon for a hand twice the size you're accustomed to. But, fine. Most of them are already cool. There should be enough for our purposes. The bows and arrows are already out; I gave a shipment to Captain Jikk last night. Not much more to do." He sipped at his coffee and glanced at Susan.

"Susan, you look lovely, considering how little sleep we've all had. How is . . ."

"Joly's fine, and so is Titania."

"Glad to hear it. I'll have to stop by and see how she's coming along. I know being away from home is hard on her."

MacDuff noticed that the coffee was awful and continued to sip at it. He ran a hand through his ever-graying hair. "Nearly three weeks since Dunsinane. I'm surprised."

"Thank the gods for small favors," said Oberon. "Whatever has been keeping him, I shouldn't think the Erl-King will wait much longer."

MacDuff shook his head. "No. An attack against him should at least be a possibility he has considered. I hope we haven't been given this time to the detriment of Julia and Douglas, either. At all events, I feel we have used the time wisely."

Oberon tapped at his pipe. "I'll agree with that."

"Another point is that, in a way, I rather hope the Erl-King doesn't wait too much longer. My men are rested and well-armed. I'd prefer to fight now, while we have our energy and our enthusiasm, for lack of a better word."

Graymalkin appeared from below and jumped to Susan's lap. "Well, little devil," said the First Sister. "We're not seeing much of you these days."

"I've seen him," remarked Oberon, "among the wolves.

It appears our feline friend is keeping Douglas' pets in line in his absence."

"Not a mean feat, I suspect," said Susan. The cat batted at the lock of hair that fell across her brow. She poured some cream into a saucer and set it down, and Graymalkin immediately turned his attention to it. It was an expensive gift, Susan reminded herself, but her familiar deserved it.

Oberon thought a moment. "Do you suppose the Erl-King knows where we are?"

MacDuff nodded. "I don't think that is too much to assume."

"Then," said Susan, "we shall be ready when he gets here." The lock fell down again. This time it was MacDuff who gingerly pushed it aside.

"Aye," he said. "And if he doesn't come . . ."

"We will go after him," Oberon sighed.

MacDuff poured himself another cup. He took a sip and winced inwardly as it burned his throat.

"No Golanlandaliay," said Belial. The Erl-King tapped the arm of his throne pensively. "Three weeks, and no wood elf attack."

The Erl-King looked up. "Where are the humans?"

Belial smiled. "Braemar, my liege. Our scouts spotted them there."

"They have moved closer to us. Perhaps they know where we are."

"You do not expect an attack from them, surely?"

"I do not know what to expect. One mad king can try anything, with humans."

Belial nodded. "In any case, they are more convenient to us. They have not been acting like they are planning an attack. The last we saw, they were playing games."

"Games?"

"Aye. They all came to the field of Braemar and played games. Some sort of native ritual, I imagine."

"Funeral games." The Erl-King tapped at the arm again. "There may be method to that."

"My liege, I have no reason to fear the humans, and I feel we have waited long enough. It is time to wipe them out, once and for all."

"I had hoped to have the boy on my side by now, but he resists me."

"Would you like me to kill the woman? Perhaps that would change his mind."

The Erl-King's eyes darted back and forth in thought. "No. Julia will be more important alive. The boy, mature as he seems, is terribly attached to his mother." A sudden tremor shook the entire structure of the tower. The Erl-King's hair crackled wildly, then dimmed a second, before returning to its normal level.

As this happened, Belial nearly swooned. He straightened himself against the table.

"What the hell was that?" said Belial. He looked around and turned back towards the throne when he heard the Erl-King say, "Wait." The throne was empty.

The Erl-King stood in his forest, but found it unfamiliar, full of black, liquid trees. A sharp wind whipped past him and made the ground lap up across his boots. "All right, children," he growled. "What is it? What is going on?"

Nothing!

The Erl-King saw the trees were losing shape, molding to the wind, threatening to fly apart and join the ground in a black, shapeless lake. Damn. For once, the Erl-King felt as if there were almost too many of them. Could there be? This was what he had feared most, he needed Douglas . . . Douglas!

"Douglas, boy, are you here? Is this your doing?" He shouted over the wind and knew that his voice did not carry.

He is not here, said the voices. *We are alone, father.*

The Erl-King was pummeled by the wind and placed his hand on one of the trees. His hand slid into it and the soulstuff wrapped around it and held on. "Enough!" He tore his hand back out. "I demand that you stop, this instant, or there will be no more games! You will all die!"

The forest was green again. The pebbles in the path sang the Erl-King's praises, as always. A gentle wind carried a few stray leaves across the path. The Erl-King turned around, then caught a figure in the corner of his eye. The boy Douglas was there, his black outfit immaculate, save the leaves that fluttered past and clung to his chest. "Hello, father."

"Douglas," the voice was slow, careful. "What are you doing?"

"Talking to my family. You want that, don't you?"

"And what is the family up to today, might I ask?"

Douglas raised an eyebrow and scratched his chin as he had seen MacDuff do. "I really can't say. They seem to have been upset. All over now, it seems."

The Erl-King tried to read his son's thoughts and hit a wall. "We've been through this before." His voice was ginger, again, serene and fatherly. "I'd ever so much prefer to accompany you if you wish to visit with your brothers and sisters. Now I should like for you to return to your quarters." He was still trying to understand how Douglas had managed to get in here without him.

"Father . . ."

"Now, Douglas. To your room."

"Very well." The boy looked around at the trees, swept the leaves off his chest, and pushed aside a few pebbles under his feet. He looked up and smiled. "Pleasant day, isn't it?" Douglas faded back into the woods and disappeared before his father could respond.

In his room, the boy sat cross-legged and bent forward, hands firmly placed on the black floor. He pulled away, and the place where the floor had molded to his hands flowed back into its original plane. Father had them scared, all right. "That is all right, my brothers," he said, crossing his arms. "Good try."

Kreen the Syth leaned against a rock and felt the water come up over his boots. He had been back at Thorfinn's for five days, keeping watch on the Dark Nest at the Old Man of Hoy. The tower had been quiet. Then, on his fifth day of watch, he finally saw something. Near the top of the Old Man, where the black tower expanded to become the support of the dome of soulstuff, something like a portal opened. The first two elves that fluttered out, their hair and skin glowing and crowlike wings shining, looked like a couple of birds from where Kreen stood. *Well. At least a couple of you are moving about.* They flew around the portal a bit. Shortly Kreen saw them joined by another Darkling, who nodded at the other two, then flew up at the portal again. He gave a huge sweep with his sword arm, turned, and flew. By the time Kreen saw the hundreds of Darklings pouring out of the whole like bees, he had already turned and begun to run south. In seconds he was skimming across the Penland Firth, making his way towards the mainland, sure he could beat the army of elves to Braemar in time to warn the allies. By the time the Darkling named Af could see and report the jet of water that flew up behind Kreen's feet, Kreen was halfway across the firth. By the time Af could wipe the blood off of his sword and look out on the dimly lit shores of northern Scotland, Kreen was dead.

Joly opened her eyes and tried to yell. Susan, who reclined on a pallet near the wall where MacDuff and Malcolm kept watch, sat up with a start. "Thane!"

MacDuff turned around to look at her as she stood up and looked over the wooden wall into the northern sky. "What?"

The tents under the net fluttered softly in the light drizzle. The net was barely visible. "Joly tried to say something," she said. Rapid footsteps could be heard from inside coming towards them. The wooden door swung back to reveal the diminutive Joly, awake and excited.

"Good Lord," said Malcolm.

Joly's throat had not completely healed, and a section still lay bare. A thin trickle of ichor ran down the orifice at her pharynx. She could not speak. One look into Susan's eyes told her Sister everything. *Now.* Ruthe came running out the door and put a cloak over Joly's shoulders.

Susan was already heading for the bell. "Here we go again," she yelled back at MacDuff as she began clanging the bell with all her strength.

"But Oberon's man . . ."

"Forget Oberon's man! My Sister is the seer; she will not be wrong." The bell clanged mercilessly in her acute ears. She looked out at the sky and began to make out the faint shimmer of elf hair. "There is not much time," she said.

MacDuff saw it, too. "Ruthe, you control the winds. Do your business. And," he levelled an eye at her and knew it was a thing she could accomplish, "make my voice heard." He looked back at Susan. "We're ready," he said. *I hope.* The fluttering flaps of the tents were opening. He made his way for the ladder down to his horse. The wind began to blow wildly in the direction that the elves were coming from. MacDuff gripped the ladder firmly as he descended. Ruthe was cooking up a storm.

Belial, down in front, took the wind into account and doubled his effort. Winds would not stop them. The Darkling general whipped his majestic black wings and swooped at full speed for the first tent he saw. He felt the cold air whip against his teeth as he held out his sword and saw the tent rapidly grow to full size.

Hunh! Belial gagged and rolled on something invisible

that hit him. *No, not invisible, you imbecile. String.* He had hit the thing at full wing and had had the wind knocked out of him. He tried to move and found his wings to be tangled. Belial looked out across the field through the mesh over his face and saw at least fifty Darklings doing exactly the same, slamming full force into a rolling sea of fishing net. He whipped his head around and saw the humans clamoring out of their tents. Belial absently counted the black feathers he saw falling to the ground as a Scot with a harpoon took aim at him.

"Darklings!" Belial yelled as he tried to wriggle his way out of the net. "Those of you in flight! Take down that net!" He winced when he felt the Scot's harpoon go through his good wing. He noticed as he reached for his dagger with his free hand that his own sword was biting into his leg. Belial managed to grab the dagger in his belt and ripped through the netting enough to wriggle out and take flight in pain. His wings hurt but were not broken. Belial looked across the billowing expanse of the net and saw that some had not been so lucky.

MacDuff was riding alongside the net with his sword out, cutting the ropes that held it up, hoping that the Scots would remember his orders. *This is for first defense only. As soon as the shiny birds hit it, it is no longer useful. Cut through it and get it out of the way.*

The Scots erupted through the net with a vengeance as the elves tore at them. As soon as the harpoonists were free of the net, they began casting. No use bringing elves down on top of the net and pinning you under, MacDuff had said, and be careful where you aim. Belial saw a harpoon fly past him and fall back to the earth, barely missing another Scot. He had seen this one before, the one who had elfblood in his long hair and fought like a dog. Out of the corner of his eye Belial saw a brother fall with an arrow in his chest. Archers. He turned his attention to the one called Dukane.

❖   ❖   ❖

Baal the Darkling was swooping in for a kill as he felt a metal-tipped shaft shove itself through his thorax. He was suddenly jerked to the ground. His wings flapped uncontrollably as he felt himself being dragged towards a human who held the rope and yanked on it, foot by foot. Baal shrieked and dug in his heels, whipping his wings to give himself backward force. The shaft ripped back out of him. He used his last ounce of energy and ichor to shove the damn thing down the dirty human's throat.

MacDuff looked up from the body of one downed elf to see another one flying in at him. In the second that it took him to draw his sword from the body, the incoming creature's head exploded. *What the hell?* The Thane of Fife slid into the saddle and looked around as the Darkling fell to the ground. A set of hooves stepped over the lifeless carcass and made the wing bones snap and mix with the netting that had been ground into the mud. The rider was female.

"Susan. Jesus."

"I am a witch, Thane."

"You'll get no complaints from me. We are still outnumbered, however." A bolt of lightning lit the sky and flashed from one end of the dome to another. The faint drizzle turned into another hard rain.

Oberon tore out a hamstring and was gone before he could hear the elf yelp. He found the archers, Syth and human, near the woods at the southwest corner of the field. Oberon could see them hurriedly notching and shooting at the elves in the air.

Dukane had lost his horse minutes ago and realized that he preferred to stick to the ground anyway. He slung back his soaked mane and saw Belial coming in. The Darkling seemed to have a hurt wing. Something about this one seemed familiar, as did the general's insignia on

Belial's tunic. "Oh, lad, I've seen you before," shouted Dukane.

"You shall never see me again," said Belial, as he slashed at Dukane with his sword. The blade was batted away by the spiked buckler that Dukane whipped at him. Belial stood ground and was parrying Dukane's first thrust when he felt a pain like nothing he had ever felt before. The horror struck him like a death blow and he looked up to see the human whose axe had disfigured him.

Dukane grinned. Abel reared up on his steed. His axe was spinning so fast that Dukane could barely see its shape. Belial screamed and tore at Abel's side, but luck had deserted him. The blow sank into leather but no flesh. Dukane raised his sword and swiped down with it, shearing off the other wing at the root.

Belial foamed at the mouth. *My wings!* The nerves in the roots of his wings were screaming at first taste of air, and little wing bones moved in the gory stumps. He stepped away from the two humans and tried to take flight *I have no wings!* and could not lift himself. He was on the ground *like a human, like a worm* and he saw that he had nothing to do but fight, for he was dead already. Suddenly, he felt himself being dragged from the fight by two other elves, who picked him up and carried him *like a human, like a worm* to safety at the edge of the field. He saw his own wings on the muddy field, drenched with rain, disappearing in the distance. *I have no wings!* "No!" he cried, as he furiously looked about him. Belial found an abandoned horse and mounted the ground-animal. He kicked its flanks and moved alongside the field.

The sky crackled and lightning clawed the red-filtered, dark sky. Illuminating the field and giving picture to the clamorous din, the torches continued to burn under their wooden covers. Dukane slapped Abel's back hard and looked him in the eye for a brief moment. *From here on out, we fight together.* And thus from then until the end of the war, and indeed for years to come, when needed, viewers of any battle would see Abel and Dukane, the giant and the farmer, fighting side-by-side. They met the enemy together, like oxen harnessed to the same plow, and no one forgot them for a long time.

Seyton was getting tired. He felt pain in his chest as he tried to catch his breath. *Too many of them.* The sky was still filled with crackling elves, though several hundred lay on the ground. Twice as many Scots lay dead. *Too old. How the hell does MacDuff carry on like this?* He saw James on foot and rode to where the boy was energetically fighting a pair of Darklings. As boys do.

Seyton charged ahead on his mount and swiped hard at one of the elves and took a chunk of its head off. James looked up at him for a second and gave him a nod. The boy pulled back his buckler and brought his sword arm around at the elf. The elf parried, then brought his sword up and down again on the boy's shoulder. Seyton was drawing back to finish off this one when another Darkling blindsided him and threw him off his horse. He went blind a moment and tried to blink the mud out of his eyes, and realized in horror that he had landed on James. He tried to move but felt his knee give. James managed to stand and slashed at his opponent. He had lost his shield.

Seyton shook his head and raised his body with his arms. He could see the Darkling that had hit him through a strange fog that made everything move slower than the life he knew. *We'll fight . . .* The tired muscles in his back screamed as he lifted himself to his knees and swung out his sword and clipped the elf's leg. The black sword came at him and his shield knocked it aside and he could barely hear the echo of the metal. *We'll fight until from our bones . . .* His right leg would not work and he remembered how small were the victims of the Erl-King and he fought on his knees.

Out of the corner of his eye he saw that the boy was

dead, and judging by the sword in the skull of the
Darkling there, James had died well. Seyton tore out with
his sword again and ripped off the crackling foot. The elf
lost balance and fell before he could take wing. Seyton
used his left leg to propel himself forward and he landed
on the elf. He batted the wing that came crashing up from
the ground on his left away with his buckler and crushed it
with his shield. *We'll fight until from our bones our flesh
be hacked . . . .* The Darkling was growling and Seyton was
watching his crackling eyes as he dropped his sword and
pulled the dagger from his belt. The monster's other wing
was flapping against the arm Seyton used to plunge the
dirk into the elven throat. He felt something he knew he
would recognize when it came, and he did not have to
take his eyes away from his opponent's to know that his
own side had just been torn through. Seyton thought of
the gray in his own hair and the crackling gray hair on the
elf's head and died.

Belial swore as he saw another elf fall with an arrow
through his chest and called out to his soldiers with his
loudest voice and raised a torch. He saw a Darkling with
one foot turn his way and fly towards him. Perth set
ground.

"Your wings . . ." The gravelly voice sounded disgusted.

"Forget it, Perth. Take the torch. I want the men to
move on the archers. Southwest corner." He thrust the
torch in Perth's hand. "Move!"

Perth took to the air and swung the torch several times
and shouted out to those who were in the air. Belial could
see by the way he whipped his head around that he was
wary of arrows. The news travelled from elf to elf quickly
and soon the greater part of them had turned and begun
flying towards the archers near the woods.

Oberon looked up and saw a flock of giant crows tearing across the field at the corner from which flew the
arrows. He nodded to himself. Good. He turned and

flashed across the field and met Captain Jikk. Jikk was already shouting the expected orders.

"One more wave and move! One more wave and move!" Another wave of arrows flew as each and every archer dropped his bow and turned tail. They ran at a human's pace.

At least forty Darklings dropped. Perth felt a shaft go through his right wing but kept flying. His eyes grew wide as he saw the garrison of archers move toward the trees. Oberon's men were poorly trained, after all. "Take the cowards!" he cried, and two hundred Darklings swooped down through the wind and rain after the fools running into the woods.

MacDuff saw the elves moving southwest but could not break away from the battle on the field. He sighed, moving with his sword, keeping himself alive. He trusted it would go as planned.

Sixty yards into the woods, Malcolm III of Scotland stepped from behind a post when he saw Oberon come running past him. The Syth king was well ahead of the rest. "Now?"

Oberon turned and looked back. "They took the bait, Canmore. Give your order on my mark."

The archers moved at a fast human's clip through the trees. The Darklings dipped into the woods and followed.

Forty yards into the woods, the runners passed a tree with a painted red trunk. The humans, the smaller part of the party, moved immediately north and buried themselves in the trees. The rest did not deviate from their westward course. They simply, to the perception of the Darklings, disappeared.

Oberon said, "Mark."

"Now!" cried Malcolm, as he brought a sword down on a tautly held rope attached to the post. A soldier at a post just like it did the same. Two trees that had been bent back nearly to the ground, tall saplings with bound extensions that gave them another twenty feet or so, flew forward at the enemy that MacDuff had known would be flying low.

Perth saw the net that came flying towards him for a split second before he hit it. Suddenly something slammed into his back and forced him closer into the mesh. He gasped for air. Another Darkling had struck him from behind. Darkling after Darkling tumbled upon one another and bent back the net as it came loose from the two catapults.

The net collapsed and the Darklings tumbled to the ground, trapped. Malcolm was the first to step forward and plunge a sword into the body of the nearest Darkling that lay squirming in the pile of feathers and crackling skin. He looked around him as the wind and rain whipped through the woods. The faint glow of the red star filtered through the treetops and blended with his wild, red hair. He thrust the sword as far as he could, twisted, and pulled it back out. Black blood flowed down the blade. From the trees he heard the voices of the Scots who had hidden there, swordsmen and spear-chuckers, and they all came forward and began slaughtering the downed Darklings.

Feet clamped to the sides of his horse, MacDuff was surrounded by the bodies of his own men and of the crow-like elves. In the dimness it was hard to make out whose limbs and wings belonged to whom. The Iron Thane felt a trickle of warmth across his forehead. *Lucky, lucky, old man,* he thought. But another, truer thought clung to him: luck had nothing to do with it. MacDuff glanced towards where the Darklings had flown into the woods for half a second and then readied himself for the next sortie. A Darkling had just downed another human and saw him, taking flight and levelling his blade at him.

The elf flew around and then down, speeding at Mac-Duff. When he got within range MacDuff threw out his shield and knocked the blade aside, bringing his own sword around. He missed the Darkling as it avoided his stroke and flew up again. *That's right. Go around for another run.*

"You are a silent one," said the Darkling as he flew up and around. "You do not yell as the others do."

MacDuff nodded. He could see the field without looking at it, the hundreds upon hundreds of men fallen, the multitudes still fighting. He felt the weight of his sword, the tiny tinge of pain in his shoulders and biceps, the cramps in his fingers from holding the threaded hilt. *I have no words . . . .* The Darkling came at him again with the black blade and slashed at him; this time MacDuff met it with his *my voice is in my* sword as he swung it across from left to right. A black wing tore loose and the elf took to the ground, enraged.

My voice is in my sword. The elf looked at his severed wing a moment and swung at MacDuff's right side. Mac-Duff brought down his sword and separated the elf's sword-hand from its arm. He looked out at the red-gray field and the fallen men and his sword moved by itself, an iron appendage that flowed through him and made him what he was. The Iron Thane took off the elf's head.

Oberon appeared by the fallen head. "MacDuff. They hit the net."

MacDuff reared back and swung around, looking out at the hundreds of men engaged in the field battle. "Men of Alba," he cried, as loudly as he could. He knew he would be heard. "Into the woods."

A soldier engaged in hand-to-hand combat is not generally accustomed to breaking loose and heading across the battlefield away from combat, but that was exactly what MacDuff was asking the men to do. Abel Galloway let his axe rest a moment and turned his horse and began pounding through the mud into the woods. The Darklings stayed on the tail of the men as they ran and rode. Dukane found himself stopping every few yards to slash at one or two. The battle itself sidewinded into the woods of the Grampian mountains. On the eastern side of the field, near the castle, Ruthe and Susan watched hundreds of black wings flying into the woods.

Abel stopped his horse by a tree and spun around, swinging his axe at a Darkling flying overhead. He saw the pile of dead elves and praised the king as the body of the Darkling passing him was cleft in two and crashed to the mud. He saw something coming at him on horseback and blinked. It was a Darkling, or seemed to be. It had huge cleavages of blood running down its sides. An elf with no wings.

Belial screamed and thundered at Abel, sword drawn and levelled. He was hunched over, as he had seen humans ride in battle. "You took my wings!"

Abel smiled. "Oh, of course. You." He swung his axe up and knocked the sword aside. Belial was caught off balance, unaccustomed to riding, and fell to the ground. He landed on his feet and spitefully plunged the ebon blade into the draft horse. Abel felt his favorite mount buckle under him and he tore his feet from the stirrups and jumped to the ground, his axe flying wildly. He drew back and swung it hard at Belial's head. Belial was still fast enough to move out of the way and the axe dug deep into a tree.

Abel stared at what he had done. *Damn!* He tugged at the axe for a moment and could barely move the forty-pound piece of iron. He saw Belial draw back for another swing. A mass of fur growled loudly as a wolf jumped up, tearing with its claws and teeth at Belial's torn side. The elf screamed.

The wolf shook his muzzle and let the tiny bits of hollow bone fall. A few of them stayed in his mouth. He dropped to the ground and sprang again, taking a mouthful of crackling flesh out of Belial.

The axe came free with a mighty tug and Abel turned

away and looked for another opponent. He got on Belial's horse and rode through the trees. Belial was still screaming.

The wolf suddenly yelped and fell, its back slashed. Af the Darkling set ground and nodded at the general. "You have no wings, my Lord."

"I can still fight," said Belial, before he felt a black sword slide through his ribs and his heart.

"No," said Af. "You have no wings."

Perth dodged a tree and prepared to set swoop on groundling when he saw another arrow fly through his wing. He looked at the ground. *I thought all the archers were gone.* A Darkling to the left cried out as another shaft flew into his chest. Just then he heard something he had not heard in ages.

Oberon looked up at the air, then farther southeast. There was song being sung. A song of a thousand voices. "MacDuff, can you hear that?"

MacDuff had no time to answer. A wave of arrows came flying through the air. Then, all at once, the woods were full of reddish-brown wings and decorated amber bodies.

"Wood elves!" cried Perth. There they were, after all this time, painted for war and firing their arrows.

The cry echoed through the forest as flying swordsmen encountered the dismal prospect of fighting flying archers. "Wood elves!"

Susan and Ruthe saw a swarm of black wings erupt from the woods, seemingly as quickly as they had disappeared. When they saw the black swarm turn reddish brown, they knew why. A horse came riding across the field. It was MacDuff.

"Susan! The wood elves! The Darklings are in retreat!" MacDuff was shouting. He stopped his horse ten yards away and tried to see through the rain and wind. When he came closer he saw that the two Sisters were gone.

The wood elves stood ground, letting the Darklings run. Oberon and Golanlandaliay came to where MacDuff stood, next to two abandoned horses.

Oberon recognized the horses. "Where are the Sisters?"

MacDuff looked at the retreating cloud of glowing crows. "I have an idea."

Susan looked sideways at her Sister. She spoke with a thought, not wishing to speak aloud or needing to. *A lot of mass.* She heaved her black wings and adjusted her vision, trying to stay in pace with the rest of the army.

I think we'll manage it, replied Ruthe.

CHAPTER 15

The slightly brighter glow of morning shone through the Erl-King's red star and woke Graymalkin immediately. It had stopped raining. The cat sat up and stretched, tonguing his teeth for a moment, and sprang to the top of the den wall. He looked over the wooden partition to get a new perspective on what he knew was there already. He could see the humans wandering the field, selecting their dead and burning them in a blazing pyre in the center. Only the night before, that place had been a symphony of noise and blood.

Blood. The smell of wounds was powerful on the field and in the den, and Graymalkin dropped to the earth and slowly padded through General Belin's sleeping troops. Not one had gone unhurt, but fully three-fourths of the canine allies remained alive to fight another day. But not, he knew, in this war. He had heard news and now found it his displeasing duty to pass it along.

Graymalkin nudged Belin's shoulder with his nose and whispered. "Belin! Belin, are you awake?"

The wolf looked terrible. Belin's nose had been gashed terribly, and in the night the blood had flowed and dried, painting his gray muzzle a dark, brownish red. But he had kept his eyes, and he had held his forces. Belin moved slightly in his sleep and let out a deep breath. He licked his chops in his sleep.

"Belin!"

An eye opened and the muzzle snapped violently at Graymalkin as the great, gray head turned towards the cat. Graymalkin jumped back a second before he saw Belin let his chin fall back on his paws. The canine warrior eyed Graymalkin fiercely. "Graymalkin." He snorted slightly and licked at the blood on his nose. "What is it?" he said, and he still sounded asleep.

"Are you quite awake, Belin?"

"Graymalkin, I have fought battles in my sleep. What is it you want? And what the hell time is it?"

"It is morning, I think."

"Wonderful days."

Graymalkin nodded and sat down, putting his own head on his paws in the way of General Belin. "I have come to say good-bye."

The wolf stared at the cat and looked around him to be sure all his soldiers were sleeping. "You're doing fine, feline. We haven't lost many. I gave you my word as a wolf that we would follow you."

"Yes, I know. And you have done well. But the war has changed. Our job here is finished."

Belin was almost hurt. "Why?"

"The allies won the battle last night, for all practical purposes. My mistress has already left for the Erl-King's fortress and, it appears, the allies are going to follow."

"Where is he?"

"The Old Man of Hoy, Belin."

The wolf nodded once, then thought a moment, then nodded slowly again. "The Orkney Islands."

Graymalkin continued. "As Paddock flies that is fifty miles from here. But the trip would be near impossible for all of us. Your wolves would be ill-used to that kind of swim. Even the human leader, the grayish one, is cutting his forces down to a select few, a little under a thousand, for the attack. With the Syth and the wood elves, that should be all he needs. As it is he will have to construct special devices in the north to carry them the rest of the way."

"He will attack the Erl-King with less than all he has?"

"There are more humans up there, from what I can gather. Forces too near to the Erl-King to act alone. The grayish one intends to meet them and attack the Old Man from the Erl-King's own back yard."

"I understand," said Belin. He licked at the blood on his nose again and expected the sting. He wanted to be terribly insulted, but even with all the pride that he carried, he knew when his usefulness had run out. He felt slightly depressed. "I understand. You are correct; we would be in the way. Our place is on the home front."

"Belin, many a Darkling lost a sortie because of your wolves. General Belial of the Darklings himself was horribly injured by a wolf and had to be slain by one of his own men."

Belin raised the corners of his mouth in pride for his second-in-command. "Aye. That was Leir. He took a mean cut across the back, but I suspect he will pull through. Nothing broken." The wolf looked over at Leir, who still slept. He would lead someday. The sound of fires and men and the stench of burning corpses filtered through the air. "We did well, didn't we?"

"Yes," said Graymalkin. No apologies. No sorry-I-took-you-hostage-back-there to be said. Only the parting of ways. "Go back to sleep. When the rest awaken, tell them the war here is over and you can all go home to your dens."

"I will tell them. I won't sleep."

Graymalkin rose and stretched his long, black body, and turned to go. He turned his head back again. "If things don't . . ."

"I'll know," said Belin. "Go and fight well."

The cat nodded, turned, and sprang over the wall and disappeared. Belin stayed where he was, content to let the blood dry.

Covering all, covering all, blackness thick as night. In his eyes, in his throat, drinking in the light.

There is a time for little boys . . .

Douglas opened his eyes. He could see nothing.

To jump and skip and play.

No movement. Douglas tried to move his legs and found them paralyzed. Or, rather, trapped.

There is a time for grown-up men . . .

He reached for his face and could not feel it, could not feel anything. He could not tell for sure if his arms had moved at all. He blinked, or thought he did, but felt nothing.

To turn and walk away.

His eyes should have been sending out light, glowing as his father's did, but there was no familiar glow to be seen. Nothing was to be seen. All was to be sensed.

There is a time for hearing tales . . .

What was that? How long had he been listening to that?

Of ghosts that walk the land,

Father.

There is a time for mothers dear

No!

To let go of your hand . . .

"Where am I?" he cried, and he did not know if he had actually heard his voice. It seemed to emanate not from his mouth, which he could not be sure had actually moved, but from his mind. He could not be sure if he had even spoken.

"You are with your father." That voice could not be mistaken.

"I cannot move, father."

"And you see, boy, there is exactly where you are wrong. You must learn your nature."

"But I cannot see!" Douglas shouted, or thought he did, and looked around, and the movement he thought he made with his head sent his whole body spinning through the void. Was he falling? Had he moved at all?

"See!" cried the Erl-King.

And Douglas saw a lake of blackness that travelled to infinity, its waves lapping and licking at one another endlessly. He saw without light, for he did not need it. He saw himself, a face, floating in the sea of darkness that rolled forever. He moved and the whole sea moved with him, and it followed his every thought.

"My son, you have never understood what you are," said the voice of his father, but the king of the Darklings did not appear.

"Why can I not see you?" asked the boy, and the waves carried his words, moving to form sound. Nothing was the way he knew it to be; sound and light and all of life were not free to stand alone, but were all one, all the darkness, all responding to his command.

"Can you not?" In the distance the figure of his father appeared, long and thin, sparkling with the light he created of himself. The figure floated in the space above the black waves. He put out a hand. "Come."

"I cannot."

"You are mistaken. Come."

The face in the waves looked at his father. "I have no body. There is nothing to stand on."

"There is whatever you wish, Douglas."

It was but a tiny thought in Douglas' mind, a wish that

he did not ponder but only thought, and made so. Slowly the waves near where stood the Erl-King subsided and a hard, black, flat plane rose like a raft of onyx. It did not bob or suffer the toss of the waves, but only stood there, as much a part of the sea as if it had been there before. As much a part of Douglas.

Douglas' face rose from the plane of black waves and they hung from him like a shroud. He thought a moment about a magician his mother had dared to take him to see once. A dove had emerged from beneath a black cloth where there had been no bird before. Most of all Douglas had been struck by the lovely shape of the cloth wrapped over the flying thing before the bird broke free, the beautiful movement of the folds as they flowed down. It looked to him like a ghost must surely look. At the time he thought it was an evil thing.

The waves broke free from the sea and hung about his face. They were his body. And now he began to move forward, and when the thought *walk* came to him, a path rose in the sea just like the platform to which it led, upon which stood the Erl-King. But Douglas had no body.

And when he thought *body* the waves formed legs, long, muscular legs like those of his father, and he stepped onto the path and began to walk, as he felt the top of his body form. The waves sifted and rippled and became a great, firm chest and back, and formed a neck and lapped up to his face to pull away and reveal it again, bonier, thinner, longer. Black hair formed and grew down past his shoulders. He had hands, alabaster and smooth. When he walked to his father he could tell that he was just as tall. And he knew that he was beautiful.

"*Sie sind kein Mensch*, Douglas," his father said. "You are not human. You are so much more. More even than myself. You could not see because you had not opened your eyes. You could not open your eyes because you did not know how. You have the power to make your own eyes, to make your own world, or destroy this one and remake it as you choose. You thought correctly a moment ago, it is all one, and that one is *this*. Not the vague, meaningless unity of order the Sisters follow so blindly but *this*, which is controlled by you. Palpable and real to you in every sense and sensation. The tastes and sights and smells and sounds are all one essence, and you control it. You *are* it. And everything you ever knew, every sound you ever heard in your life, every grizzled taste of fish brought for your supper, every stagnant drop of water, was not real in the sense that this is."

The voice was sweet and smooth as finest silk, and his father's eyes were deep and sparkling with a light all their own that bespoke uniqueness and clarity unshared by the world Douglas knew. Was it true? Of course it was. "That is the old life you knew, an imperfect and meaningless collection of unreliable sensations. This is the life that is forever, the darkness untainted by the light that men and Sisters worship because they must stoop to remain within its confines. That is the lie that has been so many times thrust upon you, that you have accepted because you have known no other way. This is the life I restore to you, that I have come so far to give to you, that you may be rescued from your captivity and become what you are destined to be."

Douglas did not blink or move, but only stood and watched his father, those crackling eyes giving off their energy and strength, that voice flowing on with sweetness and truth. "No doubts," said the Erl-King. "No hesitation. No uncertainty. No hiding in basements and wishing the world would go away. The world is of your own design. No loneliness. You are all and that is everything. No sickness. No dying. You are immortal and unbound by the rules of your old playmates.

"If you think about them, Douglas, you will know I speak the truth. You can feel them, can't you, slipping away, because you know they do not share what you have, what you are. They are a part of a different world which you can already feel yourself leaving, can't you, as it grows smaller and smaller. It cannot hold you and you do not mourn, for you have already moved away; it is done, and you have left. They are small and wrong and lost in their own meager walls of perception, and they cannot ever know what you know. And though you once thought you could never be free and would never want to be, now you find that you are and there is no sorrow, no need for acceptance, only the observation of that fact that you have moved on, and the blissful awareness that this is the life you have chosen. Because there is no other choice."

Douglas could see his father talking, and the velvet voice carried across the sea of dark waves as far as he surveyed, dancing forever. "It's true, isn't it?"

The Erl-King smiled. "Yes, my son. It is true."

Outside the coastal town of Burghead, in the north of Scotland, the wind blew over the fields but did not move the waves of grain. They lay flat, soaked with rain and starved for light. Abel Galloway sat on his horse at the side of the road and stared at the dead field. He had been here before.

The giant man heaved a great sigh and wiped the sweat off his brow. An ugly, dirty fog had set in, and his face and clothes felt filthy. He turned his gaze away from the dead fields and looked back at the group. They were following, he knew, but no one had topped the last hill yet. Abel passed the reins to his left hand and pulled his right foot from the stirrup, sliding his leg over the horse and to the damp road. He brought down the other foot and stood on his home ground for the first time in what seemed like centuries. He absently patted the horse's neck as he reached in his pouch and produced a few lumps of sugar for the animal. He could feel the rough tongue licking at his giant hand and the feeling reminded him of his old horse. This was a good horse. MacDuff had been sure to get him a large, strong mount, and Abel knew that in time, God willing he had it, he would grow to like it. He missed his old draft horse. He missed his son.

Dark and foggy and unusually hot. What wonderful days. Abel pulled the great, light brown cloak around him and wiped his hand on it as he stepped into the marshy field. He shook his head, surveying the land that he once farmed, and could barely make himself believe that at one time he had used this land, worked and sweated in it, to produce all that he needed for himself and his family. And now he turned around and looked at the flat grain and it hit him with the full stinging force of a slap from which even a strong man cannot help but hurt. His family was dead; he had known that. The town was gone. But here it was, here was proof that even the work was gone. He may as well have never been here before. And for all that was missing and all that was silent where there had once been the noise of horses' hooves and churning soil, the very silence was deafening to his ears. The farmer sat in the field·of dead grain, not even feeling the water that seeped through his cloak. He wanted to cry.

"You farmed here." It was the voice of MacDuff.

Abel looked over his shoulder to see the Thane sitting on his horse, looking out at the field. "I imagine you are going to tell me to take it like a man."

MacDuff looked at Abel for a long moment. He did not see the giant who sat ignobly on the ground, his long blond hair limp over his shoulders, his eyes betraying the slightest of tears. MacDuff was thinking about his own loss, about finding out that his house had been sacked and family slain, and how he had been able to do nothing but fall to his knees and ask why. "You must feel it as a man, Abel. That will be enough."

"They tell me," said the blond, "that you lost your family and home."

"My home I have not seen in months. It still stands, but I could not stay there. Aye, I lost my family. My wife. Two sons. Is this what you heard?"

"More or less. There is much talk about you, MacDuff, but very little said. No one knows what to make of you."

The older man squinted in the dimness, listening to the gentle wind. "Well, I never asked to be made anything of, for that matter." He saw Golanlandaliay, wings firmly packed under a cloak, approaching from the group on horseback. MacDuff's firm hand pressed a moment on Abel's shoulder. "We will continue this later. You have my word."

The past three days had been spent on the move through the Grampian hills; no time had been wasted after the surprise win at Braemar. Oberon and the Syth had quickly dispersed ahead of the rest to Burghead to begin preparations for the next phase. The extremely welcome, though fashionably tardy, wood elves had accompanied Oberon ahead of the group. Golanlandaliay, or Gol, as the Thane of Fife knew him, had remained with the slower movers to acquaint himself with, and come to terms with, MacDuff.

Abel hopped to his feet as he saw the amber king. "Not far now," he said, loud enough for Gol to hear when he approached. "I imagine there won't be much left of Burghead, however."

Gol nodded. "We don't often come this far north, but I have been in these parts."

"You'll be going much farther north before the month is up, friend," Abel said. He almost shuddered at the thought himself. Living on the northern coast was fine, but sailing into Norse territory, even with the surprising help of the Vikings themselves, did not please him. Those people were crazy. He then laughed at the thought. After all, he was the one travelling with elves and little people. And, he thought, looking up to see a feathered figure darting towards them, intelligent owls.

Paddock was distracted; it disturbed him that his mistress had suddenly flown with Mistress Susan in the company of the children of the Erl-King. Phoenix willing, they would find the woman and the little man before they were discovered. He extended his talons and touched down on the outstretched sleeve of the king of the wood elves. Paddock sang a few things to the bird-man about the flock he had just left. They were building turtles.

"Turtles?" Abel asked MacDuff when they had the boatyard in sight. Through the dense fog, they could just make out the shape of the Syth, quickly scurrying from shore to craft with wood and tools. Oberon was visible in the torchlit gloom, directing traffic, looking at plans, a thin stream of smoke emanating from the pipe he held in his mouth.

"Aye," said MacDuff, as he let his rein-weary hands rest on his lap. "It began with something Seyton said, rest his soul. We want to move a thousand humans and at least as many Syth to Thorfinn's territory. We have to do it under the Erl-King's nose, no less. What Seyton suggested was a camouflage of some sort."

"But why turtles?"

"Ah," said MacDuff, eyes twinkling. "That is what we will look like. The design we devised is oblong but, with the roofs, looks circular. Seyton remarked that they would look like about twenty-five very large turtles. Each will carry some seventy-five persons. It won't fool them, but with any luck we will not be noticed until we've already met with Thorfinn, if that soon." He lifted his right hand to pull the rein slightly and guided the horse toward Oberon.

The king of the Syth turned to him and nodded. "Hello, Fife."

"Have you seen the town?" Abel broke in.

Oberon nodded, stepping over a few pieces of timber

in his path. He patted MacDuff's horse. "Aye, lad. You were correct. There is not much left."

"But there are people."

"There are. The town will survive, Abel, provided we do our job and give it a chance." Oberon took his pipe from his mouth and blew a puff of smoke. He looked at MacDuff and said, "Let's walk for a moment." He nodded to Abel and took MacDuff aside, and the two began walking along the shore. Oberon watched the water through the fog and sucked on his pipe. "You notice, of course, that the plants are dying. And without the sun, there will be no farming for awhile. Do you realize we've been at least six weeks without direct sunlight?"

"And our rations are running low," said MacDuff, his hands placed thoughtfully at the small of his back. "The men seem to be getting weaker by the day. Perhaps it is all this travelling. But I fear if this isn't over soon, we may run the risk of starving."

"It's worse than that," said Oberon, and he let another stream of smoke escape from his mouth. The stream flowed upwards and out of sight, and MacDuff watched it disappear against the black curtain that hung across the land. There was a sparkle, an inkling of a thought, as he turned his gaze toward one of the torches nearby, with its constant outpouring of smoke.

MacDuff ran a hand through his hair and brought it down. The hand was as filthy as the air was. He took in a breath and resisted the instinct to cough. "Worse . . ."

"Aye. The men have been complaining, haven't they? Shortness of breath, weariness, all perfectly attributable to battle fatigue. But do not tell me you haven't noticed that the air . . ."

"Is getting thinner," said MacDuff, grimly. "Yes, and it surprises me. Six weeks. I had rather assumed that this dome was allowing air in from outside."

"I expect not. But the dome is huge, you know, and

we've only now become aware that we have a limited amount of air to breathe." Oberon looked out at the waves that lapped against the shore. This was going to be every bit as tough as Susan said. He took his pipe from his mouth and held it, playing with the carving on the bowl. "A limited amount of air. And it is getting hotter, too."

"Yes."

"Any notion why?" asked the king of the Syth.

"I can guess," said MacDuff, as he scratched at his beard. "Perhaps all these fires are the cause. Maybe the smoke and the dome are trapping the heat of the fires, constantly adding, no less, to the layer of smoke at the top of the dome. Soon the layer will be flat across the ground." He watched the fog. Already the smoke was getting into the moisture in the air and making it unbearable to be human.

"Aye," said Oberon. "So there you are. MacDuff, this is much more serious than had at first occurred to me. Even the immortals need air to breathe, but the Erl-King could be different, he always has been. We may have won that last battle back there, but there is a new problem greater than the comparatively simple task of jaunting to his fortress and wiping him out with new allies in tow. The real problem is that, regardless our theoretical strength, and all we hope to do . . ."

"We just may run out of time, and suffocate, and die." MacDuff was watching the sea, listening to the waves pounding against the shore. Outside the wall was the same sea, and there was air there. "I understand." He let out a sigh. "We have wasted enough time. No more dawdling. No more waiting for the Erl-King to move. Attacking him is no longer a choice; it is an imperative. That wall has to come down. Soon."

MacDuff began to walk away, then turned back, raising a hand. "And, Oberon," he said, "about that pipe . . ."

CHAPTER 16

The Erl-King stood on the enchanted rocks at the top of the Old Man of Hoy, his brilliant light casting magnificent shadows throughout the dark cave. Had there been no Dark Nest, he would have been standing on top of a natural column of sandstone four hundred and fifty feet above the rocky shore. The Old Man on the island of Hoy was fantastic by any account, but when it became the heart of the Dark Nest, it took on entirely new dimensions. The rocky sandstone floor upon which the Erl-King stood blended gradually into the black soulstuff attached to it, doubling the size of the floor. The black layer surrounded the Old Man entirely, extending the natural stack of sandstone upwards by another three hundred feet before smoothing off into the domelike envelope that covered all of Caledonia. The same layer was a virtual world in itself, extending down the full length of the Old Man in the countless tunnels and stairs that spiralled around the cylinder. In these black tunnels nested the Darklings. And

when the father called, it was to the natural platform of
the Old Man, buried deep within the Erl- King's Dark
Nest, that the Darklings flew.

The meeting had been called immediately upon the
return of the army after the battle at Braemar. The
Darklings gathered there held their faces tight, hiding the
pain they felt from the wounds they had received. They
had lost a battle. How could this happen?

"My children," said the Erl-King. The hiss was heard
throughout the room. "It will all be over soon."

A Darkling in the back frowned and whispered to her
nearest neighbor. "Is it me, or has he changed?"

Susan looked back through her adopted crystal eyes.
"Yes," she said, with a note of resignation. Eons ago,
before the humans had come, he had been different. Always chaotic, always powerful, but different. Susan looked
at the Erl-King, at his face, and could see how the beautiful, smooth white skin had gnarled like an alabaster tree.
How his hair had gone white and his eyes glowed brighter
than ever before. He was barely the same immortal she
remembered from the dawn. Although she felt sure that
he could be beaten, to see him now, after all this time,
frightened the First Sister just a little. This is what the loss
of order brings. But order could not be completely escaped: This was chaos in an ordered, powerful form.
Though she hated the word, she could only look at his
form, his perversion of himself, and call it evil. He had
grown in power, learning to steal the souls of the humans
and siphon power off of them.

Susan ran her eyes across the sea of wings and crackling
hair before letting them rest on the wings of the Erl-King.
They were tall and long, like the rest, but *made*. She knew
it, she had seen him, so long ago, had known him, as an
other like herself. How could this be his role? The Erl-
King had fashioned himself wings of the same stuff the
Dark Nest was made of, so that the children might better

recognize their father. The irony was sickening. The thousand children of the Erl-King, and they were not his children at all. He had taken the Darklings, not even his own race, and perverted them, too, until gradually they had become reflections of what he was. How, she did not know. But this was something she would never do, Susan announced to herself indignantly. She hoped.

"General Belial," he was saying, "is gone. The humans have surprised us by showing backbone. They are still worms. The Syth are but fast worms. Do not let these alarm you, my children. They were fortunate that I was not there." A wave of murmurs passed through the crowd.

"Yes, my children. I will be joining you in your fight, when the time comes. You will not have to fight alone for much longer."

"That doesn't seem right," whispered Ruthe. "Why should he want to join the battle?"

Susan nodded slightly. "Perhaps he is not so confident as he had been. It is possible he feels he now has to be there. When the time comes . . ."

"Many of you," said the Erl-King, "have holes in your wings where you have suffered the indignity of the shaft. We who fly have never used this weapon, this defiled instrument that the wood elves use. It is a weakling's plaything. It is the weapon of a coward who wishes to lie on his cot and shoot defenseless avians out of the sky without letting them see their foe."

More murmurs. "That hit a nerve," said Susan, as she nodded, mimicking the adulent congregation.

"Our cousins who fly were our allies! We had peace with them! But they have betrayed us by using such a blasphemous instrument against us!"

"Never mind that you attacked them first," Ruthe whispered.

"Something tells me," said Susan, "that he hadn't planned on that."

"But we will not be vanquished by this blasphemy! We will not be destroyed by our kin who turn against us so sinfully! Let them loose their arrows; we will still come and tear out their throats, and when we do so, we will look at them, in their eyes, in those unevolved, dull eyes in those hideous, plain faces, and we will watch them die."

Ruthe looked around. "Shouldn't we be looking for Julia and Douglas?"

Susan frowned, "Even if you turned to mist you would be noticed. We are all supposed to be here. I'm doing all I can to shield our auras, in case he was looking. I don't understand, he seems distracted, as if this is almost too much to keep track of. This wall must be putting an incredible strain on his will."

The Erl-King paused for a moment. "There comes a time in every father's life when he must make announcements of joy to his children. I have such an announcement to make. Our family, you see, is about to grow."

What? Susan thought.

"Soon you will have brothers. Even now I hear them calling, waiting to be born. I will bring them, and they will join us. And they will be ruled by one who will sit at my right hand and will lead our army as no Darkling ever has. Children, I tell you this now, and you will obey me. The one of whom I speak is very dear to me and will be your Prince."

"Oh, no," whispered Ruthe.

"My children," he said. "You have waited."

We have waited long, said the crowd, but from behind, near Susan and Ruthe, came a very different voice, silky and resonant and regal. The two Sisters turned back with the rest of the congregation to see the one that had entered, who wore a long black cloak and had black hair that ran to his shoulders. The Prince. The dark figure walked into the crowd and it parted to make way for him, opening a path to the father.

"We have watched the humans grow."

They grow in number.

The figure did not look to the side, but strode with royal bearing to the front, repeating with his subjects the responses to the father.

"But we will rule."

With you as our king.

"We will crush them."

Crush them all.

"Steal their young."

Steal them all.

"Fill them with terror and dread."

Fill them all. The Prince reached the front and lowered himself to one knee, bowing his head.

"Is that . . . that can't be," said Ruthe.

"And all will die."

"I'm afraid so," said Susan. "That is Douglas."

All will surely die.

The water was foul and full of death, and the somber, roofed boats made their way stealthily through the still darkness. The journey was not hard. What bothered Mac-Duff most, as he watched the men row, was the absence of waves and the sticky warmth that had settled on the land. By all reckoning, although he could not be sure, in two days was the Feast of St. Bride's Day, February 1. The land, however, was dead and gave no evidence of winter. The fog was filthy and full of smoke, and though MacDuff had ordered that all unnecessary torches be extinguished, he knew that the effort was a drop in a very large bucket. The damage was done. Throughout the kingdom there would be fires, he knew, and he could imagine the smoke of them, travelling up to the stopped sky, curling around like the stream of smoke from Oberon's now abandoned pipe, curling back down upon them. Choking them and heating them and filling the world with gray. Still the slightest illumination from the red star filtered through the fog, lest he for once forget that the Erl-King was still there, that they were going to meet him. That the sun was out there. Somewhere.

MacDuff stared at the water as his boat passed over it, the dead fish sliding slimily past the hull. The men were hungry, he knew. And there were fish, and they could not be eaten. He looked around him, at the other roofed boats surrounding and following. The faint sound of snoring could be heard from those who did not row. Some of them farmers, some of them soldiers. Some of them part of clans he had actually warred with in times past. Little people with magical powers. Flying men very like the enemy, too. Bird-men and dead fish and dirty smoke.

The serpent will come from the hole . . .

MacDuff's ears perked up as he heard the men singing softly. It was a hymn to St. Bride, the goddess who midwifed the child Jesus. *Although*, he thought, *if she is a saint, she must not be a goddess*. He decided absently that this was a strange question, and that one appealed to whatever might be willing to listen. *Deus Juvat*. Long before MacDuff was born, his ancestors had prayed to *Brideag*. They called her St. Bride now; she was still beyond men, and so they sang to her. Like the dead fish in the water it all flowed past him: the smallness of men, the need for gods. The sinking feeling that he was at a loss to pray to something. The realization that there was something in men, though, that made them not so small after all. They were born and passed away and lived forever through their kin, and their gods were part of them. Their lives, he thought, might, just might, be much more complex than he had imagined, and he knew that cynical dismissal might be a comfort, but it would not be true. Sisters and Syth and elves were immortal, yet men were somehow eternal through their very mortality. They were all sheep, yes, but the shearing was only a part of it.

Fathers shed their souls and lived forever in the memories of the sons. He could tell the stories of his ancestors with pride and knew that it made a difference. His children had died too early and he knew that that, too, made a difference. That was how men lived forever: glory and love and friendship. Pain and hunger and joy. To believe differently, he knew, would be to forget his children. The pain he felt for their loss verified that they had made a difference. The alternative would be easy, but he knew it would be wrong. And then, as the Thane of Fife watched the dead fish roll by the ship and tasted the terrible air, he knew his pain as good. The men still sang, hushed, to their ever-transforming deity.

> *"The serpent will come from the hole,*
> *On the brown day of Bride,*
> *Though there should be three feet of snow*
> *On the flat surface of the ground . . ."*

Deep in slumber, Abel Galloway let his arm drop to his side to retrieve his axe. In his dream, he found it. The warm, dirty fog choked him, and no wind, not even this one, could lift it. The wind whipped across the rocks at the base of the Old Man as he jumped from one craggy stone to the next, feeling the texture of the slippery rocks, thankful for the slight traction that sandstone could afford. The Campbell badge thumped against Abel's chest and echoed his heartbeat. His axe was soaked in elfblood. Still they came, the flying, alabaster men with crow's wings, and he could never see them through the damp, filthy fog until they were there, when he would meet them with his great axe. He swung his axe automatically, time and time again, goring the Darklings by the score. And then he heard a new sound, amidst all the noise. Above the crash of metal on metal, above the compounded roar of water the army splashed through, above the thumping of the badge of Campbell against his heart, he heard a word.

Father.

Jess? Abel slung back his blood-soaked hair and looked around him, seeing only the darkness and the grimy fog.

Father!

Then he heard a brassy *whish* and saw the curtain of fog shift as a lithe figure flew forward, its ebon wings flapping. He raised his axe to meet the great-winged creature before it got close enough for him to see that this was no Darkling. This was something of which he had never dreamed.

Short whispers echoed in the ebon halls as Susan and Ruthe walked quickly through the spiralling tunnels of the Dark Nest. They had managed to break away from their adopted battalion without gathering too much attention. In this they had been fortunate. Susan had worried that they would be noticed as two Darklings never seen before, or that they would be carefully held to their group. Yet so many had been lost in the last battle, and so great was the excitement, agitation and sheer confusion among the children of the Erl-King, that Susan and Ruthe were able to slip away, through and among the rest. They mimicked whatever particular expressions they saw on the Darklings around them, looked like they were more or less certain of where they were going, and moved on. They stopped in the first quiet tunnel they could find, reasonably confident that they could talk.

"We have to find Julia," said Ruthe. "She has been here too long as it is. God, I can't believe this has happened." The black walls sent off an internal light that could not be identified. Not that she would need it.

"After the meeting," said Susan, "the Erl-King retired with Douglas through a door in the back of the hall. I wonder if he retired to his own chamber."

Ruthe inwardly shuddered at the realization that this new entity was, in fact, Douglas. Her godson, as it were, was different, now. And she could only begin to imagine just how powerful the child might be. And just how much of a threat a child with that kind of power might pose. They had promised Julia that they would keep Douglas safe. They had botched it, that was certain.

"What do you think he meant by the new siblings he referred to?"

"I shudder to think," said Susan. "I fear it has something to do with the new Douglas." Susan arched an eyebrow and moved a silvery lock away from her left eye. *Haven't been able to get rid of that*, she noted absently. "The Nest is twice the size of the Old Man of Hoy. We could spend days searching and still not come up with the right room, but . . ."

"But we don't have to search like humans," continued Ruthe. "I follow you."

"You are the woman's friend, Ruthe. I assume you know her heartbeat like the back of your hand."

Ruthe laughed quietly in self-mockery. "I am sorry to tell you, but I do not."

"What? You have an immortal's memory and a built-in capacity talent for listening to these things. Even saying 'capacity' is misleading; how could you avoid hearing her heart?"

"I avoided it deliberately, Susan. It was a conscious decision."

"What the devil for?" asked the exasperated First Sister.

"I did not want to know when she would die." Ruthe stared at the black, self-illuminated wall and chastised herself for the irony. She had made the decision out of the supposition that Julia would die of old age. And now, because of that decision . . .

Susan caught herself. There was no sense in being angry. "I have warned you and warned you about the dangers of friendship with the mortals. 'Problematic' is an understatement of the difficulties. You know that she is going to die."

"Yes."

"Then why not know when?"

Ruthe looked up at her Sister and felt the slightest of tears flow through her crystal eyes. "How could I profess to love her when I knew the day of her death? How could I be her friend if I were able to prepare myself for her death? I knew what that would mean; I could see myself, slowly pulling away, because I knew her days were numbered. Distancing myself to avoid the pain of that sudden loss."

"This is exactly why we must know, to avoid that unnecessary pain."

"Without the threat of that unnecessary pain there would be no love, Susan. She is my friend, and I pledge my love to her, without thought for the cost of not knowing when she will leave me. She would never be able to become immortal, could never hope to outlive me, but I refuse to know ahead of time when she will be taken away. It was the closest I could get to mortal love. The closest, I think, to love itself. Risking that pain was crucial."

Susan watched her sister for a long while before speaking, as she let her mind wander across the millions of years they had existed. Could time even apply? Had they ever not existed? Of course. They were immortal, not eternal. And after all this time here was Ruthe, the Second Sister, trying to be mortal in her own small way. *Was it possible*, Susan thought, *that there was something they missed? Could there be comfort in an end? Could pain be worthwhile?* And did that not simply lead to the pain-worshipping Erl-King? Or was the Erl-King simply doing what Ruthe was doing, in his own perverse way, tying himself to the linear and the mortal because there was something undeniably frightening and lonely about immortality? She first wanted to say that this was exactly why Ruthe was wrong, because look at the extreme, but she could not completely rest on this conclusion. There was something about the mortals, something about a beginning and an end that fit into her circular mindframe in a shocking, comforting way that she could not completely define. Something that drew one to them and threatened to keep them when any immortal knew that it would not last, and even worse, there was no predicting the end of it, even if one could tell how many years would kill a heart or could even see into the future. There would always be unknowns with the mortals. And maybe that was why it was beautiful. And all at once she was willing to empathize with her Sister. "Yes," she said, and no more.

"MacDuff, eh?" observed Ruthe. "You've been forgetting to note a few heartbeats yourself."

Susan blinked. "We are wasting time, Sister. It is exactly this sort of analysis that will get our allies," she almost said loved ones, "killed."

Ruthe nodded and rubbed her eyes. "Since you mention it, though, there are only two remotely human hearts in this fortress. The Darklings are mortal — they can be killed — but there is only one heart that could be called mortal and degenerative."

"Right," said Susan. "Can you locate it?" She could see her Sister, eyes closed, already working on the task. Ruthe's mind was ablaze with its search through a cacophany of supernatural hearts, sifting for the one that would degenerate in the way that human hearts do.

"Yes." The eyes flew open.

"Where is she?"

"Exactly the worst place." Ruthe stood up. "She is not twenty yards from the Erl-King himself."

CHAPTER 17

The Norwegian Vikings settled in Northern Scotland, especially in the Scottish Hebride and Orkney Islands, as early as the late eighth century. It was from these points, while the Scots and Picts quarrelled, that the Vikings made their assaults on Ireland, England and the rest of Europe. Though the worshippers of Odin, most of them, were nominally Christian by the early eleventh century, it was a very *Viking* Christianity. Old habits die hard. It was nine years before the Norwegians were defeated at Stamford Bridge by the English King Harold (himself shortly to be trounced by the incorrigible Duke of Normandy) that the north of Scotland went dark. It was then, in the beguiled year of 1057, that the Norwegians in that territory lost touch for a few strange months, and a Scots chieftain named MacDuff allied with Thorfinn of the Orkneys in a last-ditch effort to end a tyranny of which history has failed to tell.

Through the smoke and red glow MacDuff saw a tall figure standing on the shore, framed by the skin roof that hung over the Thane's head. Dead waves lapped at the rock upon which the figure stood, and as the boat drew closer, MacDuff could see him more clearly. He was a big man, barrel-chested and paunchy. He stood in such a way that his girth seemed like a store of unused power, and MacDuff could tell that the weight provided no encumbrance. He wore a crown that flashed, even in the gloom, and it sliced through the smoke as he slightly moved his head. Through a mass of flowing red hair that flamed in a way that Malcolm's might someday, the eyes of Thorfinn the Mighty studied the approaching army of Scots intently.

In a matter of minutes the boat came to rest on the rocks. Immediately two or three Scots warriors jumped off to secure the vessels with ropes. MacDuff sat for a few seconds longer, listening to the splashing of the men's feet as they scurried, watching the now plain face of the king of the Orkneys.

"MacDuff," said Thorfinn. The Viking stepped forward, extending a thick, bare arm.

MacDuff grasped the offered hand and stepped out of the boat and onto the damp rock. "Thorfinn. I trust the Syth have already arrived without incident."

"Yes. They are hidden away in one of the longhouses."

The Thane of Fife nodded. He turned to watch the rest of the vessels coming to rest. Except for the men who splashed out to secure the boats, the soldiers remained in place. "I offer you my thanks for your extension of friendship on this occasion. We require . . ."

"My friend," said Thorfinn, and MacDuff noticed the wrinkles in Thorfinn's face that had appeared since last they had met, "you will have all that you require. I imagine that food and drink should be in order first, and then rest. Tell your men to come ashore."

"Realize, Thorfinn," said MacDuff, "that the moment we step on land we are in your camp, and you in our war. I cannot have it otherwise."

The Viking's eyes twinkled. "When I heard that Malcolm was taking on that demon, I thought it best to stay out of it. Not my war, after all, although I found it odd he was sitting here. When I learned that you were in command, I knew that I would be damned if you would upstage me. Bring your men into my castle. We are allied."

MacDuff gave another, graver nod, then raised a hand towards the sea. The army slowly poured out of the turtle boats. He could see Malcolm stepping out of his boat with his attendants, and a number of Thorfinn's men came down to lead the men to the castle. They stepped wearily over the rocks, and even the amber wood elves appeared thoroughly crushed by the weight of fifty miles rowing over dead, pungent water.

Thorfinn led MacDuff as they walked over the rocks in the direction everyone else was going, but separately. "I know of your troubles with MacBeth after Duncan's fall. I was sorry to hear about the Lady MacDuff."

MacDuff was momentarily taken aback by this sort of sentiment from a Viking, especially Thorfinn the Mighty. But he accepted the condolences of one warrior to another. "I killed him," said MacDuff, as if that were a proper response. It was the only one he could think of.

Thorfinn was watching the stream of warriors snaking up the hill in the darkness and smoke to his castle. In the distance was the Old Man of Hoy. "I understand you turned back the Erl-King at Braemar."

"Aye, with the help of the wood elves."

"Strange days. Syth, elves, flying monsters, stolen suns. All told, I'd rather be raiding."

"Believe me, Thorfinn, I had other plans myself. But there are new problems to contend with."

"King Oberon told me about the growing heat, not that I could help noticing. How long do we have?"

"Hard to say," said MacDuff. "Days, perhaps weeks.

Already it will be hard to fight. Very soon the Erl-King will get back his courage and attack again. The wood elves rode along with us so as not to attract attention in flight. The Erl-King is sure to attack us here if he knows this is where we are. He wanted to take us out first, possibly you next. He'll be more than happy to do both at the same time. I suppose all he really has to do is wait for us to die of heat and not suffocation."

"Then we must attack him."

"Aye. Immediately, no less." The door of Thorfinn's castle was looming close and sounds could be heard inside. Malcolm would be busy already, meeting with Thorfinn's chiefs, being official.

Thorfinn stopped in the path. "How immediately?"

"In the morning, so to speak." MacDuff was still walking.

"In less than fifteen hours you want to attack the castle? Do you have a plan?"

MacDuff turned back and looked at Thorfinn and gave a slight smile. "I will. Fifteen hours is a long time," he said. "I don't know about you, but I am hungry."

"Fine. Join me in the hall. Anything else you will need?"

"Hmm. A lot of Vikings come morning."

"I expected as much. I called an *Althing*, when I knew you were coming. We will fight. Our prayers go out to God and Odin, and whoever else may help us. Anything else?"

"I could use some coffee." The Thane and the Viking stepped into the great hall of the house of Thorfinn the Mighty and breathed easier for being indoors.

The hall was gigantic, decorated with banners and totems that told the tales of the Norsemen and their gods, Odin and Thor and company. MacDuff surveyed the embroidered tapestries on the walls. "Stone."

"Yes, MacDuff. We build with stone. There is plenty of it to go around."

"A Norman development?"

"Bite your tongue; even the Romans built with stone." Thorfinn led MacDuff through the crowds of wet, miserable men to the dining hall and the two took a seat at a long table. It was dimly lit, as only a few torches were allowed to burn on the walls, as per MacDuff's advance advice. A raise of Thorfinn's hand and a nod brought food and a fresh pot of coffee.

MacDuff picked up a lump of bread and bit off a small hunk of it. He let the bread dissolve on his tongue and tried to remember how long it had been since he had eaten. He swallowed and felt satisfied. He was requiring little these days.

Thorfinn tore into a huge fish. "We have had trouble finding fresh fish, as you may well imagine. We have some dried reserves, of course. The fish will run out soon." The red-bearded man watched MacDuff chewing another small bit of bread. "That is, you may want to enjoy the fish while you can. Surely you can eat more than that. A man your age should eat more."

"A man my age." MacDuff picked up his cup and took a sip. "I find of late that it takes little to sate my hunger. Too much food, too much flavor, these things distract me. Better to be a little hungry."

"Mad."

"Perhaps." He took another sip. He looked around and saw that King Malcolm was at another table with the other chiefs. He could see MacHenry smiling broadly at finally getting some food. A red-headed woman who MacDuff decided must be Queen Ingijbord was serving them. In the back of the hall, leaning against a stone column, was Golanlandaliay, arms folded, head covered in a hood to disguise his distracting coloring. Soon he made eye contact and MacDuff motioned for him to come over.

When Golanlandaliay reached the table MacDuff said,

"Here, sit. Take off that hood. Thorfinn, this is the king of the wood elves, Golanlandaliay."

"Wood elves," repeated Thorfinn, shaking his head and letting out a laugh. Golanlandaliay raised an eyebrow but decided that there was no offense meant. Pulling down the hood, he revealed his beautiful, amber face. He sat down by MacDuff and warily poked at the food.

"You may call me Gol," he said.

"Compared to whatever he said, King Gol," said Thorfinn, "I shall do exactly that." The green eyes crinkled cheerily at the supernatural being across from him. "The food is safe, my friend. We treat our guests and honor them, king or servant."

Who would have thought that a Viking and an elf and a Scot could sit together and talk? Could only a threat bring enemies and wary acquaintances together? MacDuff pondered these things, remembering the way he had acted in the Syth meeting at the Great Shepherd, and the way Gol had made it abundantly clear he had no love for humans, had not even bothered to properly identify himself. Yet here he was. And Thorfinn. MacDuff had met the Viking king, but circumstances may as easily have put the two in warring camps as camping together.

It was with Thorfinn that MacDuff really began to see the odd sort of irony at work. Two mortal men, pulled this way and that by forces beyond their control. They might pass laws and judgments, command armies, but they were, in the end, no more in control than one of the horses. And one day they may be levelling swords at one another; now, here they sat, two men growing older, drinking their coffee, planning battle, and wondering when they would go to be slaughtered.

Gol was talking to Thorfinn, trying to forget his apprehension of mingling with mortals. It was time for business. "Have you warned your men, Thorfinn, about the odd sort of allies alongside which they shall be fighting?"

"Winged amber men and little white fellows? As well as I can. We are under attack here, Gol, there is little time for prejudice."

"Well said," came a voice from behind, as Oberon appeared and sat at the table beside Thorfinn. Oberon fidgeted at his pouch for his pipe, then realized it was not there.

"How are you, old friend," said MacDuff, for indeed now the Syth king seemed so.

"Damned annoyed at not being able to smoke my pipe."

MacDuff shook his head and smiled. "Only essential fires."

"Bah," spat Oberon. "Look at all these torches. And there's no telling how many fires the rest of the kingdom is burning, those who don't have the fortune to listen to your advice, Thane."

"Those torches are for seeing, and seeing badly at that," said MacDuff. "I can barely see my food."

"What little he eats of it," added Thorfinn.

"And," said MacDuff, as if it were necessary, "if we used the activity of the rest of the kingdom as an excuse we would only hang ourselves faster. Even you can asphyxiate."

"When do I get my pipe back?"

"When I get the sun back."

"Damn," muttered Oberon.

"Get used to it," said MacDuff. "Here, drink some coffee."

"Well," said Oberon, taking a cup, "I guess we have to win, then."

"That's it," said Thorfinn. "Now that we all have our respective motives, let us discuss this Dark Nest monstrosity."

"Is there an entrance?" asked MacDuff.

"Aye," said Thorfinn, "at the top. They fly in and out."

"My men could reach that height, easily," said Gol.

MacDuff nodded. "But I doubt it would be useful to fly the whole army into the castle, even if you could. You would be at a disadvantage."

"It's even worse than that," said Thorfinn. "The door opens and closes magically. You can't go in if they don't want you to, even if you can reach it."

"Can we draw them out?" asked Oberon.

"We'll have to," said MacDuff. "And that will probably be Gol's move — get their attention and fight them at the base."

"We have the arrows," said Gol, smiling grimly.

"We all do now," said the Thane of Fife. "And the Vikings always begin battle with volleys of arrows. That will help tremendously. But fighting among these rocks will end up as a sword fight. The Erl-King is inside, or is guaranteed to retreat to the inside in case of danger. There is also the problem of the rescue we wish to perform: Julia and the boy are still captive." And Susan and Ruthe were in there, too, he thought. He hoped they were faring well. "There has to be a way into that . . . what did you call it?" He looked at the king of the Syth.

"Soulstuff."

"Soulstuff." MacDuff tapped the table. "The Erl-King controls it, makes it, lives in it. You can't knock it down, break through it, or cut it. Damn." Through the dim light the sweat was visible on MacDuff's face. It was going to roast and suffocate them, too.

Thorfinn leaned back. "So, what do we do?"

"All that we can do," said MacDuff. "We sleep, we wake, we start a fight."

"Sounds like Scotland," Thorfinn said.

"Aye," said the Thane of Fife. "Hope for something miraculous. St. Bride be with us. Odin be with us. Whoever feels like helping." In the feasting hall, the Scots army was treating the attendant Vikings and wood elves to their hymns. The voices were wine-worried and beautiful.

MacDuff watched Malcolm, the ruler of the people, singing with the men, looking like a hero. The chieftains remained at their table, grim in the torchlight. Armstrong threw MacDuff a glance from across the room. MacDuff nodded in response. "I am tired," he said. "There will be battle in the morning. I believe I shall sleep after all."

. . . feel it as a man, Abel . . .

Abel Galloway spurred on his steed and galloped through the green wood, his eyes entranced by the movement of the trees flying past him. He felt as though he were standing still and the forest rushed around him on all sides, but then he remembered he had somewhere to go, and continued to move with more certainty. The limbs whipped past and the sound they made in the wind was hollow, unreal, and he could barely tear his eyes away when he remembered the weight against his forearm.

Jess! He looked up again at the trees, looking for the wood to come to an end, unsure he wanted it to, feeling Jess against his arm. What was strange about that? Why was it strange to be with Jess? He felt numb, as if he were asking himself too many questions, when he should be watching the mesmerizing dance of the trees in their parade.

Father! Jess cried, and for that tiny instant the wood turned black and the wind through the tentaclelike trees tore through them made them whip about like cloth, and drops of blackness tore from the trees and flew at him. And then Jess was silent and it was green again.

Abel was lost in the trees again when he heard Jess cry *Father!* and all turned black once more. Something that Abel saw before he knew he saw it caused him to reach for his axe with his giant right arm. The horse came to a stop but the woods continued to flow. In the whipping blackness Abel heard the sound of wings unlike any he had heard before. The figure that flew towards him was no Darkling.

It was jet black and thin as a reed, not an arm's width in diameter at the waist, with arms like whips and hands like scythes. On its neck rode a long, thin head that rounded at the top and came down, beaklike, to a vicious point. Its eyes were hollow and oblong, dark recesses in a dark, scythelike head. From its thin back grew a pair of wings which resembled nothing other than dark glass, and as they flapped they made sounds like the din of battle.

Abel swung his axe at the middle of the creature and saw the blade go through, slicing the creature in half. He watched the torso reseal as soon as the blade no longer separated the parts. The thing hovered in the air, waiting for its own time to attack. The creature needed no sword. It moved its head sideways, drew back its right arm, and the scythelike limb came flying forward at Abel's throat and stopped. The long beak came close to Abel's face as the blonde man sat still. The beak dipped down and two oblong, hollow eyes came closer to him. The head swivelled, as if the creature were looking at him through one eye at a time. The head drew back again. It seemed to say something that was hard to hear.

Abel blinked and looked down at his lap and found it empty. Again he heard the raspy sound and he looked up again at the whipping black woods to see that the creature had disappeared. Suddenly there was the sound of battle din, and he saw hundreds of the glassy wings in flight through the black wood. He heard the voice again, the one that was hard to hear.

He heard it again as he sat bolt upright in bed, and felt the beads of sweat pour down his body. He listened for a moment to the darkness in the castle. Nearby he heard snoring, and remembered where he was: that would be Dukane, in the next cot. Beneath his hands Abel felt the soaked bed. Even the stuffy heat did not compare with what he had just seen. He thought about waking Dukane up and then grimaced in disbelief at such a ridiculous thought. He lay back down and tried to sleep.

Abel stared at the ceiling and tried to shake the terrible vision. Above the snoring, beyond the terrible heat, above his pounding heart, outside the world in which all these things presented themselves, Abel heard what the creature had said behind its hollow, black eyes.

Father . . .

Julia slammed her fists against the wall of her cell. In the dim light she could see her hands, gnarled and bruised. She refused to eat. She would not touch his food. And she would get out of this place.

She struck the wall again stubbornly, then collapsed against the wall. She brought her thin knees to her chest and gripped them tightly. She clamped her eyes shut in thought. She had not seen her son in . . . God, how long had it been? Days? A week? She knew where the boy was; he was with his father.

This made her draw back her head and scream in anger.

"Julia, please!"

Julia opened her eyes and looked across the dark room at the two Darklings that had somehow appeared in her cell. "How in hell did you get in here," she spat. "I want my son. Nothing else."

One of the Darklings looked down at her alabaster form and remembered the shape-shift. The body of the Darkling began to bubble and flow before reforming in seconds in the shape of Ruthe. Immediately Susan appeared in the same manner.

"We followed your heartbeat," said Ruthe. "It was a blind jump."

"Good that you're alone," said Susan. "I wouldn't want to perform a jump like that into a crowded room of onlookers."

Julia nodded slowly, digging her nails into the soulstuff floor. "Aren't we fortunate, then," she said. She looked up again at Ruthe. Her eyes were liquid and jaundiced.

Ruthe knelt before her. "You look terrible."

"Many thanks."

"The Erl-King has been starving you?"

"The Erl-King has been busy with my son. I have been starving myself." She gave a short, weak laugh, then looked back at Ruthe. "Not very useful, I imagine. But I have control over nothing else."

Ruthe touched Julia's knee and stayed intent on her friend's eyes. "We're getting you out of here," she said, and stood up as if to indicate that she meant now.

Julia did not move. "Not without Douglas."

"Julia . . ."

"Not without my son!" she cried. "If you want to help me then get me to my son! Or leave me and get him and get out of here yourself." She struck her pale forehead. "It's not safe. I never should have gone back to Oban."

"You did what you felt was right," said Susan.

"Small comfort, Sister."

"Julia," said Susan, clearing her throat a bit. "We have to get out of here. I don't think Douglas will be able to come with us."

Julia's eyes flew up to Susan's and burrowed deep to see what this meant. She looked at Ruthe intently, then back at the floor. "What does that mean?" she asked, calmly, preparing herself.

"I will explain once we are free; we came to get you . . ."

"Damn you, Susan, I want answers!" The burrowing eyes took aim again. "Tell me. Why not Douglas?" She calmed down slightly and asked, "Is my son dead? Did the bastard kill my son?"

Susan sighed. "No . . ."

"Then what the hell is this about?" The eyes turned

away. "Ruthe, you talk; your Sister never could deal with humans."

Ruthe nodded slightly and bit her lip for a second. "He's changed, Julia."

"He'll never change; he's been the same way for over a thousand years."

"Douglas has changed." Ruthe waited for this to register in Julia's face.

"What do you mean?"

"The Erl-King has taken him to his side."

"My son would never join his father."

"I'm afraid he has, Julia," said Susan. "The Erl-King can be very persuasive. Douglas is very powerful at his father's side."

"He's five years old."

"That is not relative to an immortal such as Douglas. He does not look like a five year-old anymore. He does not feel like one."

"What did the Erl-King do to him?" spat Julia, angrily keeping in the tears.

Ruthe answered, "We cannot be sure. Douglas seems to have fashioned a new form for himself. He is fully grown, and as powerful looking as he is in reality."

"He made himself big?" Julia gave a curt laugh. "As any five-year-old would."

"We must go."

"He is my son, and I will not leave him. I don't give a damn if he sprouted wings. He will listen to me!"

Susan was growing impatient. "Julia, he will not. That I can tell. He is completely sold to his father's side."

"Now you listen to me, Sister," said Julia, as she rose to her feet. "I am not going to leave Douglas with his father after I spent five years hiding him, just because you tell me I'm not going to have an easy time of it. I've never had an easy time, Susan. I'm not going anywhere without my son."

"Why, Julia," said a voice from the doorway that was not there before. "I'm glad you've decided to stay with us."

All three looked back to see the crackling form of the Erl-King. He stood still, hands firmly behind his back, as if he were a field surgeon inspecting the casualties.

Julia gave what could only be called a roar and ran at him, her nails stretched like claws in front of her. She was going to tear his lily-white throat out.

"Stop," said the Erl-King, and the black floor flowed up around her feet and held her there, scratching at him in vain. He turned away from his former bride. "Susan. Ruthe. A long time. I wish you would tell me before you plan a visit."

"Erl-King," said the First Sister, "let her go. She'll come with us and the boy can stay."

"You keep your damn bargains to yourself, Susan," snapped Julia, her eyes intent upon the Erl-King. "You give me my son, bastard."

"Give you?" The Erl-King shook his head. "Douglas can make up his own mind, Julia. He's a big boy now." He looked back at the Sisters. "Isn't he? You know, you are not the only ones who can smell an anomaly."

"I do not approve of what you have done with the boy, Erl-King," said Susan.

"He did it himself. He was bound to join me in the end; you have to realize that."

"Not if you had stayed away."

"What would you have me do?" He was almost angry. Almost. "Leave my immortal son to be raised on fish by a human? Leave him hiding in a hole? Without giving him a taste of his true nature?

"And," he turned, "my dear Julia, it is his true nature. Douglas is the son that you have borne me. For this I thank you. But he is meant to be with me. Keeping him would be . . . very wrong of you."

"Damn you."

He sighed. "I fear, Susan, that your friend will never understand. A common mortal limitation. You, on the other hand, should know better. Turning against me."

"I am tired of this, Erl-King," said Susan. "Your perversity has gone on long enough. I turned against you when you decided to kill the humans."

"You have a problem with that? I guess you must be jealous of my lack of respect for these primates. You never did like me, I recall."

"We had every reason, Erl-King. Please." This was Ruthe. "Joly has been hurt. This cannot go on."

"It will go on as long as I like. I have no real quarrel with you. Back off and all will be well."

Susan scowled. "You will be the one backing off, elf. Golanlandaliay will destroy you. You know that. And there is nothing you can do to stop him."

"Oh, ho, ho, ho. There, my Sister, is where I believe you are wrong." He looked at Julia slyly. "Susan, Ruthe, it has been a nice meeting. It is time that you left."

"You cannot get rid of us."

"I might, but I do not have to. Douglas is better at this than I am."

The figure that stepped out of the wall came like a shadow and stood by his father. Douglas looked for a moment at his mother, then looked away. All Julia could see to tell her this was her son were the eyes and the hair that he had been born with. She began to sob.

"Douglas," said the Erl-King. "Escort our guests out of the nest."

Douglas hesitated. *Mistress Ruthe, I mean no harm. It is better this way.* A thought was all that was required to bring a wall of soulstuff around the two Sisters.

Susan and Ruthe could not believe what was happening as they fought the cone of blackness that enveloped them and whipped them through the wall of the fortress. It thrust them like a magical arm clear to the outside, and when they could see again, they felt the rush of hot, thick, smoky air that enshrouded Scotland.

As flies to wanton boys, thought Susan. *As flies to wanton boys.*

MacDuff lay on the huge bed and tried in vain to sleep. It wasn't the coming battle, really, that kept him awake. It was no form of discomfort; he could sleep on stone if need be. It wasn't the lack of a bearskin rug to talk to. It was something intangible, the knowledge that this war was coming to an end and the suspicion that with it would surely end his life. He waited for death. He deserved it. Responsibility kept taking it from him.

He studied the tapestry on the wall, idly picking at the strings on the front of his nightshirt, his eyes half-open, absorbing what little light the gloom afforded. There was Odin, the Father of the Gods, with his one, all-seeing eye. He was the god of victory, of war and knowledge. He fought like the god he was but spent his greatest energies planning the battles which brought glory to his chosen peoples. He travelled with his armies on his eight-legged horse and above him, guiding him, were two ravens. These, MacDuff knew, for he knew much, were named Hugin and Munin, Thought and Memory, and they led their master subtly. If respected they led well. If misunderstood they led to failure. The success of following thought and memory depended upon the master's ability to use them wisely. *A great task*, MacDuff mused, and felt on the edge of sleep, before he became aware that there was something in the room.

Or rather, someone. It was no sound but the keen sense of an experienced man that led him to this conclusion. He was being watched by someone in the room. But somehow he felt no suspicion and lay still, watching the wall in the gloom.

Slowly, as fog rolls in, a figure materialized. A tinge of

flimsy blue material flowed down a form that stood some five and a half feet tall. The head was adorned with long, flowing auburn hair, and though MacDuff could not see the face, he could not mistake the lock of hair that lay covering the left eye.

Susan.

MacDuff sat up in the bed, slowly, and moved his legs to where he felt the floor, and stood, all in one sweeping, fluid motion. He was not fully aware that he did these things, so intent was he on this unexpected visitor.

She glanced sideways and spoke and confirmed that it was her. "MacDuff. I . . ."

"Are you all right?" he asked, holding out an arm. He could not help but feel he was talking to something like an apparition. She was immortal, a Sister, and every way he tried to relate to her seemed at first new and strange. And for all that, very quickly familiar. "We feared that you and Ruthe . . ."

"We are fine. We had to come back. We could not take Julia. Douglas is under the control of the Erl-King. Goddess, MacDuff, he threw us out like dogs. I honestly do not know what is going to happen."

"Neither do I," said the Thane of Fife, truthfully.

"I'm not used to this lack of certainty." She stepped sideways a bit, as if wanting to pace and not wanting to, as entrancing blue gossamer flowed over her body with life of its own.

A witch, this is a witch . . . MacDuff sighed. "Nothing is certain. This is what it is to be mortal. Be glad you only have a taste of it." He could not find the right thing to say, and winced at the fact that he sounded scolding. *No. Not a witch. Susan.*

"Tell me something," he said. "In the dream you sent me, you said I had . . . slipped out. I took that to mean that I should have died long ago, that something in my destiny had gone wrong. Is this correct?"

"Slipped out . . ." She closed her eyes, deep in thought. They opened again and she stared at the Thane. "It is hard to say, MacDuff. There has always been something different. Whether it is because of the nature of your birth or your essence, I cannot say. But I will tell you, I would be hard pressed to say it is something that went wrong, now."

"When the time comes, Susan, will I die? Here?"

"I do not know. For the first time I am sure of nothing."

He looked at the floor and kept his eyes there.

". . . except that Douglas is powerful, MacDuff, and with his father there, I don't know how to defeat him. We may defeat the entire Darkling army and still lose." Her voice quieted to a whisper. "How do you live in this world?"

His answer, as he took her softly in his arms, was a kiss.

CHAPTER 18

Phoenix curse the damn fool Erl-King. May he lose his wings. After Ruthe and Susan had been gone for entirely too many days, Paddock began to get nervous. The owl flew nervously about the castle, waiting for some sign of his mistress' return. He felt certain that he should have followed Mistress Ruthe, even if she had forbade him. Phoenix was being unusually silent, now, as frighteningly invisible as the mice in the sky that lit up the night. He strained to see the top of the dome. His eyes hurt from the large amount of smoke in the air. The Erl-King must surely be responsible for this, too, he and his blasphemous star. Badmice, all of it.

He swiveled his head to look at the Erl-King's Dark Nest and shuddered, then moved the rest of his body around and winged towards it. Even in the slightly red-lit smoke it was visible, huge, tall and smooth. Paddock approached the structure cautiously. Mistress Ruthe was in there, all right. When would she come out?

Enough. I shall go in after her. The tower loomed over him as it grew larger with every second. It looked like a tree trunk, out of which grew the infernal dome. It was made out of the same material, too, and Paddock knew that he could not fly through it. Yet there must be a portal.

A few strokes brought him to the top of the tower, and he began to fly alongside where it expanded into the dome. The trunk was at least one hundred and fifty spans wide if a feather, and he slowly flew about its circumference, scanning for the portal through which the elves flew in and out. They did fly in and out, didn't they?

Harumph! Nothing. Paddock ruffled his feathers angrily and dipped into a spiralling dive, scanning the rest of the dome. He stayed not six spans away and travelled around the thing, down and down, looking for the opening. Nothing. When he smelled the bad water near the bottom he pulled away and began to travel back up again. Mistress Ruthe was still in there. This was completely unfair.

And then, something happened. Paddock was beating his breast in his own peculiarly religious way when he heard a sound like the heavy bubbling of Joly's cauldron. At first, he thought that was what it was, so anxious was he to be back on the heath in the mouselight, but this was louder. He scanned the wall of the tower, flying around the outside, until he could see the anomaly.

The wall was bubbling out at one point near the top. Paddock flew quickly to it as a large bubble ballooned and then popped, startling him. A flowing orifice lay open where the bubble burst, and immediately a long tendril with a ball on the end of it exploded outward through the tunnel it had borne. Paddock was quick to recover from his surprise and too thankful to succumb to his curiosity. At the speed that the "arm" burst out, he had little time. A hole had been opened up in the wall. Paddock flew in, between the tendril and the lip of the burst bubble. Only when the soulstuff wrapped around him and the tunnel disappeared did he realize he had heard his mistress in the ball, passing him, and that she was now outside. But by that time, Ruthe was the last thing on his mind.

For an instant, as the wall closed around him, he felt as if he were flying through the soulstuff, as if it were a liquid in which he would soon drown. But now he was inside, and this was not the world Phoenix made. This went on forever.

Paddock saw an expanse before him of black water (there was no other word for it) stretching on to infinity. A slight red glow sparkled against the black, lapping waves, which moved without the aid of wind. The air was still. Paddock could not tell where the border was, and a spin around showed that there was no wall anywhere near, either. Phoenix! Was this where the Erl-King lived? No. It was deeper than that. In a way more real than anywhere else, this was where the Erl-King existed.

And somewhere, in the distance, what seemed like miles and miles away, the Erl-King was here. With his magnificent eyes Paddock could make out three figures standing on the rippling ebon lake. He flew high in the air through the faint red glow until he was close enough to attack, but for some reason he held off. He sensed immense *otherness* in Douglas, very dangerous power, and he held back. He began to drift at a height where he was unlikely to be noticed and at which he could watch them comfortably. This was what birds did. Far below, Paddock could hear the silky voice of the Erl-King.

"Now that our friends have gone, Julia, I thought you would like to see the project on which our son and I are at work."

Julia looked around. Miles and miles of nowhere. All culled from the souls of children. "Down in your workshop again, I see. Make your wings here?"

The Erl-King only smiled at her, then turned away to address Douglas. "My son?"

Douglas was standing with his hands firmly at his sides, head tilted back slightly, eyes closed, deep in concentration. "They are ready."

Julia folded her arms. "I thought you said you wouldn't be keeping my son in a cellar."

The Erl-King looked back at her. "Do you mind? If you stay quiet, you're in for a treat."

"I doubt that."

"Oh, you'll enjoy this. You and I have created before. Today we shall do so again." He stood beside Douglas and looked out on the black lake. "Come from the forest, children, come out of the woods. I have a special game for thee." The ripples increased around the trio and Julia began to hear the singing voices more clearly. The voices filled the air, the lake, the entire world.

"I give you life. We have played together, you and I, for a long time. Now you will rise up and take form and join me.

"Little MacLeod, as you were called, you are there. I know it. Douglas has told me of your talks and he wishes to see you, but you have no body. Your body was left by your old parents to rot in the woods because they chose not to care for you. Little MacLeod, I call thee Rosier and ask that you come forth."

The Erl-King glanced at Douglas, who kept his eyes closed and held out a hand toward the lake. The Dark Child breathed deeply. Soon, in the black liquid, one circular ripple began to expand and bubble in the center, as if something were pushing outward. A small mound rose half an inch from the surface.

"Come, Rosier," said Douglas. "It is good that we do this for the enemy is weak, but our brothers yet need our strength, and I long for your companionship." As the hand continued to extend over the water the mound pushed farther, stretching a few inches, then stopped again.

The Erl-King's eyes flashed. "I know that you are angry, Little MacLeod. They left you, these humans. They are so weak that they take out their frustrations on those who are weaker, their own children. You were born and they did not want you. Does this please you, Rosier? Does this not make you angry?" The mound took a cylindrical shape and pushed further, drawing itself up. Now two long, hollow eyes surfaced from the soulstuff and stopped just above the surface, staring at the Erl-King.

"Does this not infuriate you, Rosier? You were innocent and they slew you, left you to die. You and all your brothers who have become my children have been so abused; do you not desire vengeance?" The head emerged, long and scythelike, and the thin neck below it betrayed a hint of narrow shoulders. Two feet to the right and left, razor sharp tips of wings broke the surface.

Douglas' extended hand clasped into a fist which he turned palm up, pulling the soulstuff with all the strength he could summon, following the soul's lead, controlling the soulstuff, overseeing their unholy fusion.

"I give you vengeance!" the Erl-King cried, "This is our game! They have given you pain and you shall give it back ten-fold. They destroyed you when you were weak and you will destroy them in kind! This is your place, Rosier! Come to destroy your destroyers!"

All at once the surface exploded and the figure burst forth, flying up over their heads. The black creature flew in circles around them, free at last to move with its own body. Paddock made sure to draw clear of its flight, but it was not looking, anyway. Rosier was engrossed in being able to move.

"Look at him, Julia," said the Erl-King. "I want to thank you for helping make this possible."

"You need all the help you can get, Erl-King. This is not your doing. You can do nothing. You manipulate and use."

"That is enough." He placed a hand on Douglas' shoulder. "Well done, my child.

"Little MacHenry, as you were called. You have been with us for some time. Join your brother. I call thee Rimmon, come forth!"

Rimmon bubbled and burst through the surface almost immediately and began circling the three with the same glee that drove Rosier. They circled, crossing paths in opposite directions, testing their wings. With every whip of their wings a brassy whish was heard. They stretched their long, scythelike arms and darted through the air without resistance. They were bone-thin, shiny black and, as Julia could plainly see, lethal.

"This is Rimmon, Julia," said the Erl-King. "A MacHenry."

"Another exposure?" Julia's voice was beginning to tremble slightly. Those scythes were going to be hell on the field. MacDuff would be in for it.

"No. He was one of my converts."

"You took him."

"Look at him, Julia. He is happier with me, as is Douglas."

Douglas looked not so much happy as thoroughly engrossed in the task at hand. He kept his palm out over the water, manipulating the soulstuff in a way his father could never fully accomplish, making the fusion possible. And he was getting better at it.

"Children," said the Erl-King, "behold your brothers! Join me, one by one, and become my soldiers!

"Angus Campbell, as you were called, I call thee Asbeel! Taste your hunger and your fury and be born!"

The black lake erupted again and yet another scythelike creature flew out of the black water, sending tiny droplets that flashed in the eerie red light. Asbeel immediately took to flying the circle with his brothers. They circled the three with such speed that the lake began to lap more violently against the boots of the Erl-King, as he held out his arms and called for more.

"Little Moray, I call thee Azza! Join me and take wing!"

Now there were four of them, circling the water and increasing its violence. They flew so fast that Julia had trouble picking them out as they began to blur. One after another the black surface tore open and gushed another tainted soul. One after another they joined the swirling circle of shining dark warriors.

". . . Little MacBride, I call thee Murmur!

". . . John MacQueen, I call thee Carnivean!

". . . Robert Seyton, I call thee Jeqon!

". . . Little Sutherland, I call thee Marut!

". . . Barbiel!

". . . Caym!

". . . Forcas!" The lake was roaring with the sound of brassy wings cutting the air and the violent splashing of the waves as the forces circled, faster and faster until a wall of black water rose and roared about them. The circle widened as the Erl-King called out new name after name and his adoptions took their intended roles.

This was what it was about, Julia realized. All of it. Me, Douglas, all to form this. *These are no additions to his forces. These will absolutely outmode the Darklings.*

More came, birthing themselves at Douglas' hand and the Erl-King's command until there were nearly fifty of them, stripped of their human names and feeding off their warped human emotion.

The Erl-King smiled back at Julia. *You see, darling. Aren't they beautiful?* He shouted out again.

"Jess Galloway, as you were . . ."

"No!" cried Julia, grabbing his arms. *Please, not that. Anything but that. Abel . . .*

"What?" He pushed her away easily.

"You don't want that one! He is weak!"

The crackling eyes sparkled brilliantly. "He is strong! He is mine! Jess Galloway, I call thee Belphegor!"

"No! Douglas, please, this is Abel's son! You can't do this!"

The Erl-King smiled. "Ah. Douglas, do your duty."

"Douglas, stop!" Julia shouted. "I demand that you stop this instant!"

Douglas opened his eyes and looked.

"Please!"

"Douglas," cried the Erl-King, "Do not listen to this woman! She is not one of us! She is weak, like a human and like a worm, and you have no suit with her. Ignore her and bring my child! Give your brother life."

My mother . . .

"You have no mother! She is flesh and bone of different nature, born to die!"

Julia's tears stung her eyes. "Douglas, I care nothing for what you consider me to be, but I beg of you, do not bring this child. Let him remain dead and move to another."

The Erl-King took her by the shoulder and spun her around to look into her eyes with his own crackling orbs. "I want this one, Julia. Because it gives you pain and because I feel like giving you pain. You are weak and human and easily crushed. Douglas, bring Belphegor."

But . . .

The Erl-King kept his grip on Julia's shoulder. His nails drew blood. "Do my bidding. Do not listen to this woman! Think of her weakness! Her hypocrisy! No virtue goads her to stop you, but favoritism of one soul over another. She would not see this one serve us but would gladly lose another! What sort of virtue is that? I offer freedom to all! Why does she favor this child, Douglas? And why not take it if she is so weak?"

The lake exploded again and the creature that bore the soul of Jess Galloway flew into the air. It hovered a moment over Douglas' head, as if waiting for instructions.

Phoenix! Paddock the Owl hurled himself through the center of the hurricane of warriors and extended his talons angrily. Mistress Julia was in danger.

"No!" Julia cried again, and tore at the Erl-King's snow-white face with her nails. "You bastard!"

The Erl-King tasted the blood as it flowed into his mouth and his eyes flared. In one great sweep he brought his left arm across Julia's face, shutting the screaming woman up. *For good*, he thought, as her body crashed to the floor.

Douglas turned, wide-eyed, unable to move. *That was my mother. . . .*

The Erl-King looked at him for a moment, then up to see a ten-pound feathered creature's claws coming at his wounded face. The owl screeched and tore at him, flapping his wings violently.

Blasphemous Erl-King! Orderless Erl-King! Die!

The Erl-King managed to get his hands on the body of the owl and throw it back, feeling it tear away from his own face. The bird went flipping back through the air. Something glowed and oozed black ichor in its right talon. *My eye!*

The Erl-King roared in shock, clutching his face with his own hand. Douglas stood still. He did not move, but only watched his mother's lifeless body.

"My Scythelings! Finish this damned creature! Tear it to pieces!"

Douglas did not really hear the sounds he heard, the screeching of the owl as Paddock fought the Scythelings and felt himself chopped apart beyond repair. He did not hear the ranting of the infuriated, one-eyed Erl-King, who stood in the middle of the flying blades and watched, as smoke poured unceasingly from his left socket. Douglas could only stare at his mother and listen for a heartbeat that was not there.

CHAPTER 19

The first day of February is the Feast Day of Bride, when the goddess — or saint, if you please — Bride waves her white wand and restores the life of the dead land in winter. It is a symbolic winter she is said to restore. In the beguiled time, however, there were those who forever after would see the Feast of St. Bride's day with an entirely different view.

MacDuff awoke in the early morning and found his breath even shorter than the day before. The smoke was seeping throughout the castle, thick and filthy, fingering its way into the nostrils and lungs of every man, woman and child in Scotland. *Battle today. Breathe what you can.*

He sat up and reached for his red cloak and clanged the iron disk in place. MacDuff could hear Susan rising behind him. The lack of oxygen would not trouble her. As far as he knew, she did not need to breathe. He slid his calloused feet into his boots and rose, feeling his back crack into position. He enjoyed the pain, somehow. He had earned it. He walked to the window and did his best to expand his chest to bring in more air. The Old Man of Hoy brooded in the distance, barely visible in the red-filtered gray.

> *"Early on Bride's morn*
> *The serpent will come from the hole,*
> *I will not molest the serpent,*
> *Nor will the serpent molest me."*

MacDuff frowned at the Dark Nest. This time, the serpent would be molested.

He turned around to see Susan staring at him. He knew she didn't read minds; she was simply staring at him. "Let's go."

"To battle? Just like that?"

"To mass," he said.

"Do we know where they are?" The face of the Erl-King crackled more fiercely than before.

A gravelly voice answered. "Yes, my Lord. The Sisters went straight below. The allies are here, with the Vikings. We should have taken care of the Northmen first."

"Do not question my judgment, Perth. Scotland is the birthplace of my son. Scotland is my first target. The Vikings will not get in our way."

The smoke from the incense lifted and mixed with the rest of the smoke in the air. On any morning MacDuff would have heard the lapping of waves from the field where they gathered. But there was no sound. The water did not crash against the rocks which began but a stone's throw away.

The cockerel had been buried alive in honor of Bride. The ceremonial fires, which MacDuff grudgingly had allowed (it was a sacrifice, he rationalized) burnt slightly yellow through the thick air.

The serpent will come from the hole . . .

Dukane was edgy and annoyed at having to go through this. He knew the battle was coming, as did all. He clasped and unclasped his hand around the pommel of his sword.

Abel listened intently to the voices of the priests, their eyes hollow patches under robes. He prayed with them and felt certain it would help.

> *"On the brown day of Bride,*
> *Though there should be three feet of snow*
> *On the flat surface of the ground . . ."*

MacDuff stood with Thorfinn and Susan and glanced at each of them in turn. The priests made him think of the Druids, and how they were no longer. And yet, as he could think of them, they were. The hot air made the sweat flow freely from his pores. The smoke was as the Erl-King. Sneaking up. Ever present.

The hooded priests raised their arms over the incense fire and all in the congregation joined the chant.

> *"On the Feast Day of Beautiful Bride,*
> *The flocks are counted on the moor,*
> *The raven goes to prepare the nest,*
> *And again goes the rook."*

Abel crossed his massive chest and threw a glance at Dukane. The general nodded, grimly.

The wood elves who were posted on the top of the wall at Thorfinn's castle thought they saw something. They were, for a moment, not sure.

> *"Bless, O Chief of Generous Chiefs,*
> *Myself and everything near me . . ."*

MacDuff was saying the words to the God that helps when he saw Ruthe's face. Susan turned to Ruthe and they seemed to pass a thought. Did you hear . . .

Make thou me safe for ever,
Make thou me safe for ever.

"Now, Perth," an ancient voice said. "Take them."

I will not molest the serpent,
The serpent will not molest me.

Yes it will! MacDuff saw Dukane stand, his sword already out. For a moment the priests looked around in confusion as two thousand weapons were drawn. The Iron Thane was headed for his horse when he saw an army of wood elves leading the counterstrike before the attacking army had actually arrived. He looked up and saw a swarm of Darklings pouring from the Dark Nest. *No need to go to them. The serpent will come from the hole.*

The horse stood near the rocks, on the thin beach, and it began to pitch and whine when it saw the approaching army of Darklings. MacDuff never reached it. As some of the Darklings broke through, MacDuff heard the horse snort fearfully as a black blade impaled its heavy torso. *I would have taken out the horses, too. No matter. We're not going anywhere this time.*

The Darkling saw MacDuff and dove for him. Mac-Duff was used to this by now. *The sword is you; you are the sword. Do not think.* In one motion he brought his sword up, from left to right, swiping the Darkling's blade aside, and then again, deep into the creature's abdomen. He stopped to try to breathe and pulled the sword from the body. He was already tired. He tried to ignore the heat and smoke as he shoved the floating, feathered mass aside. It was going to be a long day. He jumped onto a rock and watched the sky for a moment. Something he had never seen before caught his eyes. In the red and gray sky, one Darkling crackled like no other. MacDuff smiled to himself grimly. The Erl-King was here. And from the looks of things, with nearly eight hundred flying archers under Gol's command opposed, he was losing.

Oberon and his men were spending most of their time below, dodging the bodies of the slain. Then, without announcement, but only a quick look to a few of the Syth near him, Oberon was off, running at full speed for the Old Man of Hoy. As he reached the water, avoiding those in his way, he felt the slight spray of the stream that erupted behind his feet. The wall was less than ten feet away. Then it filled his field of vision and he tilted back and kept running. Oberon was running up the side of the Dark Nest.

At fifty feet up he was still going full speed and whipped back. The world spun as he flipped through the air. The hook was out. His eyes were open. And even though he was flipping through the air at a rate of two times per second, focusing was no problem for a Syth. This was what they were built for. He opened his eyes and picked a pair of black wings and yanked one off as he sailed past the Darkling. Flipping into the sea, he saw the look of the horrified Darkling as it dropped.

Oberon the king hit the water running and sped back to the Syth. "You know the drill, lads."

"Actually, sir," said a young Syth, "I've never seen that before in my life . . ."

"Hmm. You are young." He looked at the rest. "Aim carefully! Go!"

On the rocky beach below, Thorfinn the Mighty led his men through a battle to rival those of the gods. *Great stories from this,* he thought. *Great stories.* As he stepped through the filthy water he sheathed his sword and drew his bow. He took a moment to line up his targets, being

sure to take aim only on those with *black* wings. This
proved difficult in the smoke and he repeatedly had to
wait until he could see the crackle of their eyes before
dropping them. *Stupid, stupid creatures*, he thought, as
one after another fell before him. *Damned strange, but
stupid.*

Dukane sniffed as he tore the head off of a Darkling.
He looked over his shoulder at Abel. "I think this is going
well."

The great axe swung through a crackling chest and
down, dripping black ichor into the water. Abel leaned
against a rock and tried to ignore the bodies that floated
past him, food for fish. "Aye. I fear we are outmoded by
the wood elves, however." He had seen the arrows flying,
when he had the chance to look up. The bodies falling
made splashing sounds that he found distracting. But they
were bodies with arrows in them.

"Duck!" he heard Dukane say, and he did not bother to
look. He dropped and felt the water hit his chest as
Dukane's buckler slashed the incoming black sword aside.
The Darkling stopped and dropped, holding his sword
high. Abel neatly brought up his axe and tore through the
feathered man's back. He smiled at Dukane and pushed
the body aside.

Perth flew to the Erl-King's side in a panic. "My liege!
We are being slaughtered."

The Erl-King floated in midair for a second, watching
the flapping, outmoded, shiny wings of Perth. The skin
crackled like his own but he was not one of them. *Slaughtered, yes, I see that. And do you know what? I'm not
really all that bothered by it. You have served your purpose.* He shrugged and saw Perth dart valiantly back into
battle, ever the good servant. The Erl-King looked at the
chaos, at Oberon and the Syth flipping through the air
making mincemeat of the Darklings, the wood elves filling

the sea with their arrow-filled bodies. The humans on the ground catching whatever came their way. He had expected this. He could have waited for the humans to attack, it didn't matter. He had Douglas. By the time Douglas calmed down, he would have a much greater family to present. But as it was, the stage was set. And he just didn't need the Darklings anymore. He turned his one-eyed head toward the Dark Nest and his mind toward the soulstuff and called for his *real* children.

MacDuff stopped and rested for a second, his hands upon his knees. The air was too thin. He could barely catch a breath. He looked about him. The scene was one of the roar of boots pounding through calf- and thigh-deep water, off and onto rocks. He heard the clash of metal and the screams of men and Syth and elves being torn apart.

MacDuff wiped the sweat off his brow and barely had time to see the torn wood elf that nearly fell on top of him. The elf had a hole through its middle a foot wide. What the hell could do this? Then he looked up and tried to see through the smoke. *Damn fires, we should have figured that out sooner. . . .*

There were no more Darklings in sight, or none near him. Of that he was glad. But there was something else up there.

Tether of the wood elves let his bow rest for a moment. Gol had been right, all the allies needed was the entrance of the wood elves and the struggle would be ended. He hovered awhile in the air, feeling his wings vibrate rapidly in the hot smoke. He turned around in the air and saw the amiable face of Meniel, from his own hamlet, plucking off Darklings at his leisure about twenty yards away. Tether could see the Darklings, flying about in confusion. Running scared. They would regret the day they followed the Erl-King into battle. The towering Dark Nest was nearly empty now, surely, though it loomed as impressive as ever behind Meniel's war-painted body.

Tether called out to Meniel. "How goes the war?"

Meniel looked quickly around, as Tether continued to do in his rest, and brought down his bow. "A smart lot better than your study sessions ever did," he smiled. Meniel had been Tether's tutor in history. All those stories about the Big Tree and Gol and his predecessor's and the old world. Meniel had been good at that, Tether was thinking, when he saw a flash of light glint through the smoke and an obscure figure came slicing through the air behind Meniel's back.

Tether had no time. No time to raise his bow, no time to yell there's-something-I've-never-seen-before-behind-you. No time to even raise his eyebrows all the way or utter a sound. In a story, like the ones he learned in school, he would have done something, like push his old friend out of the way after covering the distance at lightning speed. But this was real life, and all he could do was watch as in less than a second the flying Scythe flew straight through Meniel's body. Meniel was still smiling, his face still caught in that ancient mirth of good battle, as the upper half of his body tore away from the lower half and the smiling parts of him disappeared through the smoke.

"Yes!" Tether heard the Erl-King cry, from somewhere near the tower, and he could imagine the brilliant white hair and the crackling body but did not need to see the damned elf. "Well done, Rimmon! Golanlandaliay, you fleshly fool! See how well your painted elves fare against my children!"

Golanlandaliay was nowhere near the Erl-King, but he heard the call. What the hell is the old man up to? And then he saw them, at least ten near him, slicing through the air like knives. They were thin and ghostly, and when they didn't fly through you with their razorlike heads they were slicing you to ribbons with their scythelike arms. They were flying scythes. Scythelings.

Eight times. Nine. Spells and more spells. Forgotten chants. Useless. Susan tried to ignore the screams and kept her hands on the wall. She knelt and lay her forehead against the Dark Nest. *I can get in.* She looked at her Sister. There were elves screaming and humans hacking. "Ruthe, can't you move this fog south or something?"

"All of it?" Ruthe shook head. "I could, but it would asphyxiate the rest of the kingdom. The fog stays. Just get into the wall."

"I can't."

"Try again! The Scythelings are going to tear through the allies before they even know what hit them. If we get in, we can stop him. Surely."

"We don't even know that," Susan yelled. The din of metal and brassy wings was deafening. She quit yelling and thought at Ruthe instead. *What are we going to do in there? Anyway, I've tried.*

But the Erl-King is just a damned elf, how could he . . .

Hasn't it become patently obvious that we have no idea what the Erl-King is? I don't know what he can do what he does, but I know he has more power than any elf should. He probably always did.

Susan, try again.

The First Sister heard rapid footsteps plunging through the shallow water. She looked up to see the tall, gray Mac-Duff. He knelt down beside her.

"Have you seen them?"

"Aye," he said. "Is this the boy's doing?"

"No. This is the Erl-King's use of the boy."

"Small difference."

She frowned, squinting through the smoke as it curled around them. Goddess, could it actually get any hotter? "Big enough, Fife-Thane. The Erl-King will pay for this."

"Any moment that you arrive at a suggestion, I shall be happy to entertain it."

"Carnivean! Rosier! Jeqon!" cried the Erl-King. "Do not lavish your attention solely on these flying imbeciles! Fly low and destroy them all!"

The three Scythelings heard and obeyed, diving through the smoke, leading many of their brothers who sought fresh meat. Soon they saw new targets, thousands of men on the rocks below. They watched the men run in fear through the tumultuous water. They watched the stupid ones who stood and fought.

It was easy, so incredibly easy to destroy them from before or behind, and so often the men stood so dumbfounded they would not even raise a weapon to fight. After all, it would not help. The Scythelings could not be hurt. Jeqon saw a huge, red-headed man with a bow below. The man saw him and hesitated before raising the bow to let fly an arrow. Jeqon saw it fly towards him and through him as he tore through the man's side with his own weapon, his own body. For a moment he saw the pain in Thorfinn's face before moving on, and a brief sensation flashed across his mind. Something told Jeqon to ignore this. Jeqon tried.

Slice them, kill them, tear them to shreds.

The Scythelings moved as one, because Father said so. Because it was good to do. It was a good thing, they knew, all of them, as they darted to and fro through the smoke and tore up anything that did not look like themselves or like Father.

And wasn't it wonderful, all of them thought — or was it Father thinking for them, sometimes it was hard to tell — to have bodies, to move and jump and play games in the world that these humans had denied them. How could they have ever doubted?

Slice them.

In the forest they sang his praises and learned of the

glory of their older brothers. And when they had listened long enough, and their appetites had been made ripe . . .

Kill them.

They learned that they were special, more special even than their brothers who were born of wing, for they were closer to his nature. And all they must do is follow.

Tear them.

And then the new Prince had come to help Father and make it possible and they were born, in a way far greater and far more real than they had ever been born before, far back, when they had crawled like humans, like worms upon the earth. It was a special thing that even the Darklings could never share or understand. To be brought from so low to such heights, wasn't Father wondrous, wasn't . . .

To shreds.

. . . it better than life had ever been, the old way, before they joined him in his world?

It was something impossible to explain that made one Scytheling out of the fifty that had been born thus far say *no.*

Belphegor had not had his first kill yet and wasn't feeling very elated when the small thing inside of him made him envision the Erl-King and say it.

You . . .

And there were so many more of them yet to be born anew! Thousands upon thousands of their brothers still playing in the forest, watching them, waiting for their turn to come out and play.

. . . are not . . .

And when they were finished with these humans, they would move on, Father said so, and soon they would have room to play for eternity . . .

. . . my father!

It was Belphegor the Scytheling that began to look feverishly for the Scot known as Abel Galloway of the MacHenry clan. It was Jess Galloway that found him.

❖   ❖   ❖

Gol saw a wood elf body flying lifelessly at him. As it tumbled through the air he sprang and flipped over, then levelled out as it whizzed past. He made a mental note of the elf's face; he would remember the name later. He would remember them all. Gol drew an arrow from his quiver and realized he was getting low. He had to find a target. He would not refill until he had to. The army could not afford hesitation. No sooner did he have the arrow in place than he saw one of the new creatures flying towards him. The Scytheling had its blades poised for slicing. He drew back his arm and let a shaft fly. He saw it go clear through the creature's body and disappear in the distance. The Scytheling seemed to shudder. Was it hesitating? Gol wasted no time drawing another arrow and sending it through the Scytheling again. The thing stopped and hung in midair. It moved its head side to side, in confusion.

The Erl-King drew his sword out of a wood elf and looked over to see the motionless Scytheling. The Scytheling reached its blade at its chest.

What are you doing, child? Fight!

But, Father . . .

A light passed through the valleys of Gol's mind. "I have hurt you, have I not? Come at me, child, so that I may hurt you again!"

Don't be ridiculous, Barbiel. He can't hurt you. You have no body.

But I do have a body!

That doesn't mean you have pain!

Doesn't it?

Barbiel looked across the beach and saw the men, with slashes in their throats and chests, in pain. Screaming. He looked up to see another arrow flying at his face. He held up his bladelike arms. No! *The arrow flew through his arms and face and away. He wanted to scream but had no mouth.*

"I have hurt you, child! You are in pain! Feel the cut I give and my shaft as it slices through you. Though it flies through, it pains you, as if you were human, for you *are* human!"

Father it hurts it hurts it hurts it hurts . . .

Barbiel, fight him!

Barbiel threw up his arms and panicked. He swam through the air at lightning speed and dove straight into the wall and was gone.

Gol drew another arrow. "Erl-King!"

The Erl-King looked.

"A point to ponder," Gol said, drawing the arrow. "What is the difference between being in pain and *thinking* you are in pain?"

Gol saw the Erl-King's lip curl. "You tell me," he heard the Prince of the Dark Elves say, and then he suddenly felt himself being knocked what seemed like a hundred feet sideways. *What hit me?* He looked to his right to see a smiling Darkling.

"Pain, Golanlandaliay?" asked a gravelly voice. "I'll show you pain."

Golanlandaliay tried to turn to face the Darkling that had butted him when he looked down to see he had not been simply butted. He had been run through. The Darkling's hand held the hilt of the black sword, and it was buried fully through the wood Prince's right side. *They say you don't feel it until you look. They seem to be right.* Golanlandaliay began to feel groggy. *Don't black out . . .* He reached for his dagger and saw *he's twisting it, oh, God . . .* Perth smile again and then suddenly his eyes grew wide and he let go the pommel of his sword. An arrow had appeared inside of his mouth. Perth began to fall.

Gol was about to fall, too. He reached down and took the pommel of the sword. It was sticking clear through him, entering above his waist, through the external oblique, and exiting through his stomach. This was a tough one. *I won't survive this.* He corrected himself: *Yes, you will. But it will take a while to get over it.* He kept flapping his wings, coasting toward the water, in the interminable length of time it took to pull the sword out. It was actually less than a second or two, and soon he became aware that the elf who had fired the arrow at Perth was holding him by the shoulders. He looked up into his savior's eyes and let the sword drop.

"What is your name, soldier?"

"Raphael," said the wood elf.

Gol nodded. "Put me down. Go back to the fight. Tell the allies this: the Scythelings can be beaten. Tell as many as you can. The Scythelings are brand new. They are deadly, but they are children. And they feel pain, or they think they do. If you can touch them with sword or arrow before they slice through you, you can win." He breathed heavily but smoothly. *Not bad. I'll live through this.* "Leave me. My job is through here."

Raphael lay Golanlandaliay upon a stone and turned back to join the fighting. Gol lay still and tried to concentrate on controlling his pulse.

Dukane and Abel felt themselves at a loss for what to do. They stood back to back, arms ready, knowing that no enemy they could beat would come to them, they waited on the smoky rocks solemnly, for seconds that seemed like hours, for death. When a shadow passed across Abel's face and he heard the brassy swish of wings, Abel raised his axe to meet the thing, for it was all he could do. Dukane was turning around to back him up one last mortal time when something made Abel stop.

"Fight!" cried the Erl-King. "Fight! They cannot hurt you!" But he knew now that his was not the only voice to be heard.

Pain! cried Carnivean as a Viking arrow flew through his abdomen and made his mind flinch.

Pain! cried Rosier as the sword of MacHenry tore through it and cleanly out again.

The children were frenzied. They had not expected this; Father had said nothing about pain. He said this would be enjoyable, that it was a game. But they had bodies now and they were being cut in a million places. Those who had not been touched yet, who continued merrily slicing the allies to ribbons, paid no heed. Those who had been the victims of one lucky blow or another were positively folding.

Abel blinked and stared into the hollow eyes as the long, dark head tilted sideways to study him. The swish of wings. The curl of the smoke. It was not human, this thing. It was not even real. But he knew, by the tilt of the head and the studying manner and the unmistakable fact that Abel had been *recognized* that this, in some way, was his son. He knew that he was probably suffering a delusion. All in all, he did not care. The Scytheling motioned for him to follow. Abel did so.

Oberon appeared beside MacDuff and the Sisters, stopping only momentarily to watch Susan try to break into the wall with her own magic. "MacDuff," he said. "Things are bad. These Scythelings, they are destroying the wood elves. The humans are very easy targets. Gol is down. Thorfinn is down. Gol should live, from what I can tell."

"And Thorfinn?"

"A difficult call. But at this rate, if we aren't all ripped to shreds by these scythe-creatures, we will still asphyxiate."

"Can they be beaten?"

"If Susan can get into the tower, she can meet the Erl-King in his own territory. As for fighting the Scythelings in combat, we are working on that. They are children. They seem capable of getting scared and losing faith in themselves. They have low resolve and not exceptional fighting skills, and if . . ."

Oberon's voice had trailed off because he saw MacDuff suddenly turn his eyes over Oberon's shoulder. Oberon turned around to see Abel running after a Scytheling that seemed to be ambling its way towards the wall. Dukane was running behind them, obviously as confused as the rest.

The Scytheling sped up when he got near MacDuff and the rest and flew straight into the structure. Abel and Dukane came to a halt. The giant blond stared up the smooth surface.

Father . . .

Abel shook his head. "I can't!" he cried. "We cannot enter, Jess!"

But you must stop him . . .

"Jess . . ." Abel leaned against the wall and looked at MacDuff. "Disappointed child. He wants me to stop the bogey-man."

MacDuff glanced at the wall where Jess had disappeared. The black surface rippled and the head and torso slid out again and looked inquisitively at Abel. The arm with the razor-like end extended. Abel placed his hand around the rod-like section that attached to the torso. His other hand grasped his battle axe tightly. The head swiveled and stared, for some reason, at MacDuff. *And you.* The other arm extended and MacDuff took it silently. He nodded at Abel briefly and then they were being yanked, all of their weight, through the solid-and-not-so-solid wall.

On the arms of Jess they left the smoke and air of Scotland and found themselves inside a wall that could not possibly have been this expansive. The red light glistened on the ebon sea and the black water went on forever, as limitless as the sky above them. Abel found himself standing on the surface, ebon waves lapping over his feet. "Are we inside the wall?"

MacDuff shook his head. "No. More than that. Welcome to the world of the Erl-King."

Jess was gone. He had disappeared as soon as they had made the transition to the interior. What is more, they now realized, as they felt the floor lapping against their naked feet, so had their clothes, their armor, and their weapons. They were naked and alone in a world of blackness that went on forever.

No, not alone, either. Douglas was here. Looming large and omniscient, MacDuff could tell he held the world in balance. And he wanted a fair fight.

As the Erl-King flitted through the air hacking men and elves to pieces and trying to keep his new children from disgracefully turning tail, he felt a sudden, terrible disruption. He had been intruded upon. He had been *betrayed*. The elves who were nearby, dark and wood both, told later how he simply disappeared from the field, as if something of much graver importance had to be attended to. In many ways, the battle was over from there. But the real conflict had barely begun.

The lake gurgled at the feet of the two men and something began to grow from it. The liquid flowed into a small mound before beginning to take shape and protrude upward. At first Abel had the same thought that MacDuff did — Jess has returned — and they were not altogether wrong. But the object that now stood on the fine point of its own blade was a weapon. The warriors were naked. Jess was offering himself up as a sword, the only kind that would work in the Erl-King's domain. Using the Erl-King's power as the Erl-King used the souls'.

"Abel," said the Thane of Fife, "the blade is yours. It was your son that the Erl-King took, and who allowed us entrance here. If this is to be used against the Erl-King, the fight is yours."

The giant blond knelt and took the sword by its ebon

pommel and lifted it, feeling its weight in his hand. Douglas stood by, in the distance, arms folded. Abel gripped the sword firmly, then shook his head. His naked chest sank. "No."

"What?"

"No. I want him, but I cannot beat him. No amount of resolve and anger will make me proficient with a weapon I do not use. Not against a master. Not with you here." The massive arm gently slid the sword back in position in the surface of the lake. His eyes met MacDuff and locked, burning with honesty. "Yours, MacDuff. It is not out of fear that I do this."

MacDuff nodded. He lifted the sword and closed his eyes for a moment, taking in air and letting it out, feeling his hands, his arms, his body become one with the sword. He did not need to see to know that the Erl-King was here, standing on the lake, waiting. Angry. "I know," he said, opening his eyes.

For the first time at a comfortable distance, the Thane of Fife got a good look at the Erl-King.

CHAPTER 20

I am MacDuff. I hold the sword in my hand and feel its weight and know this to be the only truth, the only certainty in this beguiled time.

I am MacDuff, Thane of Fife. My voice is in my sword.

This is it, Erl-King. I have seen you in my dreams. I have heard of you all my life. I thought once that my drama was complete, but no.

I have to face you.

You have lost an eye, Erl-King. The left eye. Like the old man who told tales in my boyhood. What is it? The left eye is that which gives depth to sight and is extremely useful in battle and sword play. A weakness for you, Erl-King. But I know as well as you do that it is the right eye that truly sees.

You see. I know you do.

It's all over, Erl-King. It ends here. Not in battle, not with armies, not with thievish lies. One on one. Like to like. Erl-King, I have said these words before, and I hate them, even as I find them fit to use.

I am going to kill you. If I have anything to do about it, you are going to die.

Douglas is staying out of it, Erl-King. Why? He could destroy us, all of us, if he wanted, I can see that by the way he stands and watches. But I know why he does not, I can see it in the crackle of your one good eye.

This fight will be fair, and it is mine to fight. If Douglas can keep from using this power against you himself, if he can keep from becoming you, he wins. The sword was meant for me. I may never understand, but I know this.

I see you angry and you raise that sword and you remind me of MacBeth. I have been here before.

You raise that sword and swing it, now, and when I raise mine and our blades spark I could swear I hear the sparks cry LIAR.

You lie, Erl-King.

Douglas, I wonder if you can hear what I think as I stand here and swing this sword at your father in mortal combat. Do you know what your father is?

No Darkling, that is certain. The Darklings are a bunch of weak-willed elves who found a leader that either made himself look like them or vice-versa and gave them a direction, who lied to them and called them his own.

What are you, Erl-King? Did you make this body? Do you remember what you were, in the beginning, when you looked across the universe and realized that for all your power you were alone? Do you lie to yourself as you lie to others? Do you even know the truth anymore?

Keep that sword up, Erl-King. The cut low is a bad move. You are out of practice. I do this in my sleep.

One false move, Erl-King, one slip, and your head will bounce like the ball I sewed for my son when he was three. My son was lucky, Erl-King. He never had to be taken in by you.

LIAR!

Who said that, Erl-King?

My sword said it. The wall said it. Your dupes said it. Everyone knows and no one will pity you.

LIAR!

You coward, you treacherous, sniveling coward, you take and use and manipulate power and claim as your own when your only power, after all, is that manipulation.

How ironic. Such power. But you have to have someone to use it on, or it is no good to you. So you lie.

This dome, this contraption that traps our air and threatens to kill us all, is not yours. You borrowed it. You used. You manipulate. You hurt. You lie.

Coward, I call thee!

As I was a coward when I left my family and went to England for help and lost everything.

But no victim, Erl-King. I feel no pity for you. You are no victim like the children you steal. No one ever promised you a thing, no one used you.

Look out, Erl-King. That is your arm that is bleeding. Good block. You just keep that up.

What was it like, to be alone in the universe with no family . . . how would you put it . . . assigned to you? No Syth, no Sisters, just you and your mind and your incredible, cosmically wounded ego. How bad did you hurt that you became this?

Do you want to know something? If I were there, at the beginning of time, I might pity you, might render you my friendship and help you. But the choice was still yours, Erl-King. I pity that primordial victim. But for you I have only justice. We take responsibility, Erl-King. I have learned this and I add it to my list of things upon which to meditate when you give up and quit swinging that damned sword. As if you have a chance. This is not what I was born for. This is what I was RIPPED for.

I was created for this.

Hack. Turn. Parry. Hack. Are you getting better or angrier? Am I getting tired or old?

ARRRGH! Damn. Make a note, Erl-King. No self-doubt allowed.

It is my own eye, it is God's eye, it is the eye of the Son of God . . .

I am honored by the thought, though, and as soon as I can get over the pain my body is trying to convince me to feel and I can choke down the blood in my mouth I will find a way of thanking you for making me just a little bit more like you.

Hack. Parry. Hack. A dance, Erl-King. You and I are dancing like old partners.

Now that we see eye to eye.

I don't know why life works out as it does. I don't know why such evil has come to Scotland, or whether anything is truly evil. I don't know why a person feels so thrust upon with pain that he turns to taking life, or why he becomes something like you. You liar, you coward, you fear the truth and you will never face it.

You did not want to destroy all the humans, you did not create Douglas because he would make that task easier, you did not make countless souls your slaves because you wanted to hurt, or because you felt so incredibly superior to the Sisters and the Syth and the amber-colored, obnoxious wood elves. These things are true, but they are not the truth.

The truth is so frightening, yet so incredibly simple that you can never face it, and so benign that it sounds like a joke. Like something so powerful and weak that even the First Sister fears it more than she cherishes Order. Like something my naive little son would have said.

You son of a bitch, you want love.

You have a hell of a way of throwing a tantrum, Erl-King. No pity for you. It's over. It ends here.

Hack. Parry. Hack. The serpent will come from the hole. I will not molest the serpent, and the serpent will not molest me. You lost out, Erl-King.

Tired, Erl-King? You have more power here than anywhere else, but you are far more real here, and I am just as real to you here as anywhere else. You know what the risks are. Keep it up, Erl-King. You might last a few more minutes. You might.

I wish I had understood from the beginning, or someone had, but even then it would have been too late for you. It was too late long ago.

Tag. Do not complain; you sliced out my eye. Wouldn't bend over to pick that ear up, if I were you.

Watch this, Erl-King. Replay it when you're gone and you have lots of time. That's right, follow the sword, lose it when it goes back, try to compensate, you should be better at this . . .

. . . and could that be blood issuing in such vast quantities from that white neck of yours. Ichor? And now that you are paying attention, if I do this . . .

. . . ah, yes. As I thought. It rolls quite well, Erl-King. Crawl after it a few feet. Try to feel for the crackle of the hair before you lose consciousness. Stay there. Don't move.

Poor old Erl-King.

He lies and lies.

Gol looked up when he felt a sudden blast of cold air. "Susan!" Something was happening. A seam had opened along the bottom of the dome and was beginning to raise from the ground. As light flooded in, Gol could see the ice and snow along the coast.

Susan looked at Oberon. "Does that mean . . ."

In the air, Perth knew that the Father was gone, as did all of the Darklings. "Come," he cried, "retreat! Homeward!"

"Don't worry, Sister, they won't get far," said Gol. He tugged sharply at a knot in the cloth bandage held around his waist.

Susan stopped him, reaching out a hand to his shoulder. "No, Golanlandaliay. The Darklings are no longer a threat."

"I have lost many, Sister. I am not in the habit of letting the culprit escape."

"The culprit is dead, Gol. Those you see flying away are elves, no more, no less." The flock of black-winged creatures flew southward and disappeared in the distance. "Now," she smiled, "go lick your wounds and try not to think about your cousins."

"But . . ."

"Gol? I must warn you, if you try to wipe out the Darklings I will oppose you. Do not molest the order that has been restored."

Golanlandaliay looked into the First Sister's eyes and knew that she would do it all over again. "Aye, Sister." He thrust his sword into the ground and noticed that it was snowing.

"It is done," said the rumbling voice of the Dark Child. He looked at Abel and the bleeding MacDuff and seemed to see through them. "Leave me, MacDuff. Go. I shall undo what damage I can. The children of the Erl-King will trouble you no longer."

"Douglas," said Abel. "Your mother, Julia . . ."

"Julia is dead."

"Oh, God." Abel was silent for a long moment. He closed his eyes and crossed himself, then addressed the boy again. "Douglas, if you . . . I could . . ."

"No. Do not even ask. Just go and do not look for me or the dome when we are gone. Go. Already it is snowing outside and your men will be in need of aid and shelter." This Douglas said, before Abel and MacDuff felt themselves being scooped up and thrust out of the world of the Erl-King and the wall and the Dark Nest. They landed in three feet of snow.

"Enough. As yet
disquiet clings
about us.
Rest shall we."
—Hardy

EPILOGUE

The morning after the battle, the sun came up, which, in itself, was worth its own paragraph.

As MacDuff stood on a large balcony looking out to sea, he watched the rising sun with his one eye and praised the God that helps. The cold wind felt beautiful against his skin, and he was thankful for the slight sting. He reached up and made sure the patch was in its proper place. Susan had been very good about healing the wound, but there was no getting the eye back. He thought of the Erl-King and the talebearer, and of St. Bride and Odin and Mac-Beth. It did not surprise him to see that the column of soulstuff that had taken in the wall, the Scythelings, and the Dark Nest had disappeared, leaving only the red Old Man of Hoy. Where Douglas was, he had no real wish to know. He was slightly curious but more happy to see the sun. He wished to enjoy the leisurely feeling that had come over him, for he suspected it would not last.

With the winter setting in at full force the moment the wall came down, it was apparent that the Scots forces would be staying in Orkney until the spring came around. All settled in for what would be four months of life predominantly indoors until Malcolm could be guaranteed safe passage.

After a few days Oberon took his leave, for the Syth were not particularly bothered by the cold and were eager to be home. Within a week a scout was sent back to inform them that they had met with Titania in Braemar and that Joly was not talking but of course that was only a matter of time. Oberon himself was trying to fine Ruthe a pleasant enough replacement for Paddock, and had a few ideas of where to find one. He had his pipe — MacDuff had given it back as promised and he was quite enjoying it to Titania's chagrin. Golanlandaliay returned to the big tree when the Syth left; his mild distrust of humans was gradually returning and, with the job done, there seemed little reason to stay.

Thorfinn was slipping. He did not get out of bed the first morning nor any afterward. MacDuff sat by his bed and talked with him, two old soldiers. Thorfinn was a good man, and MacDuff felt his passing in keeping with the passing of the old Scotland.

A little time before he died Thorfinn said:

"Do you realize, MacDuff, that you mourn for very little of lasting worth? There is no 'real,' 'old' Scotland or 'old' way of life. This is a land of long-dead Picts and Celtics and Scots and wayward Vikings. And each individual, from your grandfather's grandfather to you and I, have had their own view of this land. We may even do the same thing; I may lift the hammer exactly as my father did, exactly because that is how my father did it, and yet it is still not the same. Thinking about it makes it different. And it changes, and the changes, for someone else, will become the old ways.

"And, yes, I know how they fought for the land. I understand. I have done so myself. But I wonder, when I look at this land called Alba, Caledonia and Scotland, where first there were these men and now there are those, and all that remains to call the real and the old is the grass, and not even that, some say . . .

"I wonder what any kingship really solves or creates. And I wonder if there is any truth but what the ruler and ruled decide at all. But as a ruler, MacDuff, I am content with this. I am king. This is what I know."

After funerals for all the other losses, there was room for one more.

It was apparent to all that Malcolm was going to make Thorfinn's widow his own bride and take her back with him when the time came. MacDuff reflected that Thorfinn probably couldn't have cared less and that it was Malcolm's kind of ultra-political move. It would be.

One early spring morning, when the light was sparkling on ice a little more than usual, Susan came out to find MacDuff on the balcony, as usual, staring out to the sea. She came up behind him, put her arms around him and he grasped her right arm and held it against his chest. The Iron Thane sighed. The hair on his head had gone more gray still, until now little black remained.

Susan followed his gray eyes and said, "I'll join you."

"What do you mean."

"You are leaving soon. I can tell."

"Witch."

"Wouldn't take a witch to tell that," she said, and kissed him gently on the cheek. Tender. He had never thought her to be tender.

He let out a deep breath and studied the sea. "I intended to leave in the first place."

"I remember," she said. "England."

"Well," he laughed quietly. "I doubt that."

"Good," Susan nodded. "But I can go with you. We would make a fine team."

"Susan, I am an old man."

"You are more vital than most men half your age. And you live in the Scottish climate. In Spain you would be immortal."

"I have things to learn, Susan, and to consider."

"Still trying to prove your worth?"

"No. Some things Thorfinn said have made me more at peace with reality in general, I suppose. I have no more vengeance. No, I go for a different reason. Before I die there are things I must see and know."

She pushed back the auburn lock and watched the melting ice as it sparkled in the sun. MacDuff was mortal and would die eventually, she knew. And she hated to let him go. But he was trying to sort out things that few humans had the time or the life in which to consider, and she knew he had to do it alone.

"Where are you going?"

"I am not sure. Somewhere I might avoid another war, hopefully."

She nodded, still holding her arms around him, leaning her immortal head against his shoulder. He was thousands of years younger. "If you ever need help, MacDuff . . ."

"Humph. If I need help." He considered the slight possibility that she might be right. How tempting it would be, to call her at any time. That would be difficult to live with. He accepted it anyway. "All right."

"All right, then." She chewed her lip for a second. "Ruthe and I will retrieve Joly and go back to the heath. We will be there forever, most likely. She took the brunt, you know. Losing Paddock and Julia. She always knew . . ."

"The price of love," said MacDuff. "The price is worth it." They kissed, and MacDuff held her for a long time before turning back to look at the sea. They did not say good-bye.

When she awoke the next morning to find him gone, she accepted it and headed for the heath. MacDuff had to wander.

It was, or it seemed to be, a long, long time before he turned up again.

ROGER ZELAZNY
DREAM WEAVER

"Zelazny, telling of gods and wizards, uses magical words as if he were himself a wizard. He reaches into the subconscious and invokes archetypes to make the hair rise on the back of your neck. Yet these archetypes are transmuted into a science fiction world that is as believable—and as awe-inspiring—as the world you now live in." —**Philip José Farmer**

Wizard World
Infant exile, wizard's son, Pol Detson spent his formative years in total ignorance of his heritage, trapped in the most mundane of environments: Earth. But now has come the day when his banishers must beg him to return as their savior, lest their magic kingdom become no better than Earth itself. Previously published in parts as *Changeling* and *Madwand*.
69842-7 * $3.95 _____

The Black Throne with Fred Saberhagen
One of the most remarkable exercises in the art and craft of fantasy fiction in the last decade.... As children they met and built sand castles on a beach out of space and time: Edgar Perry, little Annie, and Edgar Allan Poe.... Fifteen years later Edgar Perry has grown to manhood—and as the result of a trip through a maelstrom, he's leading a life of romantic adventure. But his alter ego, Edgar Allan, is stranded in a strange and unfriendly world where he can only write about the wonderful and mysterious reality he has lost forever....
72013-9 * $4.95 _____

The Mask of Loki with Thomas T. Thomas
It started in the 12th century when their avatars first joined in battle. On that occasion the sorcerous Hasan al Sabah, the first Assassin, won handily against Thomas Amnet, Knight Templar. There have been many duels since then, and in each the undying Arab has ended the life of Loki's avatar. The wizard thinks he's in control. The gods think that's funny.... A new novel of demigods who walk the Earth, in the tradition of *Lord of Light*.
72021-X * $4.95 _____

This Immortal
After the Three Days of War, and decades of Vegan occupation, Earth isn't doing too well. But Conrad Nimikos, if he could stop jet-setting for a minute, might just be Earth's redemption. . . . This, Zelazny's first novel, tied with *Dune* for the Hugo Award.
69848-6 * $3.95 _____

The Dream Master
When Charles Render, engineer-physician, agrees to help a blind woman learn to "see"—at least in her dreams—he is drawn into a web of powerful primal imagery. And once Render becomes one with the Dreamer, he must enter irrevocably the realm of nightmare. . . .
69874-5 * $3.50 _____

Isle of the Dead
Francis Sandow was the only non-Pei'an to complete the religious rites that allowed him to become a World-builder—and to assume the Name and Aspect of one of the Pei'an gods. And now he's one of the richest men in the galaxy. A man like that makes a lot of enemies. . . .
72011-2 * $3.50 _____

Four for Tomorrow
Featuring the Hugo winner "A Rose for Ecclesiastes" and the Nebula winner "The Doors of His Face, the Lamps of His Mouth."
72051-1 * $3.95 _____

MERCEDES LACKEY

The Hottest Fantasy Writer Today!

URBAN FANTASY

Knight of Ghosts and Shadows with Ellen Guon
Elves in L.A.? It would explain a lot, wouldn't it? Eric Banyon really needed a good cause to get his life in gear—now he's got one. With an elven prince he must raise an army to fight against the evil elf lord who seeks to conquer all of California.

Summoned to Tourney with Ellen Guon
Elves in San Francisco? Where else would an elf go when L.A. got too hot? All is well there with our elf-lord, his human companion and the mage who brought them all together—until it turns out that San Francisco is doomed to fall off the face of the continent.

Born to Run with Larry Dixon
There are elves out there. And more are coming. But even elves need money to survive in the "real" world. The good elves in South Carolina, intrigued by the thrills of stock car racing, are manufacturing new, light-weight engines (with, incidentally, very little "cold" iron); the bad elves run a kiddie-porn and snuff-film ring, with occasional forays into drugs. *Children in Peril—Elves to the Rescue.* (Book I of the SERRAted Edge series.)

Wheels of Fire with Mark Shepherd
Book II of the SERRAted Edge series.

When the Bough Breaks with Holly Lisle
Book III of the SERRAted Edge series.

HIGH FANTASY

Bardic Voices: The Lark & The Wren
Rune could be one of the greatest bards of her world, but the daughter of a tavern wench can't get much in the way of formal training. So one night she goes up to play for the Ghost of Skull Hill. She'll either fiddle till dawn to prove her skill as a bard—or die trying....

The Robin and the Kestrel: Bardic Voices II
After the affairs recounted in *The Lark and The Wren*, Robin, a gypsy lass and bard, and Kestrel, semi-fugitive heir to a throne he does not want, have married their fortunes together and travel the open road, seeking their happiness where they may find it. This is their story. It is also the story of the Ghost of Skull Hill. Together, the Robin, the Kestrel, and the Ghost will foil a plot to drive all music forever from the land....

Bardic Choices: A Cast of Corbies with Josepha Sherman

If I Pay Thee Not in Gold with Piers Anthony
A new hardcover quest fantasy, co-written by the creator of the "Xanth" series. A marvelous adult fantasy that examines the war between the sexes and the ethics of desire! Watch out for bad puns!

BARD'S TALE

Based on the bestselling computer game, *The Bard's Tale.*℠

Castle of Deception with Josepha Sherman

Fortress of Frost and Fire with Ru Emerson

Prison of Souls with Mark Shepherd

Also by Mercedes Lackey:

Reap the Whirlwind with C.J. Cherryh
Part of the Sword of Knowledge series.

The Ship Who Searched with Anne McCaffrey
The Ship Who Sang is not alone!

Wing Commander: Freedom Flight with Ellen Guon
Based on the bestselling computer game, *Wing Commander.*™

Join the Mercedes Lackey national fan club! For information send an SASE (business-size) to Queen's Own, P.O. Box 43143, Upper Montclair, NJ 07043.